Dreams on the HORIZON

Dreams on the HORIZON

PENNY ZELLER

Dedicated to all of those whom the Lord has
rescued and given a fresh start.

Thy mercy, O Lord, is in the heavens; and thy faithfulness reacheth unto the clouds.
Psalm 36:5

CHAPTER ONE

HORIZON, IDAHO, 1891

SOMETIMES THE LORD ANSWERED multiple prayers all at once.

Mae Shepherdson faced her pupils and, using sign language, dismissed them from class and promised to see them early tomorrow morning.

The students signed back to her and Mae thought her heart would explode.

Her charges were learning.

And she was making a difference.

Each student had a different story. From the ones who came from a supportive and caring home to the ones who'd been mistreated or were orphans; from those who struggled to learn to those who eagerly embraced every lesson; from the youngest to the oldest, and all those in between…all were thriving under the dedicated tutelage of Mr. and Mrs. Eddington and the Horizon School for the Deaf.

Mae's heart warmed as she watched as the children bounded from their desks, waved, and one by one, left the classroom. All except Polly, whom Mae had asked to stay after class.

Polly remained at her desk, smiling as she drummed her fingers on the worn-out wood, causing a tap-tapping vibration.

Mae reached inside her own desk and removed a wrapped parcel before walking to Polly's desk. "For you," she signed.

Polly's brown eyes lit and she reached for the parcel, opening it with all the enthusiasm a six-year-old could muster. Pulling out the dress, she stood and held it against herself for size.

The dress Mama made would fit perfectly.

Polly wrapped her thin arms around Mae's waist. She then stepped back, brought her hand to just below her mouth, and signed, "Thank you." Before allowing Mae a chance to respond, Polly scuttled from the classroom, and Mae knew the little girl would barely reach her room before trying on the garment.

God had answered Mae's prayers in so many ways. He'd blessed her with a family who loved her; He'd led her to teach at the Horizon School for the Deaf; and He'd allowed her to do something big for the least of these.

Mae turned and erased the chalkboard, including her haphazard drawings of a plow, wagon, horse, and dog. The horse, especially, lacked an artist's precision. Thankfully Lenore, another teacher at the school who taught arithmetic and history, possessed the gift of drawing.

She retrieved her wrap and stood for a moment to gaze upon her classroom. Seven well-used desks, donated by a school in Utah and hauled to Horizon on a freight wagon, crowded the meager room. The chalkboard expanded across one wall, a window was on the other, and the desk Papa and Albert had made for her for Christmas was placed at the front of the classroom. A United States flag, a picture of George Washington, and a makeshift shelf that contained a Bible, *The Book of Sign Language*, and several primers, stood not far from Mae's desk.

Had she ever believed her dream of teaching and instructing students in writing, spelling, and reading would come to fruition? And not only being a teacher— for she'd been offered a job in Horizon previously at the schoolhouse she herself had attended—but at a school for children who couldn't hear. Who may have been turned aside because they were different.

Just as she'd once been turned aside.

Gathering her belongings, Mae headed out the door of her classroom and into the hallway. "I'll see you at the meeting tonight, Mrs. Eddington."

"Yes, dear. Thank you for all your hard work today."

Mae appreciated Mrs. Eddington's gratitude. She and her husband had long dreamed of beginning a school after their son had been born deaf. God led them to Horizon four years ago, and they opened the school with the help of donations.

Mae stepped outside and walked along the front yard and out the gate. She turned to view the school. Not really a school so much as a house. Mr. Jeffler, a longtime resident of Horizon, left the home to the Eddingtons after he passed. At that time, it had been nothing more than a spacious, albeit neglected, oversized shack. With the assistance of Papa, Albert, Timothy, and several of the men from Horizon, the school received a fresh coat of paint, new wood for the porch, a new roof, and a brand-new whitewashed fence surrounding the home. Thanks to the women of Horizon, each room was scrubbed and curtains hung in the windows.

The school still required numerous repairs, and volunteers donated their time as often as they could. With the exception of a few, most folks in Horizon embraced the school.

Mae's heart warmed as she thought of the Horizon School for the Deaf and all it represented—a place of community and acceptance for children who had been turned aside from society, a place to receive a quality education and lifelong skills, and a place to learn how to live, survive, and even thrive in a hearing world.

Joy bubbled within her heart. Oh, to be a part of such a grand venture!

The school never turned any child away, even with its limited funds that barely covered the necessities.

Mae knew what it was like to be turned away.

To be unloved.

But she also knew the power of God's abounding grace and His mercy in bringing her a forever family. It was the hope that flooded her own life that had set her on the path to extending that hope to other children.

Especially those whom the world had either forgotten or worse, mocked, because they were different.

Thank You, Lord, for the school. May it never cease to be a blessing to those who need it most.

Mae took a seat beside her parents in the Horizon town hall, a recently-built clapboard structure with an unrailed porch and two windows on either side of an extra-wide door. All of her family members were in attendance, including her younger sister, Ruby, who had taken her place near the front of the building and was scribbling notes about the ongoings.

Just in case Mr. O'Kane from *The Horizon Herald* should choose to hire her to write an article about the meeting.

Mae spied the newspaper owner in a chair in the front row. The man boasted an air about him that reinforced his exaggerated sense of self. He pinched his perfectly-trimmed-and-waxed dark brown mustache, holding between his finger and thumb the flawless circular curls of each end. Fuzzy mutton chops grew from below his ears and down the side of his face, protruding to a point on either side with a shaved section between the two chops. Round spectacles rested on his nose, and piercing beady eyes scanned the proceedings.

Mama and Papa sat just to Mae's right. Her glance lingered on her parents, and a flood of warmth filled her. She marveled at how the Lord should be so very merciful to give her the parents

He had. She bit her lip at the overwhelming emotion that arrived unannounced. Papa was a good man, not like her first pa, and Mama, with her compassion and graciousness, reminded Mae of the kind of mother she hoped to someday be.

Mayor Jimmie Trabert, who owned the mercantile with his wife, Tabitha, rapped on the rectangular-shaped mahogany table at the front of the room. "If I may have your attention, please!"

The room became silent, and Mayor Trabert continued. "We are here today to discuss the recent news that Bennick Railways is fixing to lay track from Ingleville to Horizon and possibly beyond."

Murmurs echoed throughout the room, and some of the townsfolk proceeded to share their strong opinions on the matter. Pablo, a portly, elderly gent with an abundance of black hair streaked with gray, voiced his sentiments first. "Don't like change none. Not one bit."

Pablo's best friend, Leonel, the opposite of Pablo with an overly-thin stature and sparse white hair, shook his head. "Me neither. Things is just fine the way they are."

Mr. Woodham, the banker, sat erect in his chair and addressed Pablo and Leonel. "You do realize change is inevitable, do you not?"

"It would be good for our community," added Miss Greta. "Matter of fact, it would bring more business to my boarding-house, so I'm in full agreeance."

"You would be," muttered Leonel. "I remember them old times when Horizon was a one-horse town."

"It's more than just bringing business to our community," piped up Mr. Salo, the blacksmith. "It'll cause our town to grow. Are we ready for that? With that growth can come more business, which I'd welcome, but it can also cause some problems. Don't need no hoodlums setting up residence in Horizon. Sheriff, what would you say?"

"Right now, we don't have a whole lot of crime in Horizon. Of course, as a lawman, I'd like to keep it that way. As Salo mentioned, there will be good and bad that comes with a railroad. My main concern is that it is not just started, but finished. I've heard of railroad companies beginning the task, but failing to complete it."

Mr. Kent, the livery owner, stood. "We don't want our town dryin' up. I heard any town that doesn't have a railroad should just forget about existin'."

"And Horizon is one of the last towns in this area without a railroad," Papa interjected.

The stagecoach driver, a grizzled man with a booming voice, didn't hesitate to express his thoughts. "If they bring the railroad here, I'll be out of a job.

"Me too," added Mr. Weyer, the owner of the Weyer Freight Company. "Why would I want something that would take away my livelihood?"

"Here, here!" shouted the stagecoach driver.

A raucous commotion resulted then, with multiple questions and comments all at once. Some cheered. Others grumbled their discontent about the decision. Heated arguments amongst some of the townsfolk ensued. While they weren't unkind, they were spirited. Some, like Miss Greta, agreed the railroad coming to Horizon would be beneficial. Others, although in the minority, vehemently disagreed with what such a change would mean to their town. Some mentioned they didn't trust the company to finish the project they started.

From what Mae could garner, no one really had a choice about whether the railroad arrived or not.

A few men stalked in from the saloon, stumbling in drunkenness and sharing their sentiments before the sheriff escorted them from the building.

Leonel's vociferous voice sounded above the others. "The train's gonna be loud too. Anybody thought about that?"

An uneasy feeling crept into the pit of Mae's stomach and she felt as though she were smothering. The noises grew louder and panic rose in Mae's chest. Swallowing soon proved difficult, and a glance at her hands revealed trembling. She struggled for a deep breath. Her thoughts raced and she shivered. Were it not for the fact her legs felt like lead, she'd flee from the meeting.

It's only because you so strongly disliked the obtrusive sounds of the railroad when you lived in New York. And the thundering voice of her first pa, along with his stomping through the tiny apartment in the tenement where they lived.

Mae couldn't forget that.

But why did these unwanted and painful memories creep into her mind with the slightest provocation?

Her heart rate increased and she shivered. Instinctively, she briefly covered her ears with her hands and squeezed her eyes shut before realizing a few of the townsfolk were gaping at her.

Mama put an arm around her. "Mae, are you ready to go?"

She didn't want to interrupt her family's participation in the meeting so she shook her head and instead prayed the Lord would remove the memories and give her the peace she so desperately sought, even after all these years.

More questions and comments resounded.

"Where's the route gonna be?"

"When's it supposed to be finished?"

"Should we build a hotel to accommodate all the new visitors?" To which Miss Greta had a retort.

"Sure would be nice to get the mail sooner."

"I'm looking forward to traveling to Boise City to see my grandchildren."

Mayor Trabert rapped again on the table, and the crowd quieted. "Now, I know there are a lot of different opinions, and tensions are a bit high right now."

"You ain't foolin'," said Pablo.

"Here is the information I have at present. It appears the rail-way will go from Cornwall, to Ingleville, to Horizon. Cornwall has had a railroad for some time. It's just a matter of connecting it to Ingleville and Horizon. I received a telegram, and Mr. Bennick from the company will be here in a few days to discuss this matter at length. I did hear that Ingleville has given the railroad a hearty welcome."

"Don't care none what Ingleville has done," muttered Leonel. "This here is Horizon. Not Ingleville."

"True, and I ain't never much cared for Ingleville anyhow," added the stagecoach driver.

The discussion continued for well over two hours, and while the debate may never be completely resolved and the differing opinions would likely continue long after the meeting, most favored, and even anticipated, Bennick Railways bringing a railroad to Horizon.

However, as beneficial as the railroad would likely be for Horizon, an unsettled feeling firmed itself deep within Mae's chest.

Chapter Two

LANDON BENNICK ATTEMPTED TO hide his irritation at his mother's perpetual insistence that he take an interest in Orla Rothleutner. The thought of entering into matrimony was the last thing on his mind.

Especially entering into matrimony with a woman of his mother's choosing.

Not that he didn't love Mother, but her idea of whom he should marry vastly differed from his own.

"Now, Landon, need I remind you that Orla is a delight and it would bode well for you to show some interest in her when her family arrives this evening?" Mother beckoned the maid for a cup of tea.

"Agreed," added Father, taking a brief moment to lift his gaze over the newspaper he studiously perused. "As you are aware, it would be ideal if Bennick Railways were to merge with Rothleutner Industries. Your continuous refusal to take an interest in Miss Rothleutner has not escaped my attention. There are certain responsibilities a man with your social standing must adhere to."

"Yes, sir." Landon resisted the temptation to utter his disagreement at his father's tactless hints. Such a dispute would do no good. Father was set in his ways, and once he made up his mind on a matter there was no changing it. Bennick Railways consisted of a vast fortune, from both his grandfather's business and Father's company, and would allow generations of Bennicks to live a comfortable life. Without the addition of wealth from the Rothleutner family.

"Orla is a lovely young lady. I don't know why you haven't asked to court her yet." Mother clucked in disapproval. "Please do strongly consider her as a matrimonial option."

It was a similar conversation every time the Bennicks and Rothleutners would attend a social event together or whenever Mother would invite the Rothleutners to supper.

Mother patted her perfectly coifed hair. "You and Orla will have ample time to talk tonight and next week as well at the social gathering at the Kingston Estate."

If Mother had her way, he and Orla would be married by next week. Also, if Mother had her way, the Bennick family would have a social engagement each evening. For Landon, the whirlwind of constant activity proved exhausting. But as the only Bennick child, there were enormous expectations placed upon him. Father expected him to carry on not only the family name but also the family business. And to do it well. Without complaint.

As Father was fond of saying, "One can hardly run a successful company if he is a recluse." Mother would add, "Nor can one run a successful company with no wife and heir."

No, if Landon ever decided to marry, it wouldn't be to someone of his mother's choosing. It wouldn't be to unite two businesses as Father wanted. It would be for love. Landon desired someone ordinary who loved him for him, not for his family's wealth or what they hoped to gain by marrying him.

The knock at the door indicated the Rothleutner family had arrived. The butler led the family to the dining room. "Now, do remember our conversation, Landon," Mother admonished, leaving Landon to briefly wonder if she recalled he was twenty-five instead of nine.

Mother embraced Mrs. Rothleutner first, then Orla as if she hadn't just joined them yesterday for tea.

"It's such a pleasure to be invited to your home," gushed Mrs. Rothleutner, a plump woman with hair that added two inches to her height.

Mr. Rothleutner shook hands with Landon's father. "Good to see you, Bertram."

Landon glanced at Orla Rothleutner. She'd dipped her head and tossed Landon a smile that didn't quite reach her eyes.

They partook in the supper Cook prepared, and Orla fixed her attention on her food. It was likely she'd received a similar lecture about merging family fortunes.

Pleasant conversation transpired with talks of the weather, which quickly turned to upcoming plans for Landon and Father. "Landon will be traveling to Idaho in two weeks. The spur between Cornwall and Ingleville is nearly complete. Next, we will extend the spur from Ingleville to Horizon."

Mr. Rothleutner buttered his second roll. "I don't recognize the names of these towns. Are they near Boise City?"

"A fair distance away, but soon numerous towns will be connected. I'll be journeying to Horizon in the coming month to tend to matters as well."

"I've never been to Idaho," Mrs. Rothleutner declared. "I've heard it's part of the Wild West."

Mother raised her eyebrows in interest. "I'd like to someday visit. Bertram says one would ride a stagecoach from Ingleville to Horizon until the spur is complete. Can you even imagine?"

"A stagecoach? I do declare. I suppose there are no modern conveniences to be had in such a place." Mrs. Rothleutner shivered. "It's nearly the next century. Poor souls who are without contemporary conveniences. Whyever would you wish to ride on a stagecoach? I've heard they're dreadful."

"It will be an adventure for certain. I would like to see this area that Bertram and Landon are so fond of discussing.

"Speaking of topics of interest, did you hear about poor Mrs. Sewell?"

Father and Mr. Rothleutner had no qualms about listening to Mother and Mrs. Rothleutner discuss the latest gossip, as they immediately ceased their quiet conversation about silver prices.

"I did not hear about her. Do share what you know."

"Yes, well, her son, Gene, went off and supposedly fell in love with that dreadful girl who works as a seamstress at the millinery on Ninth Street."

Mother gasped. She and Father exchanged a private glance before Mrs. Rothleutner continued.

"Yes, so scandalous. Both Mr. and Mrs. Sewell wanted desperately for Gene to marry a girl from the Burge family. Instead, he chose someone far below his station. I can only imagine what would have happened to all of the Sewell family money had Mr. Sewell not disowned Gene. Such a shame." Mrs. Rothleutner fanned herself. "It's disgraceful, is what it is."

"I don't agree with the decision to disown Gene," said Father. "But neither do I agree with his choice to deliberately go against his parents' wishes."

Mother placed a hand on her heart. "Indeed. The Sewells are one of the wealthiest and highest-principled families in Denver, if not the entire state of Colorado. Tsk, tsk."

After dessert was served, everyone retreated to the parlor. "Landon, why don't you and Orla take a stroll?"

"Indeed," agreed Mrs. Rothleutner. "The evening is rather pleasant."

Landon rose from the sofa and directed his attention to Orla. "Would you care for your wrap?"

"Yes, please."

"Take your time, darlings," Mother said. To Mrs. Rothleutner, who sat beside her, Mother murmured just loud enough for everyone to hear, "I do hope that son of mine will settle down someday and provide me with a grandchild."

Landon offered his arm to Orla, and together they strolled down the tree-lined street past the many extravagant homes on Aldworth Avenue. The sunset cast a breathtaking orange-and-purple hue, and the air smelled of supper cooking somewhere in the prominent neighborhood. A carriage drove by, the horses clip-clopping in perfect time.

Orla sighed. "It seems our parents are set on arranging a courtship and subsequent marriage for us."

"They've been planning that for some time."

Orla gazed into the distance, her expression unreadable. "I've attempted to tell Mother and Father that we aren't suited for each other to no avail."

Her words shocked him. "You have?"

"Indeed. Unfortunately, they have yet to understand my position on the matter."

"My parents as well."

"Landon..." Orla faced him, and her brow crinkled. "We have known each other for years, ever since your parents purchased their home here in Denver. You are a kind man, and I have appreciated our friendship. However..."

"I agree with you, Orla."

"You do?"

"I do."

The rigidity of Orla's shoulders eased, and she exhaled. "I'm so grateful. I've been working myself into a dither over this continual matchmaking scheme in which our parents have collaborated."

"I'm rather relieved myself. While I appreciate our longstanding friendship, for me that is all it would ever have been."

"Yes. Especially since I am fond of another."

Landon grinned. "Might I ask who that could be?"

Orla's face reddened. "Sylvester Wagner."

"The vice president of Wagner Bank?"

"Yes. And while his family is not as wealthy as yours, Sylvester has accumulated quite a fortune."

"Have you mentioned this to your parents?"

"Not yet." Orla wrung her hands. "They are so set on combining the Rothleutner and Bennick fortunes they can think of nothing else. But if you are in agreement that we aren't suited for each other, I can now tell them."

"I am in full agreement."

Orla placed a hand on his arm. "Thank you."

"You're welcome."

"Do you fancy anyone?"

"Can't say that I do. I've recently been learning a lot about God and that He has a plan for our lives. I wonder if it might behoove me to pray about who I might someday marry."

"That's brave to have so much trust." Orla's hazel eyes widened. "Who you marry is of utmost importance."

"It is." He shrugged. "I still have a lot to learn, but I've been attending services whenever I'm in Denver."

"As opposed to just at Christmas and Easter?"

"Indeed."

Her eyes shone with gratitude. "Thank you, Landon, for your agreeance."

"You're welcome. Our parents will be disappointed."

"They will be. But Father already knows Sylvester and his strong work ethic, and I do believe Mother will like him. He is a kindly gent with a brilliant mind."

While Mother and Father would indeed be disappointed, Landon felt freer than he had in a long time.

CHAPTER THREE

LANDON HAD NEVER RIDDEN in a stagecoach before, and the experience proved amusing. He'd spent numerous hours aboard trains throughout the United States. He'd boarded a streetcar more times than he could count. He'd been transported by buggy, had once driven a wagon, and frequently rode his horse. But the stagecoach was altogether a different matter. Thankfully it was a relatively short distance between Cornwall to Horizon. The completion of the rail from Cornwall to Ingleville, and then from Ingleville to Horizon couldn't come quickly enough.

He'd never considered himself as having a weak stomach, but then he'd only eaten the most delectable of food. Anyone not achieving Father's level of standards regarding meals was efficiently relieved of employment at the Bennick household.

Therefore, Landon was entirely unprepared for the meal served during the second of the two stage stops.

Weariness overtook him, but Landon heeded the driver's admonition to avoid falling asleep and resting your head on a fellow passenger's shoulder. His stomach growled at least fifty times in the last ten minutes, and his trousers and jacket were covered with three inches of dust. The stage stop between Ingleville and Horizon was nothing more than a dilapidated building emitting a peculiar aroma that reminded Landon of the time while staying at the Bennick estate in New York when the new driver had gotten lost and they inadvertently found themselves in the Hilyard slum region. The squalid conditions, including piles of garbage, a burned building that was never cleaned up and removed, and the unsafe, teetering, derelict tenements were the opposite of the neighborhood on Vanderburg Hill where Landon's family owned one of their three homes.

And now as the stagecoach passengers unloaded at the final stop before Horizon, Landon inhaled, smelling again that day in the Hilyard slums.

The odor caused his stomach to lurch, so opposite from the hunger he'd experienced just minutes ago.

One of the other three passengers on the stage, a rotund man who'd been repeatedly admonished for attempting to fall asleep and rest his bald head on his wife's shoulder, apparently didn't mind the pungent odor. "I sure am hungry," he said, rubbing his protruding belly.

Two dogs and a cat roamed around the stop. A woman emerged from the building and took a moment to pet the dogs and cat and pat the flank of one of the stagecoach horses before inviting the passengers inside for a noonday meal. "Just finishing up some bread," she said. A man, presumably her husband, assisted the stagecoach driver with the horses.

Inside was an open area with an oven, fireplace, baking table, and three shelves of food items. Four chairs surrounded a square table that boasted one leg shorter than the other three. "Have a seat," the woman invited. "I'll be gettin' you all some food."

She pootled toward the baking table. "Gotta set this last bit of dough to risin' first," she muttered more to herself than her guests. A cat scurried after a mouse that zipped across the floor before the plump tabby purred and rubbed against the woman's leg. She leaned down, patted its smooth fur, then immersed her hands in the dough, continuing to knead it even as cat hairs flitted from her hand.

Landon never considered himself one to have a weak stomach, but at that moment, he retched. Whatever hunger he'd had prior, left him, and his loss of appetite was further confirmed when the woman later plopped bowls of an unknown substance on the table and invited the passengers to eat.

"I'll be outside." Landon turned to leave the room, willing his stomach to retain the remaining food from breakfast.

"You all right with it if I have your portion?" the robust man asked.

"By all means, help yourself."

Landon figured Horizon would be similar to the other towns he'd encountered during his family's extensive travels during his childhood and as an adult working for Father. However, the small town struck him as different from the moment he disembarked from the stage. For one, folks seemed friendlier. For two, the town was cleaner and better kept than some he'd seen.

A tall, thickset man with an abundance of reddish hair and graying sideburns approached him. "Do you know where you're going?"

Landon peered about him. Apparently, the other three passengers were either staying with folks or resided in Horizon. "Yes, sir. Just looking for the hotel."

The man's expression remained stoic. "You'll find no hotels in Horizon. At least not yet. Miss Greta's boardinghouse is your best bet unless you've got some family or friends to stay with."

"Miss Greta's?"

"Yes, it's right down the road. I'll take you there."

Without waiting for Landon to respond, the man grabbed one of Landon's three bags and hoisted it into the back of a wagon. "You gonna walk?" he asked.

"No, sir." Landon climbed onto the buckboard.

"Name's the Lieutenant."

"Landon Bennick. Much obliged for you taking me to Miss Greta's boardinghouse."

The Lieutenant beckoned the horses. "Figured you looked out of sorts standin' there twiddling your thumbs."

Landon wasn't sure "twiddling your thumbs" accurately described him holding two pieces of luggage while peering about, but he didn't argue with the man.

"Visiting someone?"

"No, sir. I'm with Bennick Railways."

The Lieutenant narrowed his eyes and scrutinized Landon. He transferred the reins to one hand and scratched his red-bearded chin. "Hmm."

Most of the time, towns sprung around railroads, but in the few instances where spurs connected already-built towns, Landon had received his share of diverse responses when revealing his identity. "We're hoping to finish the Cornwall to Ingleville spur soon as well as begin on the line connecting Ingleville to Horizon."

"I see. Did you have a hand in the Ingleville spur?"

"I did. I visited the town before we began construction. However, one of my colleagues is now in charge of that project while I will be responsible for the one in Horizon."

The Lieutenant returned his gaze to the road and slowed the horses. "I can tell just from your speaking you ain't from around here. Where is it you come from?"

Sharing with curious strangers that his parents owned three homes didn't usually bode well. Landon found that the best answer when discussing such matters with those in more uncivilized areas was to mention his home in Colorado. "Denver."

"Denver, eh? Never been there and don't plan to go."

Landon wasn't sure how to respond to the man's brusque way of things, so he instead perused the town. Several passersby waved as the Lieutenant passed. Horizon boasted a church, mercantile, livery stable, two saloons, a barber, a millinery, a doctor's office, and a school. The entire town could fit inside his Denver neighborhood.

"I will warn you that folks have their opinions about the railroad coming here."

"I'm aware of that."

"Lucky for you, Miss Greta and most of the others want the railroad. Unlucky for you, some folks won't look kindly on some outsider coming to town with a mind to change things."

Landon shifted. After sitting for so many hours on the stage and now the wagon, his legs begged to walk about. "I do not incline to change things. The railroad will be a valuable addition to your fine town. It will bring commerce and money to Horizon and make it easier to ship goods in and out."

"Humph. Depends on who you ask."

The Lieutenant stopped the wagon in front of a well-tended two-story home with an expansive front porch, numerous flower gardens, and two enormous trees on either side.

"Much obliged for the ride. What is the charge?"

"The charge?"

"For delivering me here from the station."

"Guess I never really gave much thought to that. I always bring folks here to, well…" The Lieutenant stopped mid-sentence and stared at the porch where an older woman had emerged with a broom.

"Sir?"

"Sorry. I was just taking a gander—" The Lieutenant cleared his throat.

Landon extracted several coins from his pocket and handed them to the man. "Would this suffice?"

"Well, I'll be. Yes, yes, that will do nicely. Thank you." The Lieutenant pocketed the money. "If you need anything else, be sure to say so."

"I will. Thank you."

The one thing Landon did need was to have peace about presenting the information regarding the spur to the townsfolk. The reasons such presentations oftentimes caused trepidation were twofold. For one, some people weren't amenable to change. And for two, Father expected perfection from Landon. A requirement he sometimes failed to meet.

A few minutes later, Landon removed his hat and prepared to greet the woman on the porch, but it was clear her attention was not on a potential new boarder, but rather on the Lieutenant. She pressed the wrinkles in her skirt with her free hand.

"Ma'am?"

"Pardon?"

Several seconds ticked by before the woman focused her attention on Landon. "What is it you want?"

"I was wondering if you have any rooms available."

"Depends on who's askin'."

"I am, ma'am. I would need to board for a few months."

The woman set the broom against the wall of the house. "Come along inside. I'm Miss Greta, the proprietress of this fine establishment."

"Pleasure to meet you, ma'am. Landon Bennick. I'm here with the railroad."

Miss Greta arched a pointy eyebrow. "The railroad, you say?"

"Yes. We're building the spur from Ingleville to Horizon."

"We do have some rules for this fine establishment."

"I wouldn't expect any less." Landon peered around at the tasteful, if not sparse, furnishings.

Miss Greta led him to a desk in the corner of the foyer. "Your name again?"

"Landon Bennick."

With large and precise strokes, the woman wrote the date in the far left column, his name in the next column, and the charge in the third column. "Pay your rent of ten dollars a week on time, don't cause trouble, no smoking or alcohol in the house, don't argue with the proprietress—that's me—about ridiculous things as you won't win, keep your room tidy, and maintain a cheerful disposition. When a meal is served, be there to eat it or forget about it altogether and find yourself somewhere else to eat. If you're accustomed to newfangled conveniences, you'll find none of those here. The outhouse is out back." She squinted at him. "There is no hotel in this town, so unless you got family or friends, you'll have nowhere to stay if you don't abide by the rules."

"Yes, ma'am."

"One other important rule," Miss Greta held her pencil midair. "Accept what's for supper because I don't aim to be makin' any special meals for anyone. Now. You want the finest room available or a less expensive one? If the latter, I can offer you one of the attic rooms."

Money was not a concern, and Landon knew from previous stays at boardinghouses that attic rooms, while less expensive, were painfully warm in the summer. "Your finest room available suits me."

"That's what I thought. You don't seem like poor folk." She handed him a key. "You'll be in the Wildflower Room. Up the stairs, first room on your right."

"Thank you."

"I'll ring the bell to announce breakfast and supper. If you don't hasten to the dining room quickly, the food will likely be gone, and I won't be cookin' any more of it for that day."

Landon nodded. "I understand all of these things, and thank you for arranging a room for me in your fine establishment."

Miss Greta stood straighter. "You are welcome."

Landon unlocked the door to his room. Miss Greta's name for it was accurate as there wasn't a blank space on the wall not covered in blue, yellow, pink, and purple flowered wallpaper. A rug on the worn wood floor boasted more flowers. He set his bags on the floor, washed his face, and prepared to visit the town before supper.

Mae entered the post office to secure a few stamps for Mrs. Eddington. Mr. Kleiber, the stooped postmaster, handed her four letters. "Busy day for the school."

She flipped through the letters, noting three were from families of the students at the school. Hopefully, when they arrived to visit their children, the parents would be able to make a payment. Mae overheard Mr. Eddington mention to his wife that funds were paltry this month. Thankfully the school was self-sufficient and able to raise their own food. However, some necessities couldn't be grown on their small farm, along with wages for Mae and Lenore.

Despite the struggle the school recently experienced, no student would ever be turned away due to lack of funds.

"That reminds me." Mr. Kleiber reached behind the counter and produced a basket of numerous squares of brightly-colored fabric. "The missus wanted me to ask if you could use these for the school's upcoming charity event. She, Maribel, and the rest of the sewing circle collected them over the years."

"Oh, yes, we most definitely could!" Mae set the letters on the counter and rifled through the material. "There is so much we could do with these. But are you certain the sewing circle doesn't need them?"

The elderly postmaster smiled. "She had a feeling you would ask that. No, they don't need them. You know how they are—always wanting to bless others and such."

"Thank you so much. These will be put to good use."

Mae placed the envelopes on top of the fabric and left the post office. If the charity event were successful, perhaps the school wouldn't struggle so. She appreciated the townsfolk's continued benevolence. Except for a few, most supported the school.

She stepped out of the post office, and a brief, gusty breeze swirled her skirts and caused a dust devil in the street. She clutched the basket tighter in her hand. A glimpse heavenward indicated blue skies and nary a cloud.

A tap on her shoulder drew her attention from the weather. She turned to face a man of about her age of twenty-three, holding a letter. "I believe you dropped this, miss."

The man was rather handsome and no one she had seen before. Mae attempted not to stare into his blue-green eyes, but instead focus on the correspondence in his hand. "Yes, I believe I did. Thank you."

He handed it to her with a smile, and she dipped her head, attempting to hide the rosy hue that surely stained her cheeks.

They stood for a moment as if time halted.

He removed his hat. "I'm Landon Bennick."

The name sounded familiar, but she couldn't place why. Mae opened her mouth to respond, but for the briefest moment, no sound emerged. If only she was more gregarious like Ruby or lively like Lucy rather than shy and timid.

Mr. Bennick awaited her answer.

Perhaps she ought to find her voice again. "I'm Mae."

"Mae?"

Where were her manners? "Forgive me. Mae Shepherdson."

"Well, Miss Shepherdson, it is a pleasure to make your acquaintance."

"And yours as well."

An awkward silence passed between them before Mr. Bennick hiked a thumb toward the mercantile. "I best be on my way."

"Yes. I, as well."

Obviously, Mr. Bennick was not from Horizon as Mae knew just about everyone in town. Was he visiting a relative? Opening a new business in town? Working at the bank? From what she could ascertain, he wasn't a farmer, miner, or one who would work at the livery given his attire. She watched him duck into the mercantile before she hastened to her horse, a peculiar thought floating through her mind.

Would she see the dapper stranger again?

CHAPTER FOUR

THE NEXT DAY, LANDON finished unpacking his clothes. He stuffed them into the lone bureau in the Wildflower Room at Miss Greta's boardinghouse. A piece of paper slipped from between two shirts the servants had packed for him. Landon set the paper on the bureau and stowed his bags beneath the bed, then stood and arched his back. He hadn't slept well on the thin mattress last night.

He welcomed the day when constant travel to various places slowed.

Landon wandered to the window, Mae Shepherdson, the woman he'd met yesterday on his mind. How could he forget her with her long brown hair, dark blue eyes, and a sweet smile that did something peculiar to his insides? Did she reside in Horizon? In another town nearby? Perhaps he would see her again.

The view from his window encompassed nearly all of Horizon's main street, allowing him to see a reasonable distance. A father and his young son—perhaps three or four years old—strolled down the boardwalk. The boy held his father's hand while intermittently jumping up and down and pointing to various things.

A stab of envy permeated through him. His own father ensured Landon would never be without the necessities of a man of his station. The sprawling bedrooms in each of his parents' three homes, the finest of clothes, the gold pocket watch, the best horses, and a secure future. But Landon had never held on to Father's hand and moseyed down the boardwalk. Father had never expressed exuberance like the boy's father when Landon said something amusing.

He temporarily shoved the thought aside and completed the task of organizing his room. He positioned his Bible on the nightstand next to a lamp and wash basin. His attention veered again to the folded piece of paper that had fallen earlier from between the two shirts. Curiosity got the better of him, and Landon unfolded and flattened the stationery to see Father's precise handwriting with his faultlessly-spaced penmanship.

Landon,

Best of luck in Horizon. Do remember to represent Bennick Railways with the utmost of care. Be diligent in your presentations so as to avoid bringing any such blight upon the Bennick name. I am counting on you to handle this matter with perfection.

Father

Anger meshed with frustration, hurt, and disappointment caused a pain in his chest he couldn't articulate. Landon gritted his teeth and refolded the letter. Hiding it would transitorily remove it from his vision, but doing so would not remove it from his memory.

At least he wished you good luck. That's more than it could have been.

But even Father's best wishes couldn't remove the ache. Not when the remainder of the letter provoked a sting not remedied by anything except perhaps prayer.

That was, *if* the Lord wasn't the same type of father.

Ever since Landon could remember, Father's high expectations had been nearly impossible to attain. He loved Father and felt honored to work at a business as esteemed as Bennick

Railways. But he'd gladly relinquish his birthright to hear Father say he loved him. Or was proud of him.

Landon attempted to swallow the sorrow. Perhaps a walk would do him some good. He tucked the letter beneath his stack of clothes in the bureau and left the room. As he advanced down the stairs, the aroma of roast beef lingered in the air. Should he notify Miss Greta of his decision to go for a walk? At home, he would always let Cook know he would be out for a while so she'd wait to set a supper plate for him.

Miss Greta hummed as she bustled about the kitchen.

"Ma'am?"

She turned swiftly, a glower lining her face when she saw him. "What do you want? Can't you see I'm busy?"

"I just wanted to let you know I'm going for a walk."

She firmed her hands on her ample hips. "Do I look like one who would be concerned about your comings and goings?"

After Father's letter, he preferred not to deal with a cantankerous landlord. "I may be late for supper."

"And as I mentioned when you first arrived, there will be no waiting for you to eat at your leisure. Eat a meal when it's served or forget about it altogether."

"Yes, ma'am." He turned to leave before Miss Greta beckoned him.

"Mr. Bennick?"

"Yes?"

Miss Greta wiped her hands on her skirt and pressed her lips together. "You have to understand that if I make allowances for folks, I'll be feeding them all day long. No one has time for that."

"I understand."

She opened her mouth to say more, but then quickly shut it.

"I best be on my way." Without waiting, Landon continued out the door and onto the porch of the boardinghouse. The late afternoon weather was a reprieve from the temperatures earlier in the day, and he ambled down the street, walking the length of the main thoroughfare before turning around.

Folks nodded or waved, and friendly faces abounded in the small town. Hopefully, the residents would continue to exhibit kindness if something went awry with the railroad. Like it had in a town in California.

Landon hadn't wanted to remember the horror of what happened that day. Yet, the memory stuck in his mind as if it happened just yesterday.

The fact that it occurred on his watch made it all the worse.

The steep incline where the workers removed undergrowth, rocks, and trees made the work dangerous as did preparing the area for explosives. Landon suggested that the field engineers find a different location for the route; however, options were limited. Two men, both hardworking fellows by the names of Kuang and Manos, died when an accidental explosion killed them both instantly.

Landon had been the one to deliver the news to their fam ilies.Father had been the one to blame Landon for carelessly overseeing the project.

But Landon knew he hadn't been careless at all. Rather, he'd done all he could to prevent the accident.

To no avail.

Landon found himself in front of the church, and he trudged up the stairs of the humble building and stepped inside. Noticing no one around, he settled into the back pew, his ruminations weighing heavily on him.

Things had never been easy with Father. Not even when Landon was a youngster. He put his head in his hands and stared at his boots. Both Mother and Father had determined to decide whom Landon would marry, when he would marry, where he would live, and what occupation he would choose.

Was God the same way? Dictating what Landon ought to do with his life?

I've never lived up to my father's expectations.

Was God the same way with an abundance of rules? Insisting His children remain steadfast in those rules with perfection? What happened when one failed?

The heaviness weighed on him. He couldn't please his father, let alone a Holy God in whom he'd recently placed his trust.

Failure lurked around each corner, waiting to devour any sentience of peace. The desire for acceptance for who he was, not who he *should* be, burned in his chest.

If the Lord demanded flawless obedience, Landon would fail.

Just like he routinely failed Father.

"Hello?"

Landon lifted his head to see a man standing next to him. "My apologies. I was just taking my leave." Landon prepared to stand just as the man took a seat.

"Is something weighing heavily on your heart?"

"That is an understatement."

The man extended his hand and offered a firm handshake. "I'm Pastor Albert."

"Landon Bennick."

"Nice to meet you, Landon. Are you new in town?"

"Yes, sir. I'm here to represent Bennick Railways, the company building the spur from Ingleville to Horizon."

"There's been much discussion about the railroad."

"That would come as no surprise. Tell me, have the townsfolk eagerly accepted the news, or...?"

Pastor Albert studied him. "I would say most of the townsfolk eagerly accepted the news at our meeting last week. Some vehemently disagree." The reverend shrugged. "But you can't please everyone."

"And you? Where do you stand on the issue?"

"I believe it will bring commerce to Horizon. I also believe it will provide opportunities for me, as a man of the cloth, to share the Gospel."

Landon released the breath he'd been holding. "That's good to hear that most are amenable. It makes things easier. And, yes, you are correct when you say you can't please everyone."

"So is the prospect of bringing the railroad to Horizon what's got you concerned?"

The man was frank. Landon would give him that.

"Somewhat."

"I see. Well, if there's anything I can do to help, please let me know."

Landon figured the man would go on his way after saying his piece, but Pastor Albert did just the opposite. He remained sitting next to Landon. "If it's not an imposition, I would like to ask something—a religious inquiry."

"I tend to get those types of questions on occasion." His mouth twitched into a smile.

"Forgive me for asking, but you seem too young to be a pastor."

"No offense taken—I am younger than some. God placed the calling on my life before I was grown, a tug so forceful there was no way I could resist. I humbly remain a student of the Word, and I will never know all there is to know this side of Heaven. However, if a question burdens you, I'll do my best to answer it."

Landon studied the man beside him. Would Pastor Albert consider his query absurd? Toss him from the church for lack of knowledge? Offer ridicule? "I can ask another time. I should be going."

"You can ask another time or you can ask now."

Indecision arose, and Landon tapped his finger on his thigh. "I'm just wondering about the Lord, is all."

"You're in the right place."

"I don't know a lot about Him. Yet. Last month at my church in Denver, the pastor prayed with me to surrender my life to Christ. I have a hunger I've never had before when it comes to reading and studying the Bible. There's so much in there I don't understand." Landon stared at the wooden cross at the front of the church. "I know Jesus died for my sins, but my family and I have only really ever attended church on Easter and Christmas. For appearances. As an obligation. So Father could put some cash in the plate in front of others and attempt to best them at who could give more during those holidays."

A trapped breath solidified in Landon's lungs. Would Pastor Albert think him inferior for handling his faith with such indifference? Landon waited for a response and hazarded a glimpse from the corner of his eye.

But there was no judgment, no disdain, and no condemnation in Pastor Albert's expression.

Should he continue?

Before he thought of the matter more, his mouth opened and the words emerged. "I imagine God is like my father."

"In what way?"

"One wrong step and we taste His wrath? One wrong step and He expresses His profound irritation and disappointment? Are His expectations so outlandish and so extreme that we can do nothing but fail?"

"God is a God of justice. And of wrath."

The disappointment hit him like a punch to his stomach. "I figured that to be the case."

"He is a Holy God who cannot look upon sin. His anger and wrath are always warranted. However, there is good news. That wrath fell upon Jesus when He went to the cross. There's a verse in Romans that states, *'Much more then, being justified by his blood, we shall be saved from wrath through him.'* If we've put our faith and trust in Jesus, we don't have to fear God's wrath."

The tension in Landon's shoulders released. "That is good news. But what about when we don't obey? Is He, like my father, watching us constantly, waiting for us to make a mess of things?"

"His eyes *are* on us, but not to catch us in an error. God is also a God of love. Only a God who loves us beyond our comprehension would send His innocent Son to take the penalty for our sins. As we grow in Him, we become more like Jesus." Pastor Albert's brow furrowed. "As a father, I seek to love my sons the way God loves me. To love unconditionally, to be there for them whenever they need me, and to teach them the right way of things. I also have to teach my sons about obedience. They are twins, and what one doesn't think of, the other one does—and if I allowed them to partake in some of the shenanigans they concoct, they'd either get hurt or hurt others."

"But does He demand perfection?"

"Not at all. He knows we are fallible human beings. He created us and knows our struggles and everything about us. If we were perfect, we wouldn't need Jesus. And if we were perfect, we wouldn't need forgiveness, which God offers abundantly."

Landon knew he'd be thinking about all that Pastor Albert said far into the night. "Thank you for answering my questions."

"It sounds like your pa can be a hard man. I've found the best thing to do when struggling with others is to lift them to the Lord. Can I pray for your pa?"

Landon wasn't sure it would do much good given Father's stubbornness, but he agreed and bowed his head as Pastor Albert prayed.

"Do you have plans for supper?" He asked after leading the prayer.

"Just ensuring I arrive at the boardinghouse in time to eat."

"Ah, yes, Miss Greta. Well, you're welcome to join my family for supper tonight if you'd like."

"I wouldn't want to impose."

"It's not imposing. And Velma, my wife, is a good cook." Pastor Albert rubbed his stomach.

"All right. I'll join your family. Thank you, Pastor Albert."

"Please, call me Albert."

Landon followed the pastor to the parsonage next to the church. The modest whitewashed house boasted a humble porch with two rocking chairs. The pastor opened the door, and an appetizing aroma of pot roast and fresh bread lingered in the air. Within seconds, two tiny boys ran to Albert, and he lifted one in each arm. He planted a kiss on each of the boys' chubby cheeks and told them he'd missed them.

Father had never been that excited to see Landon, and Landon for certain hadn't fervently embraced Father when he arrived home from work. When he returned home from boarding school, Father sent the coachman to retrieve him from the train station. While Father did inquire about Landon's time at school, such discussions were brief and likely only a matter of formality. Mother would occasionally glance up from planning the latest social gathering and interject a word or two.

But they never missed him.

Not like Albert missed his boys after only being mere hours from them.

A longing took up residence in Landon's heart. If the Lord called him to be a father someday, would he be a distant one like his own or a loving one like the pastor?

Albert released the boys, and they clamored around him, both speaking at once at an overly enthusiastic pace, their childlike gibberish bringing a smile to their father's face.

A woman who'd been tending the stove meandered toward them. The pastor wrapped an arm around her shoulders. "I missed you today, Vel."

"And I missed you. How was your day?"

"Before I share about the ongoings, I'd like you to meet Landon." Pastor Albert turned aside. "Landon, this is my wife, Velma. Velma, this is Landon. The boys are our twin sons, Simon and Sherman."

Velma smiled, her small, squinty eyes disappearing into round cheeks as she did so. "Pleasure to meet you, Landon. Will you be joining us for supper?"

"Yes, ma'am. If it's all right."

"It most assuredly is."

Should he ask if Velma needed assistance with preparing the table? At home, the cook and servants cared for every detail. But Horizon, Idaho, was far from home. He stood idly by for a moment watching the happenings around him. Simon and Sherman had climbed into chairs, their short statures allowing them to barely reach the table. They poked at each other and laughed. Albert kissed his wife's cheek, and she giggled before retrieving the pot roast from the oven.

Landon never saw his parents being affectionate. It was as if their marriage was a business rather than a union of love and affection. It was clear from what Landon witnessed that Albert and Velma loved each other and their children.

The exuberant chaos ensuing in the parsonage would never have been allowed in Landon's home. He was to sit perfectly still at the supper table. Mother sat at one end, and Father at the other. Two servants stood nearby tending to every need. On several occasions, Father requested his food item be altered, recooked, or replaced with another meal.

Even when he sat down to supper, Father was never content. Never satisfied with what was given him.

Yet here at the pastor's house, everyone seemed content, even though the home was small, crowded, noisy, and the furniture tattered and worn.

Landon marveled at the revelation. Mother demanded only the finest quality of items, and Father happily obliged. The mismatched dishes on the table differed greatly from the blue willow pattern china at his parents' Denver home.

Albert led a prayer thanking the Lord for the food. Father never led prayers before supper.

Velma passed him the plate of bread. "Are you visiting Horizon for long?"

"Yes, ma'am. I plan to be here a couple of months at the least. I'm working for the new railroad."

Landon shared some of the plans with Albert and Velma that he would be sharing at the town meeting next week. An hour later, he prepared to leave. "Thank you for the fine meal, ma'am."

"You're most welcome."

Albert clapped him on the back. "Our big family, with my parents and brother and sisters, are having their weekly supper Friday evening. Would you care to join us?"

Landon welcomed the idea of having supper with Albert's family again. Odd since he never anticipated Mother's constant scheduling of suppers and other events. "I might just do that."

Chapter Five

There was something about having the entire family around the dinner table that warmed Mae's heart. She knew she wasn't the only one. Timothy rushed in from helping Papa. "Lucy's here!"

Mama placed a hand on Mae's shoulder. "Go ahead. Ruby and I will finish tending to supper."

"Are you sure?"

"More than sure." Mama nearly pushed Mae out of the kitchen.

But Mae didn't need any prodding. She stepped out into the sunshine just as Lucy and Hans rounded the driveway.

Becky, the youngest of Lucy's two daughters at age three, wrapped her arms around Mae's neck. "Hi, Aunt Mae-Mae."

Mae planted a kiss on Becky's forehead. "How's my favorite little Becky?"

"I fine."

Becky didn't stay long in Mae's arms. She wiggled free and attempted to skip, with one leg in front, more reminiscent of a gallop. "I learning to skip like Carrie."

"That's not skipping," said Carrie. "Skipping is like this. Watch me, Aunt Mae-Mae." Carrie bounded across the dirt in a near-perfect leap.

Becky's eyebrows knitted together, and she folded her arms across her chest and pouted.

"It's all right, Becky. You'll learn to skip soon." Mae gently patted her niece on the back before turning her attention to Lucy. "I'm so glad you're here."

Lucy returned Mae's hug. "I look forward to this each month. Care for a walk?"

Hans, a tall, lanky, blond fellow climbed from the wagon. "As much as I'd care for a walk, I'll have to pass. I think I'll join the menfolk." A teasing glint danced in his eyes before he deposited a kiss on Lucy's cheek. "See you at supper, *kjæreste*."

Years ago when Lucy and Hans were first married, Mae asked what *kjæreste* meant, to which Hans answered, "sweetheart". And, very likely, Lucy had been Hans's sweetheart since shortly after they'd met in school. Now married with two adorable daughters and a baby soon to be born, their love for each other had only grown with time.

Becky and Carrie ran ahead of Mae and Lucy as they walked down the road, past the barn and corrals, and adjacent to Papa's freshly planted corn. "How have you been?" Mae asked.

Lucy rested a hand on her swollen belly. "This little one is far more active than Becky and Carrie were. The kicking keeps me awake at night sometimes, but I'm so grateful for the opportunity to bring another life into the world."

"Are you any closer to determining names?"

"No. While Hans and I concur on most things, we haven't come to an agreement on a name. Hans is certain the baby is a girl, while I tend to believe we may have ourselves a boy this time."

Lucy hooked her elbow through Mae's. "And how have you been? How is school?"

"Busy. We now have twelve pupils. I've been attempting to assist Mrs. Eddington and Lenore with charity event preparations. Maribel and Mrs. Kleiber from the sewing circle donated dozens of fabric squares. A couple of the girls are becoming adept at sewing, so I believe we'll be able to stitch together some lovely quilts for the townsfolk to bid on."

"I'm looking forward to the event. Don't forget that Hans and I will be donating a table."

"That is so generous of you. Thank you. Hans does amazing woodwork."

Lucy smiled. "Yes, he does. But I might be a bit biased. Later Becky and Carrie will have to show you how well they've come along with the sign language you've taught them. I think you'll be impressed."

"I can't wait to see that. Thank you for practicing with them. It will be such a delightful surprise for Polly when they can communicate with her."

"You're really doing an amazing job at the school, Mae. We are all so proud of you."

"Thank you. Your compliment means a lot to me."

"Of course. Besides, it's true. You are making a difference, just as you set your mind to do."

They walked arm-in-arm for some time as the girls inspected flowers, caterpillars, and rocks. Ever so often, their glee at a new discovery emanated through the air. "Do you ever think about those days before we became Shepherdsons?" Mae asked.

"Not often. It seems like a lifetime ago."

They stopped while the girls giggled at a ladybug's travels along Carrie's arm.

"Do you often think of those days in New York?"

Mae twisted her hands together. "At times, yes. Sometimes something will happen, and it's as if I'm right back in those days when…" she swallowed the emotion that threatened to rise to the surface. "Where would we have been if God hadn't seen fit to bless us with our parents?"

Lucy patted Mae's arm. "He is a faithful God, and He cares deeply for the orphans. Would you care to discuss it?"

Mae hadn't spoken much of her days with her first pa or subsequently as an orphan. She'd kept the bulk of it trapped inside so that not even Lucy or Mama knew much of what happened back then. For some curious reason, it felt safer to confine the pain of the past. Guilt played a role in that, for why should she ever entertain such dismal thoughts when the Lord had blessed her so richly? "No, I'm fine."

Concern lit Lucy's large and compassionate brown eyes. "If you're sure."

"I'm sure. I suppose we should return to the house. Supper will be ready soon."

Lucy hesitated a moment before again looping her arm through Mae's. "Come along, girls. It's time to turn back."

"Can we take the ladybug with us?" Carrie asked.

"I want to hold the ladybug. Please, Ma?"

"Little girls shouldn't hold ladybugs," insisted Carrie. "They're very fwagile."

Becky glowered at her sister and pouted again. "I can hold a ladybug. I can."

Lucy offered Mae a knowing glance. "Did we ever argue like that?"

"No, not us," giggled Mae. "But Ruby and Timothy do."

"True. Poor Mama." She focused her attention on her children. "Carrie, do allow Becky to hold the ladybug, but, Becky, you have to be very careful."

"I will. I pwomise." Becky's former grouchy countenance was quickly replaced with a jovial one when her sister allowed the insect to crawl on her arm.

Dust plumed in the distance from a wagon traveling down the road. "I believe that would be Albert and Velma," said Lucy.

"And there's someone on a horse behind him." Mae squinted. The rider looked somewhat familiar. "Oh!"

"Do you know him?"

"I believe that's Mr. Bennick."

"Mr. Bennick?"

As they drew closer, Mae's suspicions were confirmed. It was indeed the handsome gentleman from town earlier that week. She watched as he dismounted his horse and joined Albert, Velma, and their sons.

He was visiting for supper?

Who invited him? Albert?

A case of nerves settled over her.

"Mae?"

Lucy's voice interrupted her apprehension. "Yes?"

"Tell me more about Mr. Bennick."

Her sister cocked her head into Mae's line of vision, unmistakable expectation in her gaze.

"I—well, he's just a man I met in town."

"Yes, you mentioned that."

Lucy was relentless. "I met him when he retrieved a letter I accidentally dropped."

"Oh, really?"

Mae had known Lucy a long time, and those words always raised suspicion. "Yes, really."

"Hmm." Her sister gave her a smug look. "Are you blushing, Mae?"

She reached a hand toward her face while simultaneously jabbing Lucy gently in the shoulder with her opposite elbow. "Say not a word, dear sister."

Lucy pretended to button her lips. "Your secret is safe with me."

Thankfully Lucy was generally reliable when it came to serious matters such as these. Thank goodness it wasn't Ruby who'd witnessed Mae's discomfiture.

"I suppose we should join the family and Mr. Bennick before someone comes to look for us."

Lucy corralled her daughters, reminding them to wash before supper.

As they returned home, the question remained on Mae's mind: what was Mr. Bennick doing at her family's farm?

Albert introduced Landon to several members of his family. While Mother and Father too often hosted and attended—and encouraged him to attend—events, charity balls, and the like, the folks at those events hadn't been as welcoming as the Shepherdson family.

Not even close.

As a matter of fact, from the moment Landon entered the home, he felt as though he were a treasured guest rather than a man landing on their doorstep due to one person's invitation.

Landon stepped aside to allow Albert and several members of his family to bustle about with food arrangements.

The humble home boasted a shelf that contained a collection of six or seven books. It sharply contrasted the floor-to-ceiling bookshelves in each of Landon's parents' homes. The one in Maryland left only one wall of the library free of bookshelves. As a child, Landon climbed into one of the ornate chairs and delved into reading the books. It kept him occupied for hours, although Mother and Father still saw fit to send him away for his education and so they could "travel freely without a child underfoot".

Mrs. Shepherdson brought a pitcher of milk to the table. "Do you enjoy reading, Mr. Bennick?"

"I do."

"Please feel free to borrow any books on the shelf. They're well-used, but still have much life left in them."

"Thank you, ma'am." Landon returned Mrs. Shepherdson's gracious smile. Ruby, Albert's sister, ensured everyone had silverware. A thought struck him then that perhaps he ought to help with supper preparations. "Might I assist with setting the table?" He knew little about how to do such things as servants always carried out these sorts of tasks, but he wanted to be a courteous guest.

"I believe we're about ready to eat," said Mrs. Shepherdson.

Velma ushered one of her sons into a highchair at the table, while Albert hoisted Sherman into his arms. "What say you and I round up Grandpa and the others and let them know it's time to eat?"

Sherman giggled and nestled into his father's shoulder.

Had Father ever hoisted Landon into his arms? Had Landon ever affectionately hugged his father?

Not that he could recall on either account.

Albert introduced Mr. Shepherdson, his younger brother, Timothy, and his brother-in-law, Hans. A moment later, two women and two small girls entered the house.

And Landon immediately recognized one of them as the woman he'd encountered in town a few days ago.

"These are my other sisters, Lucy and Mae, and my nieces, Becky and Carrie."

"Miss Shepherdson is your sister?" He uttered the words before giving them thorough consideration, and one of Albert's eyebrows lifted.

"You know Mae?"

Landon and Miss Shepherdson answered at the same time, their voices chorusing together in answer to Albert's inquiry. "We met in town."

To which Landon added, "And please, everyone, call me Landon."

"And call us by our given names as well," said Albert. Although Landon wasn't sure he would be able to refer to Mr. and Mrs. Shepherdson as such due to the etiquette rules Mother so aptly reminded him about on a regular basis.

They took a seat at the table then with Miss Shepherdson—Mae—directly across from him. She was as beautiful as
he remembered her. What were the chances that she was the
pastor's sister?

After Mr. Shepherdson led the prayer, commotion ensued.
Landon had never seen anything like it. Joy was on nearly
every face, save for Simon's because his mother refused him
a cookie until he finished his supper. It amazed Landon that
everyone fit around the table, especially with two high chairs
and an extra person.

Mr. Shepherdson who sat at the far end of the table beside
his wife was the first to address him. "Mr. Bennick—Landon—what brings you to Horizon?"

"I work for Bennick Railways." He held his breath a moment, waiting to see what type of response he would receive
after his declaration.

Hans reached for the potatoes. "We hear there's a new spur
connecting Horizon with Ingleville."

"Yes, sir. We aim to make travel much easier to more distant parts of Idaho. I'll be addressing the community Monday
and updating them on the details."

"You're from Bennick Railways?" This from Ruby, Albert's
youngest sister. She inclined from across the table where she
sat beside Miss Shepherdson—Mae. "Can I interview you?"

"Ruby has aspirations to work for *The Horizon Herald*
someday," the other sister whose name he believed to be
Lucy, said.

"I *will* work for *The Horizon Herald* someday."

"That's Rube for you," said Timothy. "When she has her
mind set on something, nothing can stop her."

Ruby scrunched her nose. "That's better than having no
ambition."

"I have ambition." Timothy sat up straighter in his chair.

"Eating far too many cookies, cakes, and desserts all day?"

Timothy narrowed his gaze at his sister. "Not so. I plan to do that *and* work hard."

As an only child, Landon had never known the rivalry that he'd heard of—and now witnessed—between brothers and sisters.

"Humph," said Ruby. "Anyhow, Mr…Landon…may I someday interview you?"

Albert, who sat on Landon's left side, tilted his head toward Landon. "Rube likes to interview just about everyone she can."

"It's true. I plan to write such amazing interviews that Mr. O'Kane will have no option but to hire me as one of his reporters."

"His only reporter," offered Timothy.

"I'd be honored to be interviewed." Landon wasn't sure what he could tell her that would be of interest. The Shepherdson family was far more compelling than he was.

"Thank you." To Timothy, she sent a smug smirk to emphasize her thoughts on the matter.

Mrs. Shepherdson passed the bread to Mae. "From where do you hail, Landon?"

"Mostly Denver. This is my first time in Horizon, although I spent some time in Ingleville while we were determining the placement for that spur." Landon gazed across the table at Mae, who quietly buttered a piece of bread. Should he ask her a question? He did want to know more about her. But what should he ask? He didn't want to sound presumptuous. Perhaps he should rather just inquire of the group. "Have you all always resided in Horizon?"

Mr. Shepherdson shook his head. "No, most of us have lived elsewhere before Horizon, with the exception of Ruby and Timothy."

There was something in Mae's countenance that indicated she might have more to add to the conversation, but she remained silent. Conversation amongst the family continued, and Timothy announced it was time for dessert.

Mrs. Shepherdson sliced pieces of cake. "Landon, would you care for some cookies, shoo-fly cake, or both?"

"Can't say as I agree with Mae-Mae on everything," said Timothy, "but I do agree with how she makes shoo-fly cake. Mmm. Mmm." He patted his stomach.

Ruby eyed her brother. "Better serve everyone else before you serve Timothy. We all know he has no willpower when it comes to sweets."

Hans handed a cookie to Simon. "I became a member of the Shepherdson family after Lucy and I married. I have to agree that if you want dessert, claim it before Timothy does." Hans playfully slugged Timothy in the shoulder.

"Especially Mae's shoo-fly cake. Landon, have you ever eaten shoo-fly cake before?" Lucy handed her two daughters each a cookie.

"Can't say as I have. I've eaten shoo-fly pie many times, but never shoo-fly cake. I'd like to try some, please." Mrs. Shepherdson set a piece on his plate. He took a bite and allowed the cinnamon-molasses confection to melt on his tongue.

"Well, what do you think?" Mr. Shepherdson asked, forking his own bite.

"It's delicious. I've always been partial to cinnamon. When I was a boy I once snuck into the kitchen and devoured the entire cinnamon-and-sugar mixture from the sizable container on the shelf."

"Did your ma have your hide and then some?" Timothy reached for seconds, only to be rewarded with a swat on the hand from his mother.

"Well..." Mother hadn't even known of his tomfoolery, but Cook had. Numerous pairs of eyes, including Mae's, stared at him awaiting his answer. "Well, my mother didn't know, but..."

"Lucky you. Mama knows all my shenanigans. I can't get away with anything. Of course, it doesn't help that we have a tattletale among us." Timothy glowered at Ruby.

"If you don't want to be in trouble, then behave yourself. Please do continue, Landon."

"Well, my mother didn't know, but the woman who prepared our meals was suspicious when she arranged to make cinnamon rolls and the canister holding the cinnamon-and-sugar mixture was empty. Didn't help that there were remnants all over my face, which revealed my secret."

His gaze connected with Mae's and he noticed her sweet smile.

"Then what happened?" asked one of Lucy's daughters.

Landon had nearly forgotten he was in the middle of telling a story, so enthralled was he with Mae. "I, well, I was put in the corner and was excluded from partaking in dessert that evening. Cinnamon rolls are among my favorite desserts, so the punishment was not worth my sneaky behavior." He took another bite of the cake, closed his eyes, and savored it. "This is delicious, Mae."

A pleasing blush crept up her cheeks, and Mae dipped her head. Had he embarrassed her? He was about to apologize when he noticed several sets of eyes watching him. Best he say nothing to avoid embarrassing her further. Perhaps he could apologize later.

More conversation continued as everyone cleared their dishes. Not wishing to overstay his welcome, Landon thanked Mr. and Mrs. Shepherdson for their hospitality.

Mrs. Shepherdson mentioned he was welcome to join them for supper again, and Albert offered to walk him to his horse.

"Your family is very hospitable. Thank you for inviting me."

"Yes, they are. Mama especially enjoys cooking for others."

They stood in silence for a moment near the horse Landon borrowed from the livery. "You're a blessed man to have your family."

"That I am."

Mae emerged from the house then, a pail in her hand. She handed it to Landon. "Mama thought you might like this for later."

"Is it the shoo-fly cake?"

"It is."

Even in the dim light of the sunset, he was captivated by her lovely smile. "Thank you, Mae. I'll enjoy every bite of it."

She nodded and then returned to the house as he watched after her.

"Landon?"

He begrudgingly stole his attention from Mae and reverted it to her brother. "Yes?"

"We are protective of Mae. I just thought you should know."

"Protective of her?"

"Yes." Albert shoved his hands in his pockets, and awkward seconds ticked by until Landon again spoke.

"Well, I best be on my way. Thank you again for inviting me, and please thank your family."

Landon mounted his horse even as a question played over again in his mind. Why were they protective of Mae?

Mae aided Lucy with the girls and walked outside with her to the wagon. "What an enjoyable evening. I'll see you on Sunday," said Lucy.

Mae worried her bottom lip. "I sure wish I was more verbose and sociable like you and Mama and more vivacious like Ruby."

Lucy took a step back. "There's nothing wrong with being reticent."

"I just wish I could more readily think of things to say."

"Usually you're quite talkative at our family suppers. Unless it has something to do with a certain guest."

Mae was grateful for the impending darkness so her sister couldn't once again witness her embarrassment. "It might."

"Just as I thought. Well, for what it's worth, I thought he seemed an affable fellow." Lucy aided Carrie into the wagon. "Mae, we love you as you are. If God made all of us verbose and sociable like Mama and me or vivacious like Rube, everyone would be competing for a chance to speak. We need quieter sorts."

"Thank you, Lucy."

"Always." She hugged Mae before climbing into the wagon herself. "Men have a tendency to say that we womenfolk are a chatty sort. But there my husband is chatting the night away with Papa, Albert, and Timothy. I might be a year older by the time we reach home." Lucy giggled and Mae joined in her sister's amusement.

It had been a wonderful evening, but Mae knew she'd find it difficult to sleep with her mind settled on tonight's handsome guest.

CHAPTER SIX

LANDON RUBBED HIS PALMS together in anticipation of delivering a speech to the townsfolk of Horizon, Idaho. At least he'd met several who would be in attendance, including Miss Greta, the Lieutenant, and the Shepherdson family.

People crowded the town hall, wall-to-wall, with many standing as the seats were taken. Most people appeared jovial in spirit. A good sign, at least, that this may be an easier crowd to convince. Hopefully, he would have no problem persuading them of the spur's benefits.

Mayor Trabert, a stout man with blond hair and a full beard, took his place beside Landon. "Good evening, everyone. Mr. Landon Bennick from Bennick Railways is here with us today. He'll be discussing his company's plans to build the spur connecting Ingleville with Horizon." Mayor Trabert stepped aside and took a seat in the front row.

"Thank you, Mayor. It is my pleasure to be here today to discuss the upcoming implementation of our project."

"I'm Mr. Woodham, and I work at the bank here in Horizon. I must say I, for one, am encouraged by the possibilities the spur will bring to our town."

Several others voiced their enthusiasm, and Landon felt a release of some of the tension in his shoulders. "Thank you, Mr. Woodham. As most of you know, the construction of this spur will allow ease of travel as residents will be able to travel by rail from Horizon to Cornwall and beyond. It will increase commerce and enable easier shipment of commodities.”

A tall, imposing man in his forties stood, nearly knocking his chair over. “The way we was shipping commodities, as you call them, was just fine before you came along. We ain’t interested in the railroad.”

Two elderly men shouted their agreement.

“Sirs, if I may...”

The men quieted, and Landon continued. “I understand...”

“You don’t understand a thing,” yelled the tall, imposing man. “You’re some wealthy cad from the city.”

Landon took a deep breath and prayed for guidance from the One he’d recently come to know. “Sir, may I ask your name?”

“Weyer of Weyer Freight Company. I haul goods from here to Cornwall in that direction, and from here to Varner City thataway.” He pointed to the south. “When you bring the spur here, it’ll take my livelihood. How am I supposed to feed a wife and four kids on nothin’?”

“What you have offered to the public is a worthwhile service, Mr. Weyer.”

“Is this where you attempt to cajole me into seein’ things your way? If so, I ain’t havin’ any of it.”

“No, sir. That is not my intent. It is reasonable to expect that you and I will not agree on this matter. If that transpires, then so be it so long as we are each respectful in our opinions. However...”

The man’s face turned red, and sweat beaded his brow. “Easy for you to say as you ain’t losing the ability to provide for your family. You’ll go along to the next town after you’re done here.”

Landon waited for the man to finish and for his two comrades to say their piece before he spoke again. “Mr. Weyer, have you considered how your freight company might increase its business because of the spur?”

A flash of indecision crossed his face. “Increase its business?”

"Yes sir. Bennick Railways will be building a depot. There will also be a loading dock to load and unload goods from the train. Yes, there will be some who will retrieve their orders from the train. But what of those who need goods delivered? What of those in outlying areas? Would a freight wagon be instrumental in providing that service?"

"Reckon I never thought of that."

Landon drummed his fingers on the scratched and faded rectangle table, apprehension overtaking him as he determined to choose his next words wisely. "It is not my wish to see any business fail due to the spur. Rather, it is my objective to assist folks in finding ways to use the railroad to their benefit. Things will change, yes."

"And we don't like change," growled an elderly man with tar-black-and-gray hair.

"Change can be challenging, yes," said Landon. "However, change can be beneficial as well."

Miss Greta raised her hand, then spoke before waiting to be called on. "I'm lookin' forward to the railroad bringing me more customers."

"Name's Mr. Kent, and I own the livery. I'm glad for the spur coming to Horizon. It's long past due. Do you know when it will be completed?"

"We don't have a completion date as of yet, but our workers operate with efficiency. I will be staying at Miss Greta's for the duration of the project, and my workers will be setting up camp near the construction area."

"Name's Mr. Salo, and I am the blacksmith. Say, will you be hiring men from Horizon?"

Landon nodded. "While we have a full crew of workers, we may need supplemental help. In addition, we will be hiring men to build the new depot."

That started everyone speaking at once with a majority in favor of the railroad.

A frantic voice interrupted the meeting, and Mae turned to see Lenore in the doorway waving frantically as she perused the room. "Is Doc here?"

Doc stood and rushed to the back of the room. "What is it, Lenore?"

"You must come quickly. It's Mr. and Mrs. Eddington and the children. They're all sick." Lenore exhaled a shaky breath. "So very sick."

"Let me grab my bag, and I will be at the school posthaste."

The room stilled except for a few hushed whispers.

Mae stood, but her legs threatened to buckle beneath her. Mama placed a hand on Mae's arm. "It might be best if you waited to hear what Doc says before rushing to the school."

Mama knew her well. "I have to go. What if Polly and the others..."

She hesitated to voice her fears.

In an instant, Papa was beside her. "I'll take you."

Wilhemina and Tabitha cornered them. "Please," said Wilhemina, "let us know if you need anything at all."

"I will."

Mae and Papa hurried from the building and started toward the school.

A thousand questions flooded Mae's mind. "Papa, what do you think happened?"

"Reckon I don't know what it could be, seeing as how everyone is ill."

"Except Lenore and me."

Mae saw Papa's worried expression. But he didn't request they turn around. Instead, they beckoned the horses as fast as they could safely go. The wind whipped through Mae's hair, and she thought she felt a raindrop.

"Try not to worry, Mae-Mae," said Papa, as if to read her mind.

"I'm trying, but it's not easy."

"Your ma would say the best thing to do is pray rather than fret."

Mae could hear Mama's voice in her head as she said those exact words. Mae offered another prayer heavenward.

Doc's buggy was parked outside the fence, and he and Lenore disappeared from the porch and into the house. Mae barely gave the horse time to stop before dismounting. She lifted her skirts and hastened to the school and up the stairs to the rooms.

Lenore stood just outside of the bedroom the girls shared, her arms folded across her chest and her cheeks dampened from tears. "I don't know what happened. The children were tending to their chores, and I was assisting Mrs. Eddington with supper preparations. After I finished baking the bread, I asked Mrs. Eddington if I might visit my sister in town. She agreed. On the way, I delivered Odin to his parents' home. I ate supper with my sister." Lenore's shoulders shook. "When I returned, I entered the house and no one was about. The supper dishes had been cleared, but not washed. It was eerily quiet, and when I called for Mr. or Mrs. Eddington, I received no immediate response. I rushed up the stairs, and Mrs. Eddington, who was attempting to tend to the children, was not doing well. She said everyone fell sick after supper, and I assisted her to her bed before finding Mr. Eddington in the barn. He, too, was not doing well. After helping him upstairs, I rode into town to fetch Doc."

Mae embraced her friend, her own tears flowing freely. She took a step back, and together they edged their way into the room.

But Mae was not prepared for the sight that awaited her.

The five girls were all in their beds, their normally energetic selves lethargic. Mae knelt beside the eldest girl's bed and signed the words asking what had happened.

Ginerva gave a sluggish shrug of her shoulders, lifted her right hand, and tapped her forehead with her middle finger to indicate the word, "Sick."

Polly, on the other side of the room, groaned, and Mae assisted her to a sitting position just as the little girl vomited. "Oh, Polly." Mae held her close and gently patted her on the head.

Doc arrived a few moments later and sent Papa to fetch water. "Since everyone fell ill at the same time, I believe it may be food poisoning. There have been instances of this condition attributed to canned food."

"We don't eat canned food. Everything we eat is from here at the school. We raise our own crops and have cows, chickens, and pigs. Mr. Eddington and the two older boys hunt for rabbit, deer, and pheasant."

Doc moved to the next child. "Do all of the children live at the school?"

Mae shook her head. "No, Odin doesn't. Mr. and Mrs. Eddington and Lenore stay here, but I go home each night as well."

"Except for tonight," interjected Lenore. "As you know, my sister has been having difficulties with her pregnancy. I went to her house tonight and made supper for us, her husband, and my nephew."

Mae followed Doc and Lenore to the boys' room. "Will everyone be all right?"

"Prayer is in order. We'll also need more help caring for them."

CHAPTER SEVEN

MAE RODE INTO TOWN while Papa and Lenore assisted Doc. Most everyone had already left town hall, but she was still able to secure the promise of several of the towns-folk, including Albert, Tabitha, Mayor Trabert, Wilhelmina, and Sheriff Zembrodt. Tomorrow, Mama, Ruby, and Timothy would switch places and relieve some of the others.

Mae then rushed to the boardinghouse.

"I'm sorry I can't leave the boardinghouse for long," said Miss Greta. "But I can send whatever food you might need."

"Thank you. Do you know of anyone else who might be able to assist?"

"I can help."

"Mr. Bennick—Landon. Yes, we would very much appreciate your help."

A moment of awkwardness followed before Miss Greta ushered them to the door. "Take my horse, Landon. You'll find it in the barn."

The sun began to set as Mae, Albert, and Landon rode to the school. Wilhelmina assigned everyone tasks, and Mae and Lenore served as translators for the children. Everyone bustled about emptying buckets of vomit, providing water, changing and washing bedding, and tending to the Edding-tons and the children. Albert led several prayers, and Mayor Trabert rode to Odin's house to see if he'd taken ill as well.

One of the little boys, Hosea, and Ginerva seemed to be doing the best. Mr. Eddington, Polly, and two other children, the worst. Doc pulled her and Lenore aside.

"I know how close you both are to Mr. and Mrs. Eddington and the pupils."

Mae's heart lurched. What was he about to say? "Doc, please tell us you have no bad news to impart."

"No bad news. However, there is a chance a few of our patients might not fully recover."

Lenore gasped. "But surely, eating a bad bite of food can't be so detrimental."

"That is only a hunch on my part. However, now knowing that Odin didn't fall ill either makes me nearly certain of the accuracy of my diagnosis. You three were elsewhere when supper was served. It must have been the food."

"Ginerva mentioned they ate the leftover ham and bean soup," said Mae. "Lenore, Odin, and I had that yesterday for the noonday meal, and all was well."

Doc stroked his chin. "That is most curious. However, it could be something else they ate. In the meantime, I think we should all attempt to get some rest."

Mae knew sleep would evade her tonight. For how could one garner some shuteye when several of those for whom she cared deeply were so ill?

Polly and the two other children were so young with their entire lives ahead of them. Mr. Eddington, one of the kindest men she'd ever met, had seemed so strong and healthy. How could it be that the Lord would see fit to take any of them Home so soon?

Tears stung her eyes. Perhaps some time outside in God's Creation would settle her spirit somewhat before retiring for the night. Mae stood on the porch and wrapped her arms around herself. An owl hooted from a nearby tree and crickets chirped.

Worries consumed her thoughts. She peered up at the stars, beseeching the Lord once again to heal the ones who had come to mean so much to her and thanking Him for the healing that had begun in others.

She was particularly close to Polly, the little girl with her bright smile, long blonde braids, and sensitive countenance. Mae would need to send a telegram to Polly's grandfather in Cornwall and apprise him of the situation. Not that he was well enough to travel, for he wasn't. But he needed to know.

Landon emerged from the house with a pile of soiled blankets in his arms. "Are you all right, Mae?"

Her innermost thoughts spilled from her mouth before she had the wherewithal to stop them. "I'm worried. Especially about the ones who are the sickest."

"I'm far from being a theologian or even a man well-versed in God's Word, although I am learning more each day. However, I do know that He hears every prayer we utter."

"That is true." But did she believe it? Did she believe God heard every prayer?

Yes. Yes, she did. She shoved any doubts aside, for He had heard all of her prayers over the years. He was a faithful God.

"I don't understand how they all fell ill. Doc says it was something they ate."

"It's possible. I must go, but I will be available to aid tomorrow after tending to some work details. In the meantime, I'll be praying for the afflicted."

While she couldn't see him well, she imagined his eyes to hold compassion, for the tone of his voice was considerate. "Thank you."

"Good night, Mae."

Just before midnight after considerable tossing and turning, Mae finally fell asleep.

Landon strode to the boardinghouse, stopping just long enough to check his pocket watch. He couldn't ascertain the numbers, but he surmised it to be after midnight. Landon placed it back in his pocket and sighed. It had been a long day working for the company, followed by the town hall meeting, then assisting with the sick at the school. Not that he would not have wanted to help, but even now, weariness tugged at every part of him.

At least once Bennick Railways completed the spurs between Cornwall and Ingleville and Ingleville and Horizon, travel would be easier and less cumbersome. No more stagecoaches and lengthy trips between the meager towns.

Landon gripped the railing and took the steps two at a time to his room. His legs throbbed, his back ached from leaning over the table computing figures earlier, and he could barely keep his eyes open. An enormous amount of work awaited him tomorrow. For that he must be alert. For that, he would need a good night's sleep.

Father always demanded he make a good impression. Would he have been appreciative of Landon's efforts tonight at the meeting? That by the time it concluded, nearly all of the folks, save the two elderly gentlemen and the stagecoach driver, were responsive to the railroad arriving in their town?

Landon struggled to recall if Father had ever been appreciative of Landon's efforts.

No such memory filled his mind.

He sat on the edge of the bed, then swung his legs over and rested his head on the straw pillow. But sleep wouldn't come. Landon tossed and turned on the hard bed. He laced his fingers behind his head and stared at the ceiling, recounting the day's events. This morning when he awoke, he hoped he'd see the lovely young Mae Shepherdson at the meeting, but he hadn't hoped to see her with tear stains on her beautiful face when she heard the news of those who'd fallen ill at the school. She obviously cared deeply for those who were sick.

He offered a prayer for those at the school. As he'd mentioned to Mae, he believed God heard every prayer. But it hadn't always been that way for him. Mother and Father prided themselves on faithfully attending church twice a year and consistently donating to worthwhile charities, including the church, the poor house, and the orphanages in Denver.

Before last year, Landon, too, thought that those "good works" of dedicated financial philanthropy, in addition to attending church on the two most important Christian holidays, would earn him a place in Heaven. Now he knew differently.

Albert had suggested that Landon pray for his father. Since God heard all prayers, Landon knew He'd hear those as well.

CHAPTER EIGHT

MAE AWOKE WITH A startle at the sound of men's voices and the aroma of bacon. She peered around her at the walls with chipped paint and the numerous beds with children, and for a moment, confusion settled over her.

Where was she?

She sat up and instantly bemoaned her stiff back and neck from sleeping on the floor on a thin blanket. She rubbed her neck.

The school. She was at the school.

Mae stood and pulled her wrap around her shoulders. She tiptoed to the door, fully opened it, and stepped out into the hallway. She peered over the staircase and saw glimpses of Papa, Sheriff Zembrodt, and Doc.

"It doesn't make sense that the colt died," Papa was saying. "The cow, I understand after having seen the bite, but why the colt?"

The sheriff took a drink of coffee. "It's something to ask Mr. Eddington once he feels well enough to speak. Maybe Mae or Lenore can translate for me while I ask one of the boys if they noticed anything suspicious."

Mae returned to the room and changed into her dress. If Sheriff Zembrodt needed her help, she wanted to be there to offer it. What had Papa meant by the colt dying? And apparently the cow as well?

She hurried down the steps and to the dining room.

"Good morning, Mae. You're up early."

Mae leaned against Papa and he placed his arm around her. "I heard you talking about a colt?"

"Yes, I went out to the barn to milk the cow and discovered it was dead. A colt too."

"The children will be so dismayed."

Sheriff Zembrodt poured himself another cup of coffee. "The cow was bitten by a rattler."

"A rattler?"

"Yes, but we have no idea how the colt died. It showed no signs of being bitten."

Mae cupped her hand to her mouth. "A rattler? You saw the fang marks?"

"Yes, and the swelling." Doc shook his head. "That rattler is still around here somewhere, so the children will need to be made aware once they're able to go outside again."

"Mae," said the sheriff, "I need you to ask the boys once they awaken if they noticed anything peculiar."

"Yes, sir. I, too, wonder how the colt died."

"We aim to get to the bottom of it."

The smell of bacon waffled through the dining room. "I best see if I can assist with breakfast. Once the boys are awake, I'd be happy to translate." Mae entered the kitchen to see Mama and Lucy at the stove.

Mama wrapped her into a hug. "We were worried you might get sick as well until Doc explained it was some type of food poisoning."

"Lenore, Odin, and I were the only ones who didn't partake in supper last night. Something everyone else ate made them sick."

"And there's a dead cow and colt in the barn." Lucy flipped a pancake with the spatula. "Makes no sense."

Mama added more bacon to the frying pan. "Once we discovered about the food poisoning, Doc suggested no one eat any of the food here. Miss Greta and Wilhelmina donated the ingredients for breakfast."

"I haven't yet checked on the children, but all of the girls were still sleeping when I left their room a few minutes ago."

Mae assisted Mama and Lucy with breakfast before again checking on all of the children. Several had improved, but Polly, Mr. Eddington, and two of the other children remained critically ill.

She slid next to Polly's bed and held the girl's small hand in her own. *Lord, please heal her.* Polly moaned and Mae reached for the glass of water on the bureau. Polly sipped the tiniest of sips before clutching her stomach and falling back on the pillow. Mae stayed several minutes longer before leaving the room and returning to the boys' room.

The sheriff and Doc joined her, and Mae's fingers flew as she signed the questions Sheriff Zembrodt asked. When Grover, one of the eldest boys answered, she relayed his message.

"Grover says he was tasked with milking the cow last night. It was dark by that time."

"Can you ask him if the colt was alive when he went to milk the cow?"

Mae asked Grover Doc's question, and Grover signed, "Yes".

Sheriff Zembrodt leaned forward in his chair. "Does he remember anything else about the colt?"

"Yes, he remembers that Mr. Eddington asked Millard to feed the colt some cow's milk. He did so hastily, and they immediately left the barn once the colt finished eating. Grover said he and Millard were already in trouble for dilly-dallying and not getting their chores done, so they rushed away to the house with the pail of milk."

"Interesting," said Doc. "Does he remember seeing the rattler?"

Grover's eyes widened as he asked about the snake, and he shook his head.

"So Grover and Millard went to the barn. It was already dark so they likely didn't realize the cow had been bitten. Grover milked the cow and poured some of it into the bottle for the colt, which Millard fed. They then left and immediately returned to the house with the milk. When did they have supper?"

Mae translated. "Grover says supper was served later than usual because Mrs. Eddington was busy helping the girls with a stitching project."

Sheriff Zembrodt stroked his jaw. "And Lenore mentioned before that they ate the ham and beans for supper. Did they eat anything else?"

"Grover says those who finished supper also ate a piece of apple pie."

"Had you had any apple pie?"

Mae nodded. "Yes. Both Lenore and I had apple pie earlier that day after the noonday meal. I'm not sure about Odin."

"Please ask Grover if they had anything else to eat or to drink with supper."

Mae did as directed. "He says that the only other thing was a glass of milk."

"And was it the milk from the cow Grover milked?"

"Grover says it was mixed with the remainder of the milk from Bessie, the other cow, who'd been milked earlier in the day."

Doc's jaw went slack. "So the milk from the cow Grover milked and Bessie's milk were combined and served at supper?"

Mae signed, and Grover used the hand signal for "yes".

Sheriff Zembrodt sighed. "The milk is what made everyone sick. I presume the colt died prit near immediately, and that if the two different milks had not been mixed, we may have had a worse situation."

The following afternoon, Polly's pale face showed no expression as Mae entered the room Polly shared with the other girls. Mae took Polly's hand in hers, and when Polly's eyes fluttered open, she blinked, a slight recognition in her brown eyes.

Mae assisted her to a sitting position and gave her a sip of water.

Doc's voice sounded from the doorway. "Mae, can I speak with you for a moment?"

She rose and followed the doctor outside the door. The same doctor whom Mae had known ever since she'd first arrived in Horizon all those years ago.

"We need to discuss Polly."

"Yes?" her voice sounded somber in her own ears.

"She continues to grow weaker, likely due to the fact she is unable to retain any food or water."

"I've been diligent in ensuring she has been sipping water. The broth she ate…"

Doc rested a hand on her arm. "I know, Mae. I know you've been trying. I've given her medicine to prevent complications to no avail."

The tears fell freely, and Mae hastily swiped at them. "You don't understand, Doc. It is as if she were my own child."

"Being a pa myself, I do understand what it's like to love a child. There is a chance she will recover, but things look bleak."

"Why is it that she became the sickest?"

Doc shrugged. "I'm not sure. Perhaps she drank more of the milk or the milk she did drink was more highly concentrated with the venom from the bitten cow. Perhaps it wasn't mixed as well with Bessie's milk. It could be that Polly wasn't as healthy as the others before falling ill. I don't honestly know."

"I have been praying."

"That is the best remedy of all."

Mae's shoulders shook. "Please, Doc. You have to do something to save her. She's so young."

"Did you send a telegram to her grandfather?"

"Yes, earlier today. He's elderly and isn't well enough to travel, but I do know he loves and cares for her. I'm not giving up, Doc."

"No, and I wouldn't expect you to. We will have faith that the Lord will heal her fully. However, sometimes it's not in His plan to do so for reasons we don't understand."

Mae choked back the sob that threatened. "Thank you, Doc, for all you're doing."

"I will continue to do all I can to help her recover."

The tears fogged her vision. "May I go back now?"

"Yes, and I'll return to check on her soon after I see to the others. I would be remiss if I didn't remind you to be sure to get some sleep tonight. You'll do Polly no good if you are sick yourself."

Mae would do her best, but she doubted she'd get much sleep again tonight.

That evening, Mae joined the other townsfolk at the church for a prayer meeting Albert had arranged to pray for those who were ill. Most were doing much better, with the exception of some lingering weakness.

Polly continued to struggle with vomiting, nausea, stomach cramps, and fatigue.

"Thank you all for coming. We are gathered here today to lift up those to the Lord who are still suffering from sickness at the Horizon School for the Deaf. Before we pray, Doc will answer any questions." Albert stepped aside and Doc took his place at the front of the church.

"We believe the reason for the illness is the accidental ingestion of rattlesnake venom." When many in the pews gasped, Doc explained how the ingestion happened.

"Is it contagious?" someone asked.

"It is not contagious. You would only have fallen ill if you drank the poisoned milk."

When no other questions were asked, Doc took a seat, and Albert led everyone in prayer. "Dear Heavenly Father, we lift those up to You who remain ill from this unfortunate mishap. We praise You for good health and are even more appreciative of the times our bodies are strong when things such as this occur. Please, Father, heal those who continue to suffer, and we ask that Your healing hand be placed upon them. Give those caring for them wisdom, and give those who love them peace in knowing You are the Great Physician. We especially pray for Polly, who remains the sickest of all. In Jesus' Name we pray, Amen."

Those in attendance chorused their "amens", and many asked if there was anything they could do to assist those already caring for the sick.

Mr. Kleiber, the postmaster, stopped Mae on her way from the church and handed her an envelope. "This came for you today."

"Thank you." Mae didn't recognize the sender's name and tucked it into her pocket.

"Why don't you come home tonight and get some sleep," Mama suggested.

Mae shook her head. "Mama, I must stay with Polly. She needs me."

Mama tucked a stray hair that had fallen from Mae's bun behind her ear. "I know how much you love and care for her."

The thick emotion clogged Mae's throat. "It's as if she were my own."

"I understand. I'll return tomorrow to help."

After Mae arrived at the school, she entered the girls' room and sat beside Polly's bedside. The little girl slept, her mouth open and exposing the gap where two front teeth were just last week. Her blonde hair was plastered to her head, and her thin arms rested at her sides.

She reminded Mae so much of herself before she became a Shepherdson. Mae had been so fragile and petite, so frightened and scared. Just like Polly most of the time.

And just like Polly, Mae hadn't been able to speak as a young child. But unlike Polly, Mae could hear.

Mae fell asleep that night, her constant prayers lifted heavenward.

CHAPTER NINE

MAE HAD JUST FINISHED reading to Polly, translating with sign language and plenty of fingerspelling when she heard a familiar voice downstairs conversing with Mrs. Eddington.

"She's upstairs with Polly. That dear little one still has not fully recovered. I'll take you up to see them."

Mae set the book on the chair, signed to Polly that she would return in a moment, then met Landon just outside the door.

"Hello, Mae."

He was every bit as handsome as she remembered. "Hello, Landon."

"I'm sorry I wasn't here for the prayer meeting. I had some crucial business in Cornwall."

"All is well I trust?"

"We experienced a few setbacks, but nothing that wasn't remedied."

Mrs. Eddington checked Polly's forehead for fever. "She seems to be doing a little better today."

"With your permission, I'd like to take Polly outside."

"While I believe it's a grand idea, she is rather frail."

"I thought we could set her in a chair and surround her with pillows. The fresh air would be so beneficial."

"Indeed."

Mae reached for a chair near the wall. "I'll carry this, and Landon, would you mind transporting Polly? Mrs. Eddington, would you gather the pillows?"

Fifteen minutes later, Polly was settled on the porch. Her head lolled to one side, but for the first time since she'd taken ill, Mae noticed her face brightened slightly.

The sun shone brightly, and the children played in the yard for recess. Landon retreated to the dining area before returning with a lemon."

"I brought an entire crate of these from my recent visit to Cornwall. A peddler there was selling them, and I thought the children would enjoy some lemonade."

"What a delightful idea! I haven't had lemonade since last year when my family traveled to Cornwall for our annual visit to the ice cream parlor. It's somewhat of a tradition, and this most recent time, I ordered a lemonade rather than ice cream. It was wonderful, and I dare say I enjoyed it even more than ice cream."

Landon grinned, and Mae's pulse skittered. She'd missed him in his time away from Horizon. Lenore offered to watch Polly while she and Mrs. Eddington prepared the lemonade. Polly's refusal to eat or drink much would perchance change when she sipped a sample of the delectable beverage.

She had just exited the house with a tray of lemonade when Hosea bolted up the stairs with something in his hands. He perched beside Landon, his eyes sparkling. A tiny chirp sounded, and Hosea pulled his right hand back slightly to reveal a baby chick.

The fluffy buttery-colored bird tilted its head from side to side, and Hosea laughed. Polly reached a weak hand forward and attempted to sign.

In response, Hosea held the bird with an outstretched hand. Polly's face illuminated with joy for the first time in a week as she petted the chick's fluffy head. When offered lemonade moments later, Polly had no qualms about having a small glass.

And on that day as Polly began to heal, God answered yet another prayer.

It was the following Wednesday when Mae remembered the envelope she'd received from Mr. Kleiber at the prayer meeting.

Her family had just finished supper and dishes when she'd returned to the room she shared with Ruby and found the envelope in her top bureau drawer. With all that had occurred in recent days, she'd overlooked it. Mae scrutinized the return names—Mr. and Mrs. Teague—names she did not recognize. She opened the envelope and unfolded the paper inside.

Dear Miss Shepherdson,

We found correspondence from you to Mr. Underwood regarding his granddaughter, Polly, and determined we must contact you immediately. In an unfortunate event, Mr. Underwood passed last week from pneumonia. Would you please let Polly know?

Please accept our condolences.

Sincerely,

Mr. and Mrs. Teague, neighbors of Mr. Underwood

Mae gasped and re-read the letter. Mr. Underwood had passed? Polly was now truly without anyone? Her heart broke for the little girl. While the elderly man's passing was not completely unexpected, it was sorrowful nonetheless. She refolded the correspondence and returned it to the envelope, then prayed for God's wisdom and guidance on how and when to tell Polly. Surely such news should wait as the girl had recently nearly lost her life to the tainted milk.

Ruby entered their room with her usual boisterous movements. "Mae? Is everything all right?"

"Polly's grandfather passed."

"I'm so sorry." Ruby embraced her in a warm hug. "The poor dear, and after all she's been through."

"I don't even think I can tell her yet."

Ruby worried her bottom lip. "Were they close?"

"He'd only been able to visit once since delivering Polly to the school, but yes, I do think they were somewhat close. They were all each other had."

Mae plopped down on the edge of her bed, and Ruby took a seat beside her. "Is Polly doing better since the illness?"

"She still struggles with weakness and tires more easily, but that hasn't stopped her from joining other children at recess. Her appetite has not fully returned, but Doc says that's to be expected. Landon was sweet to bring lemons for lemonade last week, and I think Polly would only drink that if given the chance."

"Sounds like two girls I know who begged Papa for more ice cream during our travels to Cornwall each year. Remember when we discovered we could have two scoops, one of each kind?"

"I do remember and have fond memories of making up games for that lengthy journey to Cornwall. It's an event I wouldn't want to miss."

"Less tedious now with the spur from Ingleville to Cornwall." Ruby reached for Mae's hand. "I'll pray that the Lord will give you the opportunity to tell Polly and for peace and comfort for her."

"Thank you, Rube."

"Certainly."

"Some good news occurred yesterday in that Odin's parents have decided to adopt one of our other orphans. Mr. and Mrs. Eddington, Lenore, and I pray each morning for the children. That those without parents would find permanent homes is one of our prayers." Mae sighed. "Sadly, we will now be adding Polly to those prayers."

"That's wonderful! Odin's parents are kind folks. God has a plan for Polly's life. Perhaps there is a couple that will adopt her."

"You're right. God does have a plan for her life, but it's just so heartbreaking with her losing her only remaining family member."

"It is. I can't imagine. While I know it's not the same, it's a blessing she has you, the Eddingtons, and Lenore. A child couldn't ask for more compassionate teachers."

"Thank you, Ruby. I appreciate that."

"On another topic, that was awfully sweet of Landon to bring lemons to the school." Ruby quirked a brow and tossed Mae a suspicious grin.

"Yes, it was. He purchased them from a peddler during his trip to Cornwall."

"And he just so happened to think of Mae and her students. Definitely a consequential occurrence."

Mae elbowed her sister. "A consequential occurrence? Spoken like a true writer, perhaps?"

"Perhaps. But I do think he fancies you."

"Or he's just a generous, thoughtful, and considerate man."

Ruby shrugged. "That too."

"Regarding being a writer…any news from Mr. O'Kane on your recent articles?"

"Unfortunately, yes. He denied them all. Each and every one." Ruby pursed her lips. "What does a writer have to write to be accepted by the recalcitrant Mr. O'Kane?"

Mae laughed at Ruby's exaggerated presentation. "He is either blinded to exceptional writing, has no funds in the budget to hire someone, or is perhaps a dullard."

"A dullard indeed." Ruby released a dramatic sigh. "I have submitted no less than fifty articles. I am more than willing to fix any issues that need correcting, but he offers no evaluation or assessments."

"Do not give up, Rube. You are a talented writer, and someday, Mr. O'Kane will see that."

"Before or after I'm one hundred and five years old?"

"Preferably before."

She and Ruby laughed again, and Mae was grateful for the temporary diversion from the news of Polly's grandfather.

CHAPTER TEN

RUBY GESTURED FOR MAE to take her seat at the far end of the church pew where her family sat each Sunday. "Age before beauty," quipped Ruby, a favorite saying of hers ever since she'd heard Miss Greta use the line several years ago.

Timothy groaned. "You always say that, Rube. You should think of something new."

"I think it's rather humorous."

"You would."

Mae rolled her eyes. Those two could argue about a blade of grass if given the chance. As the saying went, they were as thick as thieves and always had been, but they rarely agreed on much.

A suspicious grin erupted on Ruby's face. "There's Landon," she whispered.

Mae knew years ago that if she and Ruby ever had to undertake a secret mission, it would not remain secret for long. Not with Ruby's inability to mask her feelings and thoughts. Her eyes sparkled and the dimple in her chin became more prominent.

Mae's eyes met Landon's, and she quickly busied herself as the heat traveled up her cheeks. However, she didn't miss the clandestine glance between her two younger siblings.

"Hi, Landon."

"Hello, Timothy."

"You should go around to the other side and sit on the opposite edge of our pew. Papa likes to sit on this edge next to Mama, who sits next to Ruby, who sits next to me, and I sit next to Mae. But you could sit on the other side."

Leave it to Timothy to underhandedly decide the seating arrangements, even if they'd been the same since Lucy married Hans.

Prior to today, Mae noticed that Landon sat in the far back pew with Miss Greta, the Lieutenant, and two other townsfolk whom Mae did not know well.

Landon offered Timothy a lopsided grin. "I can sit where I sat last week and the week before and the week before that if that would be a more feasible plan."

"Oh, that's not necessary. The seat next to Mae is available," chirped Ruby. "Please, by all means, ambulate to the other side and sit on the edge."

Ambulate?

Just because Ruby fancied herself a writer, she made it her mission to use uncommon words.

Landon's eye again met Mae's, and she nodded. They were friends, after all, and she would welcome the chance to sit by him. Hopefully, her face was no longer the color of a red strawberry. Something about Ruby's and Timothy's insistence on dictating where Landon sat had caused a moment of embarrassment.

Landon took a seat next to her. "Figured I might sit here today. Miss Greta's pew is full of boarders." He tipped his head toward the far back row. Mae turned her attention that way as well and noticed there wasn't an ounce of space left for anyone to sit with the collection of people. "It's good to see that she invited the entire boardinghouse to services today." But when Mae attempted to turn around and face the front of the church again, her head nearly collided with Landon's when he opted to do the same thing.

"Oh!"

Landon chuckled, a pleasing low rumble that she found she liked. Yes, they had become friends since his help when Polly and the other school residents were ill, him surprising them with lemons, and, of course, his spending time eating supper at her parents' home. But sometimes Mae allowed her imagination to drift and she thought of what it would be like for someone like Landon Bennick to fancy her.

Not that he did.

But she would always welcome a new friend. Such treasures weren't always easy to come by, especially for someone more reserved such as herself.

After things settled, Landon faced her again. "I'm looking forward to another of Pastor Albert's informative sermons."

Mae focused her attention on Albert, who was greeting some townsfolk in the aisle. Never had anyone imagined that her rambunctious and at times ornery older brother would become a reverend. He'd engaged in several pranks in school, necessitating Mama and Papa's constant meetings with the teacher. None of his pranks were dangerous or of a criminal sort, but he did fancy himself on finding ways to cause mischief in those days.

Then one day when he was seventeen, things changed. While he'd always loved singing hymns even while not at church—and he'd had a penchant for memorizing large swaths of Scripture—after a meeting with Reverend Marshall, he'd decided to enter the ministry. Two months later, he'd made his intentions known to Velma, Lucy's best friend. Intentions not only to become a pastor, but plans to court her.

Velma agreed without hesitation. Mae recalled overhearing her declare to Lucy her fondness for Albert when she and Lucy were thirteen. Albert denied it when asked by Lucy, but Mae suspected he'd been smitten with Velma for several years as well.

Now Albert and Velma were married with two little ones, and if one didn't *know* Albert's past, they wouldn't know.

Papa stood tall and proud every time he introduced his eldest son and everyone, even those who'd known the Lord for years, asked Albert for biblical guidance because the Lord had ignited a hunger in Albert for His Word. A hunger that caused Albert to read and learn all he could about his Savior. And then share that knowledge with others.

Albert's transformation was just another way of proving miracles still happened.

CHAPTER ELEVEN

"PSST."

Landon turned to see The Lieutenant motioning at him. Before Landon could say a word, the man leaned toward him and said none too quietly, "See that woman over there? She shore is a pretty one."

Landon peered in the direction the man pointed. The only woman in his view was Miss Greta. She swept the boardinghouse porch, the broomcorn scraping across the wood. He gazed in the other direction. Mayor Trabert visited with Hubert from the restaurant. His attention landed on Miss Greta once again. Surely…

"Miss Greta?" he finally asked.

"She'd be the one."

The Lieutenant stood still, his focus solely on the woman as if he were mesmerized.

Landon had heard the saying that beauty was in the eyes of the beholder. Never more did he believe it than he did at this moment. Miss Greta paused and swiped a stray reddish-gray hair from her face.

The Lieutenant held a thick palm to his chest. "She is a sight to behold. Someday I aim to win her heart."

Landon looked from the Lieutenant to Miss Greta, then back to the Lieutenant, who was still swooning.

"She is so purdy and has such a pleasing wit."

Miss Greta had a wit, all right. The woman was as sarcastic as they came.

"And her smile is beautiful."

"Miss Greta has a smile?"

The Lieutenant tossed him a puzzled look, and his gray brows raised into his forehead. "You haven't seen it?"

Landon couldn't say for sure that he had. Her cantankerous personality overwhelmed whatever smile she might have.

"I know I sound like a lovelorn fool, and if you mention this to anyone…" The man squared his shoulders and cracked his knuckles. "Just don't mention it to anyone."

"I won't." Who would Landon tell? Besides, he'd never been one to gossip.

The Lieutenant cocked his head to one side. "You married, kid?"

"No, sir."

The older man scratched his chin. "Reckon you probably don't know much then about how to win a woman's heart."

Mae's image flashed through his mind. What would it be like to win her heart?

Landon was drawn to Mae in a way he couldn't explain. Her compassionate heart, gentle spirit, soft-spoken ways, and love for the Lord intrigued him. Her golden brown hair and full lips captured his attention. The way her sparkling dark blue eyes lit up when she spoke about her family and the fact he'd never met anyone like her before—not at University, in all his travels, and certainly not through Mother's incessant matchmaking activities.

Not that someone like Mae Shepherdson would ever be interested in him. She was as though a rare gem. He recalled sitting beside her in church last Sunday and how that was far more preferable than sitting in Miss Greta's boardinghouse pew. Their heads had nearly collided when they'd turned at the same time…

The Lieutenant socked Landon in the shoulder, nearly knocking him off his feet and interrupting his musings about a lovely brown-haired beauty. "Oh, no. I think she just saw us." The Lieutenant tilted his head and simultaneously whistled while pretending to gaze at a nonexistent cloud in the sky.

Miss Greta briefly ceased sweeping and glowered at them.

The Lieutenant spun Landon around in the opposite direction so fast that Landon nearly lost his balance. "Act like you don't see her."

Landon resisted the urge to look over his shoulder and see if Miss Greta remained glaring in their direction.

"Just walk along normally like nothing is amiss." The Lieutenant gave him a shove forward.

Surely Miss Greta would notice their bizarre behavior, but Landon didn't mention as much.

"Why don't you make your intentions known?"

The Lieutenant's jaw dropped. "Make my intentions known?"

"Yes. How else will she know you fancy her?"

This time the Lieutenant scratched his chin. "Don't rightfully know. Any ideas on how to get her attention?"

Landon didn't mention that the Lieutenant pointing, nodding, and staring at her likely already captured Miss Greta's attention. Although probably not in a good way. The Lieutenant gaped at Landon, his eyes never blinking, while he awaited Landon's answer.

"You could do nice things for her." Landon tugged on his collar, the heat climbing his neck in response to the Lieutenant's intense scrutiny.

The Lieutenant frowned. "I already do nice things for her." He lowered his voice. "Just between us, I do odd jobs around the boardinghouse and deliver customers to her directly from the Horizon stagecoach station in exchange for three square meals a day."

Hadn't Miss Greta informed Landon that only breakfast and supper would be served?

"Does that count as doing nice things for her?"

"I suppose it does."

The Lieutenant flexed his arm muscle, a muscle that was likely brawnier in the man's younger years, and tapped Landon's chest with his finger. "Now don't you tell a soul. Miss Greta made a special provision for me. She doesn't do that for just anyone."

"Your secret is safe."

"Good." The Lieutenant lowered his arm. "Now what other advice do you have for me?"

Landon cleared his throat. "Well, besides doing nice things, maybe you could spend time with her."

"You mean besides at meals?"

"At meals, everyone is there and there's a lot of commotion. Maybe you could take her on a picnic or on a buggy ride."

"Do I look like I take buggy rides?"

The Lieutenant *was* more of a wagon or horseback-type of individual. Landon stood straighter. "Sometimes we have to do things we wouldn't normally do to win the heart of a woman we care about."

"You sure are a smart one." The respect in the Lieutenant's eyes did something to Landon he couldn't explain. "Did you have proper schooling?"

It depended on what one perceived as "proper schooling". At an expensive boarding school all of his formative years with a strict headmaster and scant time for anything but studying and baseball during recess times, then yes, he'd had proper schooling.

"Probably attended a university or such."

Landon had graduated from the prestigious university of which his parents spent a considerable amount of tuition. He'd made it a priority to study hard to earn top grades enabling him to graduate first in his class and make Father proud.

But Father hadn't said a word when Landon graduated.

Not only had Landon not had time for nonacademic activities, but he'd for sure never had time for courtship. Not even to court Orla, whom his parents had planned for him to marry.

"Lost in thought, kid?"

"Uh…" Landon's attention returned to the Lieutenant. "Ask Miss Greta on a picnic."

"And if she says no?"

Landon could envision Miss Greta saying no. She was a cranky one.

"I heard she once loved someone. What if she still loves him?" The Lieutenant shifted from one foot to the other. "I was engaged once. Didn't work out. But that might be a good thing seeing as how Miss Greta has come into my life after all these years. I wouldn't have thought so then, but…" he peered over his shoulder in Miss Greta's direction.

The Lieutenant was smitten. That much was certain. He puffed out his chest and smoothed his beard with a rough, calloused hand that boasted a scar near his thumb. "I might take your advice, kid, and ask her on a picnic. If you see her, would you mind putting in a good word for me?"

Landon wasn't sure he would have any influence over Miss Greta. The woman rarely spoke to him other than to ask questions about when the railroad spur would be completed or to remind him of the boardinghouse rules.

"You will put in a good word for me, won't you?"

Landon wasn't sure Miss Greta would care about his opinion on any matter, but he would help the Lieutenant however he could. "Yes."

"Much obliged for that. Well, as much as I'd like to stand here and chat the day away, I've never been one to chin-wag, so I best be on my way.

The Lieutenant might not *think* he was one to chin-wag, but Landon figured he could chatter a man's ear off just discussing his feelings for Miss Greta.

A thought entered Landon's mind. If he suggested the Lieutenant ask Miss Greta on a picnic, perhaps he should do the same and ask Mae if she'd like to accompany him on one as well.

At the mercantile, Mae innocently perused the sundries when Miss Greta yanked her behind the shelves. "Do you see the Lieutenant over there inspecting the cups, saucers, bowls, and small platters?"

She stretched her neck to the left, and sure enough, the older man examined the area where Tabitha stocked an impressive variety of dishes. Or at least, she thought it was him. Mae squinted for a better look. "I believe so, yes."

"You mustn't allow him to see me." Miss Greta shifted Mae directly in front of her.

Mae wasn't sure Miss Greta's method of hiding would be effective as the woman was twice Mae's width.

"Has he proceeded on his way?"

"No, he's still looking at the dishes, but now he's also speaking with Mayor Trabert."

"Hmmf. Those two could talk until the next century. He needs to move along." Miss Greta crouched behind Mae. "My knees are far too old for this type of adventure," she muttered.

Mae turned her head to face Miss Greta. "Why don't you want him to see you?"

"Ssh! Don't turn this way. Keep your head straight forward."

She did as she was told but repeated her question in a whisper only Miss Greta could hear. "He sees you every day when he's assisting you with errands at the boardinghouse."

"That's different," Miss Greta hissed.

"How so?"

Mae felt Miss Greta's warm breath on her neck and imagined the woman becoming irritated at her numerous inquiries. "I'll tell you forthwith. For now, just make sure you keep me from his view."

Easier said than done as the Lieutenant shifted around the dishes section and meandered toward her and Miss Greta. There was definitely something different about the man. He was clean-shaven, wore new spectacles, and his clothing wasn't the usual long-sleeved tattered military shirt. "Hello, Miss Mae. Good to see you today."

Miss Greta jerked Mae slightly to the left.

"Oh, hello, Lieutenant. Good to see you as well."

"Can he see me behind the shelves?" Miss Greta spoke so quietly that Mae barely heard her.

"I—I'm not sure."

"Pardon?" asked the Lieutenant.

"Oh, nothing, just trying to remind myself what I came into town for." Would he notice her nervous untruth? Well, not entirely an untruth. Miss Greta had temporarily interrupted the mission Mrs. Eddington sent her on.

"You're too young to have memory lapses," grunted the Lieutenant.

Miss Greta murmured, "Ask him if he'll be leaving soon."

"I can't ask him that."

"Yes, you can."

"Miss Mae, no offense meant by this, but you talking to yourself has me rightly concerned." The Lieutenant removed his hat and scratched his head. "You all right?"

"Oh, yes, I am. So, are you about finished here at the mercantile?"

"Yes, just have to take my purchase to the counter, then I'll be on my way. Why do you ask?"

Mae couldn't think of a reasonable response.

"Tell him he's been here too long," snapped Miss Greta.

"I can't tell him that. That would be unbecoming of me."

The Lieutenant narrowed his eyes at her. "You might should go see Doc, Mae. Something ain't quite right with you today."

"Thank you. I will consider that."

With a tilt of his head, he studied her a moment longer before bidding her goodbye. Mae watched as he retrieved a parcel Tabitha wrapped for him. He paid the proprietress, scrutinized Mae one more time, then left the mercantile.

Miss Greta released an enormous breath. "That was nerve-wracking."

"Please do tell me why you didn't want him to see you."

Miss Greta patted her messy coiffure. "I hadn't the time to properly prepare when I left the boardinghouse. I came here to retrieve some spices for tonight's supper and had not contemplated the real possibility of seeing the Lieutenant."

"You see him every day."

"But not looking like this. Mussed from the winds outside. A soiled skirt because I was tending to my flowers, and tired eyes from not sleeping well. What would he think? A man of his handsomeness." She swooned while simultaneously peeking her head to the side and watching the Lieutenant traipse down the boardwalk.

"Dealing with matters of the heart sure ain't for cowards," Miss Greta muttered.

Several days later, Landon entered the foyer of Miss Greta's when he saw the woman standing to the side of the front window peering out. She'd gripped the curtain in one hand and tipped her head toward the window perhaps to get a better look.

"Miss Greta?"

"Ssh!" Miss Greta replaced the curtain and stepped to the side. Her jaw hung suspended and her eyes rounded.

"Is something amiss?" he whispered.

She motioned at him to join her at the window. "Some peculiar man is lurking about on the boardinghouse grounds."

Landon pressed forward for a better view of the yard. "All I see is a squirrel scampering up the oak tree."

Miss Greta scowled at him, the wrinkles lining the area around her mouth becoming more prominent. "Pshaw. I know what I saw. Probably some hoodlum fixing to rob me blind."

"Would you like me to scour the grounds to be sure?"

The woman placed her hands on her wide hips. "That would make me feel better. Either that or fetch the sheriff."

Landon doubted the person outside was causing any mischief, but he'd gladly offer his assistance to ease Miss Greta's apprehension. He left the house and started in the front yard, then rounded the right side. No one. He moseyed to the back, and finally to the left side. Nothing was awry. He'd just stride back into the house and reassure Miss Greta all was well.

Until he felt a hard grip on his shoulder, which nearly toppled him off his feet.

"Aah!" Landon jumped as his heartbeat escalated.

"Scared you, did I?"

He turned slowly to see the Lieutenant standing behind him.

"Yes, you did. How about calling out to me first? You shouldn't be sneaking up on a man like that."

The Lieutenant reluctantly agreed. "You might be right."

Something about the man was different. "Are you attempting to be incognito?"

"Incognito?"

"In disguise?"

"Oh!" The Lieutenant slapped his thigh with a meaty hand. "No. Not trying to be in disguise. Just want to do some impressing is all."

"Impressing?"

"Yes." He leaned closer to Landon and whispered. "I want to impress Miss Greta."

"I see."

"Do you like the new hat and the new plaid shirt?"

Landon had never seen the Lieutenant in anything but his old coat from the war. Before he could answer, the Lieutenant continued. "Got me some new spectacles too, as you can see." He chuckled and playfully slugged Landon in the shoulder again nearly knocking him off his feet. "As you can see. He he."

Round wire spectacles rested on the Lieutenant's nose. Spectacles that didn't fit his overly round and leathery face. "When did you get those?"

"Just yesterday. Was seeing things all fuzzy-like so I went to see Doc. He gave me these." He shook his head. "I thought Miss Greta was a pretty woman before, but after seeing her more clearly, she truly is a lovely sight. Spied her by the window peeking out a few minutes ago and almost couldn't take my eyes off her."

So the Lieutenant *had been* the one lurking around the boardinghouse grounds. Miss Greta hadn't recognized him with his new hat pulled lower on his head, his new shirt, and his spectacles. Unless, of course, she needed spectacles too. "Have you asked Miss Greta on a picnic yet?"

The Lieutenant lowered his head. "Naw. Not yet. Too afraid she'll say no."

"How will you know if you don't ask?"

"Can't expect a young kid like you to understand this, but when a man enters his seventh decade, things change." He patted his rotund stomach. "I'm not as—what's the word—svelte? Yeah, that's it. I'm not as svelte as I once was. There's more of me now."

"I don't think Miss Greta will concern herself about that."

"That's not my only worry. She'll likely say she can't leave the boardinghouse to go on a picnic, what with folks needing her and all."

The Lieutenant's furrowed brow told of his many worries. Who knew such an otherwise confident, somewhat arrogant man would have doubts about anything? "It's only for a few hours. Surely she can be away for that long."

"And what if..." the older man tossed a wistful gaze at the house.

Landon followed his gaze and noticed Miss Greta again peering out the window.

"She shore is a pretty thing. What if she'll not consider someone like me?"

"You're a war hero, are you not?"

The Lieutenant puffed out his chest. "I am."

"You're generous and do your best to help others, right?"

"I try."

"She may already like you."

"You think so?" The spectacles slipped further down the Lieutenant's narrow nose.

"Yes, I do. But you'll never know what she thinks of you if you don't ask her on a picnic."

The man's eyes darted to Miss Greta, then back to Landon, then to Miss Greta again. "She does seem to be staring at me with interest."

Oh, it's with interest all right. She's afraid you'll commit a theft and steal all she owns. But Landon didn't verbalize his thoughts. "I would take her a small gift and ask her."

"A small gift?"

"Yes, something that will make her more inclined to agree to your suggestion."

The Lieutenant squinted. "You talking about a bribe? I don't agree with bribes."

"Not a bribe. Just something to let her know you're thinking of her."

"You sure are wise for your age, kid. What would you suggest?"

"Something that would mean something to her. Nothing big, just a token of your affection."

The older man waved a hand at Landon. "You might be one of those romantic sorts, but not me."

"You want to win Miss Greta's heart, do you not?"

"I do."

"Then take my advice." While Landon attempted to be self-assured about the counsel he offered the Lieutenant, there was a degree of trepidation in offering guidance on a topic he himself knew little about.

"All right. I think I can figure something out. Thanks for your help, kid."

"Anytime."

The Lieutenant rushed away, and Landon pondered how he'd answer Miss Greta's inquiry about the hoodlum on the boardinghouse grounds.

Chapter Twelve

Mae couldn't sleep. She replayed in her mind over and over Landon asking her to join him for a picnic. She welcomed the thought of spending more time with him. And now, at eleven o'clock at night with a full day at school ahead of her tomorrow, she found sleep difficult to attain.

She left the room she shared with Ruby and shuffled to the kitchen for a glass of water. As she was about to tiptoe toward the pitcher on the table, she noticed Mama and Papa on the sofa in front of the fireplace. Papa's arm was draped around Mama, and she snuggled into him.

Tears misted her eyes. These two people had adopted her as their daughter. A little girl who, for some time, couldn't find words to speak. A little girl no one else wanted.

Mae recalled the dozen or so times when she, Lucy, and Albert had been taken to a variety of towns between New York and Idaho in the hopes they would find a family to adopt them. There were three times when Mae watched as folks attempted to adopt Lucy and Albert. Both times, Lucy had grabbed Albert's and Mae's hands, stuck out her bottom lip, and dug her heels into the church's floor. "We are adopted together or we ain't adopted at all," she'd said.

Potential parents were dismayed by her lack of respect and haughty tongue. And as such, all three times, they chose other children.

And while Mae hadn't realized it then, God had blessed her with a sister and brother who would always be there for her.

When their second parents adopted them and died soon after, it affected Mae more than she, at four years old, had realized at the time. Mama and Papa then adopted them, but Mae fretted they might die as well.

It would be several years before she would fully allow herself to be loved by her forever parents.

Now, as she stood, unbeknownst to them, watching and listening to their conversation, the tears slid down her cheeks. How could it be that the Lord had been so good to her? Not only had He seen fit to allow her the blessing of Mama and Papa, but also another brother and sister.

Mae plodded closer as Mama spoke.

"She is a grown woman of twenty-three."

"I know, Paisley. I just…with Mae, it's different. We've always felt the need to protect her more so than the others. Lucy and Ruby, they are so…"

"Independent? Strong? Of course, who knows what may happen when a man decides to pursue Ruby."

Papa chuckled. "True. He might be in for a surprise seeing as how opinionated our youngest daughter can be."

"And, of course, you'll be ensuring he's the right one for our vibrant redhead."

"You're right. But still, it's different with Mae."

"It's because Mae's our tender one. Our delicate little bird. Our one who loves deeply and feels the hurts of others as if it were her own pain."

It wasn't the first time Mae had heard Mama and Papa refer to her as their "delicate little bird". She'd always found love, protection, and security in them. Mae knew she wasn't independent and outspoken like Lucy or self-sufficient and capable like Albert. She knew she wasn't funloving, vivacious, and a bit obstinate at times like Ruby or composed, yet stubborn like

Timothy. She was more fragile and sensitive than her sisters and brothers. But not fragile in a feeble way, but more so in a vulnerable way.

"That's true," said Papa. "Do you remember when she first became ours?"

Mama snuggled deeper into Papa's arm. "I do."

"We just don't know a lot about Landon."

"We didn't know much about Hans at first."

Papa leaned his head to the side and rested it against Mama's. "Yes, but he and Lucy had a lengthy courtship, and he was here nearly every evening for supper."

"He missed his family something awful. But look at what a wonderful husband and father he is. I'm so thankful Lucy and Albert both found godly spouses. Besides, just because Landon asks if he might take Mae on a picnic doesn't mean he'll be asking for her hand in courtship or marriage."

"That's one of the many things I love about you, Paisley. Your wisdom."

Mama's light laughter brought a smile to Mae's face as well. While Mama was often what Papa would term "the voice of wisdom", everyone knew Mama worried just as much as Papa did about things, if not more.

"And one of the many things I love about you is your protective nature when it comes to our children."

Papa placed a kiss on the top of Mama's head. "I reckon you're right about me not worrying *yet* about Landon's intentions. But he doesn't permanently live here and likely has a wanderlust that will take him to many places for many years before he marries and has children. What of Mae when he decides to leave?"

"Perhaps he doesn't have the wanderlust some young men possess."

"I once possessed that restlessness. But then I found the best blessing God could give a man. You."

It was Mama's turn to plant a kiss on Papa's cheek, and Mae slid out of view in case Mama saw her from her side-eye. "And I am blessed to have you."

Mae had never known her father to be such a romantic sort, but she supposed he would be seeing as how he and Mama had a solid and godly marriage. Not a perfect marriage, but a faithful one.

Silence ensued for a few moments before Mama spoke. "I, too, worry about Mae's tender heart being broken, but hopefully that won't be the case. I think Landon is an upstanding young man."

"An upstanding young man who might be in love with our daughter."

Mama's low laughter floated in the air again. "That may well be the case. But he'll do well to mind himself if he wants the approval of a strong and protective father. I mentioned to Ruby and Timothy that we would like them to accompany Mae."

"And let me guess…Ruby said she would be happy to as it would give her another chance to interview Landon about his travels for an upcoming story she hopes to submit to Mr. O'Kane."

"As a matter of fact, she did mention that. And our son grumbled a bit at my request."

Mae slithered into the kitchen, poured a glass of water from the pitcher, and snuck back to bed, although she knew she was no closer to being able to fall asleep due to the anticipation of spending time with Landon Bennick.

Was it common for a man to be slightly nervous when he took a woman he fancied on a picnic? Or was it the mere fact that the woman's younger sister and brother would be accompanying them and likely ensuring he was suitable for their sister?

Either way, if Landon continued to tap on his knee the entire time while maneuvering the buggy one-handed to the Shepherdson farm, he'd soon wear a hole in his trousers.

The house came into sight, and Landon slowed the four-seated buggy he'd rented from the livery. Would he think of enough things to say to maintain the conversation? Would Mae think him a dolt? And why was he nervous anyhow? This wasn't the first time they'd met or even conversed.

He wanted to impress her. Wanted her to think he was worthy of her. Not in a courtship way as it was far too soon to entertain such a thought. But Landon did want Mae to hold him in high esteem.

No wonder the Lieutenant suffered a severe case of apprehension at asking Miss Greta on a picnic and hadn't yet done so.

Landon was no different.

Mae's brother, Timothy, stood outside the house resembling a lanky sentinel. Landon had the urge to salute him.

He doubted the young man anticipated the chore of accompanying his sister on a picnic.

"Hello, Timothy."

"Hi, Landon. I'll retrieve the women."

Timothy disappeared into the house. Ruby followed him out all the while batting at him because Timothy was tugging on her hair ribbon.

Landon chuckled to himself. If his parents had decided to have a daughter, would Landon pester her the way Timothy pestered Ruby?

Timothy hoisted a basket into the buggy, and the two younger Shepherdsons climbed aboard, Ruby seemingly giving Timothy a stern lecture.

Mae opened the house door, called something to her mother, then stepped outside.

Her beauty stole his breath, and Landon had to force his starved lungs to draw air.

"Uh, Mae, hello, Mae." In his own ears he sounded like a dullard with only empty space between his ears. He persuaded his legs to heed the command of climbing from the buggy to assist her.

"Hello, Landon."

Her voice. So gentle. So sweet.

"Allow me." He assisted her into the buggy, then walked around to his side. "I have just the place in mind for our picnic." Good. He'd found his vocal cords again.

"Really?"

The anticipation in her deep blue eyes commanded his attention as he beckoned the horses. Her smile, so lovely and so dainty, captivated him. As though this were the first time he'd ever laid eyes on her.

The result of Landon's ridiculous inattentiveness caused the buggy to veer to the left off the side of the road and into the field. It bumped along, jostling its passengers. Mae gripped his arm with one hand and the side of the buggy with the other as the wheels connected with lumps of hardened earth and bounced to and fro. So distracted was he that it took Landon far longer than it should have to attempt to right the buggy. "Whoa!" he tried slowing the horses, but they bumbled along as if this were the grandest of adventures, tottering right into the ditch.

The buggy slanted to the left as gravity threatened.

"Should I jump out and help right the buggy?" Timothy asked. Without waiting for Landon's reply, he clambered from the buggy.

Meanwhile, Mae slid toward him as the buggy drove half in the ditch and half out, its spindly wheels trudging laboriously through the caked mud and shallow water from last night's rain.

"This would make a riveting story," quipped Ruby, who was likely the only one not bothered by the current events.

"Whoa!" he beckoned the horses again, and this time, they obeyed. The buggy stopped, severely angled into the ditch. "We best disembark." Ruby leaped from the back, and in one fell swoop, Landon encircled Mae's waist with his hands and rescued her just as the buggy tipped completely over into the trench.

One minute she was bouncing along in the buggy seat attempting not to career overboard, and the next she was swooped into strong arms and set firmly on solid ground.

Landon's hands were planted firmly on her waist, holding her safely from the danger of the murky ditch water. She peered into his eyes, her breath quickening at their closeness. "Thank." She attempted to utter the completion of the statement, but her words lodged in her throat as a swarm of butterflies caused her stomach to flutter.

"Pardon me." Landon released her and took a step back.

"I've never nearly tipped over in a buggy before," said Ruby. She'd retrieved her notebook and was writing furiously with her pencil. "Once upon a time…"

"Once upon a time?" Timothy shook his head. "This isn't a dime novel." He scowled at Ruby before addressing Landon. "I think we can pull the buggy from the mud."

"If it isn't too entrenched."

"Oh, dear." Mae noticed two soggy sandwiches submerged in the muddy water.

Timothy scrambled to the basket. "Are the cookies all right?"

"Leave it to Timothy to be far more concerned than necessary about cookies." Ruby continued to write, the scratching of the pencil competing with the sounds of cows lowing nearby.

Landon rescued the basket. "The blanket needs a good washing, but two pails are still inside." He rested it safely away from the ditch. "Ready, Timothy?"

Timothy joined him, and together they attempted to push the buggy from its upended position. After several endeavors, they succeeded. Mud caked both men's trousers and boots.

"This might be as good a place as any for our picnic." Landon pointed to a shady grove of oak trees. "Would that be amenable to you, Mae?"

"I reckon it would suffice," muttered Timothy.

"Since Landon was speaking to Mae and not to you..." Ruby ribbed her brother, and he responded with a glower.

"Yes, this would be fine."

"Timothy, let's relocate those large rocks to an area beneath the trees for the ladies to sit on."

While the men moved the rocks, Mae and Ruby salvaged what they could from the basket, and using it as a table, set four place settings atop it. After Timothy led the prayer, they ate the apple slices and cookies.

"This will certainly be a noonday meal to remember." Mae wasn't sure she'd ever eaten just cookies and apple slices for a meal.

Landon grinned at her, and her heartbeat raced. Why was it that today she was more nervous around him? "Yes, that's true. Did you get enough cookies, Timothy?"

Her brother stuffed his final allotment into his mouth and wiped the crumbs from his hands. When he'd finished chewing, he nodded. "It'll do."

"Timothy would only eat cookies if given the chance." Mae playfully jabbed her brother in the shoulder.

"There's nothing wrong with that. Mama says I'm a growing boy, and I need my sustenance."

Ruby ate another apple slice. "Someday you'll be one of those one types of men."

"What types of men?"

"The types with skinny limbs and a rotund stomach."

Mae inclined toward Landon on her right. "Leave it to Ruby to accurately describe one's physical appearance."

"It's what happens when you're a writer. You're constantly looking for different ways to describe one's attributes, and the best way to do that is to become adept at watching folks."

"And staring. Like you are always doing," Timothy admonished.

"I don't stare. Do I stare, Mae-Mae?"

"Actually, yes. It all started when you were a young'un. I suppose even then you were looking for characters for your short stories."

Ruby shrugged. "You could be right. When I write articles—articles I surely wish Mr. O'Kane would accept for *The Horizon Herald*—I pen a complete characterization of those real people. However, when it's a fictional piece, I have no choice but to take certain attributes from unsuspecting individuals and write them into my future novel."

Her sister's serious demeanor caused a round of laughter. Landon took a bite of his last cookie. "Spoken like a true writer. Ruby, don't give up on Mr. O'Kane accepting your work. Unfortunately, some editors don't at first see the value in an article."

"Thank you, Landon."

"I would encourage you to continue writing your articles and to continue submitting them. I have a friend from University—who, finally after much diligence—had his first piece accepted."

"I suppose I'm slightly hindered by the fact that I wish to remain in Horizon rather than live elsewhere."

"Perhaps so."

Mae appreciated Landon's assistance with Ruby's heartfelt dream. "I don't think there's a Shepherdson who doesn't wish to remain in Horizon. We all love it here."

"I can see why. It's a pleasant town. I know Mae's dream has come to fruition with working at the school. But what about you, Timothy? What are your ambitions?"

"To eat cookies, cakes, pies, pastries, and the like," offered Ruby.

Timothy ate a crumb that had fallen on the basket. "For once you're right, Ruby. I do aspire to eat. However, I also hope to be a farmer like Pa. My dream is to purchase a spread of land and plant corn and spuds."

"That'll work well," said Landon, "because with the railroad, you'll be able to ship your crops to market easier."

"To market?"

"Yes. You'll likely produce more than you can use. Folks in cities will need the fine corn and potatoes you can provide."

Timothy sat up straighter. "Reckon you're right. Thanks, Landon."

"And in the midst of it all, someday you'll fall in love." Ruby placed a hand to her heart and swooned.

"Absolutely not. I'll be too busy farming to fall in love. You're the one who's always swooning, Rube."

That caused another round of laughter before Ruby eyed Mae, then Landon. "Come along, Timothy Tyler Shepherdson. Let's pick some dandelions for Mama's jelly."

"Men don't pick flowers."

"You will be. Besides, someday you'll pick them for some girl you set your cap for. Might as well get some practice."

"Like I said, I'll be too busy farming to set my cap for anyone, and I'll for sure be too busy to pick flowers. Besides, I'm too old for such ridiculous chores. You sure are bossy."

"That's because I'm the eldest."

"You're not the oldest. Albert's the oldest."

Ruby jutted her chin toward their brother. "I'm the eldest of the two of us, and no matter how tall you grow, you'll always be my little brother."

Timothy crossed his arms. "You're impossible, Rube."

Ruby stood. "Come along, Timothy. No time for wasting. Grab a pail."

Mae discerned that Ruby was attempting to give her and Landon some time alone while they stayed nearby picking dandelions. It would be a welcome gesture to have some time with Landon without the constant bickering between her sister and brother.

"All right, all right. I don't understand why you're so bossy. If you ever become smitten with some man, he'll run the other way."

"There is no one in Horizon that has captivated me." Ruby lifted her head in pride.

The two walked to the far edge of the area where plentiful yellow flowers peeped above the grass and weeds.

"Those two. Please do excuse their quarreling."

"I don't have sisters and brothers, so they're somewhat of a novelty."

Mae giggled. "Oh, they're a novelty all right. I suppose it doesn't help that they're only fourteen months apart. Ruby is eighteen and Timothy just turned seventeen a few months ago."

"I'm curious. Why does your family call you Mae-Mae?"

"It's an affectionate name my parents gave me years ago, and it somehow remained even after all this time."

The corners of his eyes crinkled with his broad grin.

Oh, but Landon Bennick was a handsome sort! Far beyond her station and would likely never be interested in a woman such as herself, but he was dapper. And kind too. "Thank you for encouraging Ruby with her writing and Timothy with his farming."

"My pleasure. I believe everyone needs a bit of encouragement from time to time." Something indiscernible crossed his face. Sadness, perhaps? "My apologies for the buggy incident. I was hoping to have a much smoother ride."

"No harm done, and it makes for fond memories."

And as she said the words, Mae knew she would never forget this day.

CHAPTER THIRTEEN

LANDON REQUIRED A BREAK from reading the map, studying grade steepness, and preparing numbers and figures for the business. He pushed himself away from the makeshift desk at Miss Greta's and stood and stretched. The conclusive plans were to continue the line from Ingleville to Horizon, making it possible to travel all the way from the other side of Cornwall to Horizon by rail. The tentative plans were to extend the line from Horizon to the next town on the map—Humboldt. There had also been discussion of creating a spur at the crossroads of Horizon and Varner City.

Even if only the Humboldt line progressed, Landon would be working in the area into next year at the very least. He would undertake other duties for Bennick Railways during the winter months but would return to Idaho next spring. In that case, he would appreciate a place to reside while conducting business in this part of the state. Not that he minded staying at Miss Greta's. The meals sufficed and the humble room with overly-wallpapered flowery walls wasn't so bad.

But perhaps he ought to purchase a temporary home, then when he moved away from Idaho for good, he could sell the property.

Father would expect Landon to be ambitious and industrious and to plan for the future.

Landon greeted passersby as he strode down the board-walk to the bank. He'd met Mr. Woodham, the banker, only once when Landon addressed the town.

"Mr. Bennick, what can I do for you?"

"I need to discuss a private matter with you."

"Oh?" Mr. Woodham's fuzzy single eyebrow rose into his wrinkled forehead.

"Yes, but first, I would need your assurance that what we speak of will remain between us."

"Absolutely. What can I help you with?"

"Do you have any property for sale?"

Mr. Woodham scrutinized Landon a moment before responding. "You planning to move to Horizon?"

"Not permanently, sir. However, I have business in the area at least until the end of next year and perchance into the unforeseeable future."

"You don't cotton to staying at Miss Greta's?"

"It's a fine place to stay, but if I'm to reside here temporarily for such an expanse of time, a home might better serve me. When Bennick Railways has completed their undertakings, I will sell the property." Landon didn't wish for his plans to cause an uproar with Miss Greta or in the community.

"I see. Well, interesting you should ask because I do have a couple of properties available. Three, in fact. One is a foreclosure. Regrettably, I do not have many available as Bennick Railways has purchased a great deal of land in recent months for the railroad."

"I'd be interested in hearing of the opportunities you do have available."

The banker gave a clipped nod. "Very well, then. The first is a foreclosure just south of town. It consists of one hundred and sixty acres and includes a frame dwelling farmhouse, barn, corral, and fifty acres under cultivation. The owners were unable to make the payments. Unfortunately, there was some damage to the home and barn before the residents left town."

"How much damage?"

"Significant. Mr. Gangi possessed a volatile temper, and while I did my utmost best within the constraints of my job to co-operate with him, he would have none of it. When the bank foreclosed after several months of nonpayment, Mr. Gangi took it upon himself to break windows in the house, uproot crops, and put holes in the barn walls."

"Seeing as how I'll be occupied with my work for the railways, I won't have sufficient time to mend or oversee the mending of the property. What else do you have for sale?"

"The second one may suit your purposes much better. The Toscano property is just past the livery on the right-hand side of the street and includes a 60'x20' lot with a modest dwelling that includes all household goods and two fruit trees. Mr. Toscano recently passed, and his son, who resides in Montana, wishes to sell the property at the cheap price of $800. Would you care to see it?"

"Would that be the white house with a porch on two sides?"

"That would be the one."

While such a place might be suitable, Landon had more in mind. "And the third one?"

"This one might be more to your preference. Are you familiar with the Shepherdson farm?"

Landon's stomach plummeted. "The Shepherdson Farm? Surely that's not for sale?" He thought of how hard the family worked. Were they unable to afford to remain there?

"No, it's not. Although if it were, I'd likely sell it a dozen times over. Rather, the Hill property is one mile past the Shepherdson farm.

He drew out a lengthy exhale of relief. "One mile past?"

"Yes. Mrs. Hill, a mail-order bride, met Mr. Hill through an advertisement and subsequent correspondence. Mr. Hill purchased the 160-acre property and built the house some six years ago and did his best to provide a welcoming place Mrs. Hill would be proud to call home." Mr. Woodham pressed the sleeve of his jacket. "I don't wish to be a chattering hen, but it's probably best you know the circumstances behind the availability of this farm. Mrs. Hill, who hailed from Massachusetts, did not cotton to what she termed as the 'dreary hovel in an uncivilized town'. Mr. Hill could have annulled the marriage, and his wife could have returned to Massachusetts, but he was besotted with her and instead left Horizon and moved with her back East."

"Interesting story."

"Indeed. So while the farm is pricier than most, it offers much. It consists of 150 fruit-bearing prune and apple trees, raspberry bushes, thirty acres of timothy hay, and thirty-two acres of wheat. If one would like, they could cultivate more than the already-cultivated acres and grow spuds or corn. The Horizon River runs adjacent to the property on the southernmost end. The land reaches the face of the mountains, and it boasts a small house, barn, some livestock, a granary, cattle shed, and a cellar beneath the house. It is priced at $4,000. Would you care to see it?"

The steep price was attainable, and this acreage was by far the best that Mr. Woodham had thus presented. "Yes, sir, I would like to see it."

"As I mentioned, it is a mile past the Shepherdson farm. If you reach a yellow house on the left, you've gone too far."

"Thank you, Mr. Woodham." Landon shook the man's hand. "Please don't tell anyone about this."

"You have my word. Do let me know your contemplations and if you would be interested in purchasing it."

"I will. Thank you for your time."

Landon drove the buggy east of Horizon as Mr. Woodham indicated. When he arrived at the farm, he slowed, parked, and climbed from the buggy, eager to see the land.

Tucked near a grove of aspens was a small cabin. Well-maintained with a porch, an attic, and shutters on the two side windows, the home had a welcoming charm. He stepped onto the lone step, then to the porch, and peered inside. Mostly empty, but tidy, it boasted only an old round table and two open shelves, on one of which sat a can of peaches.

A shame Mrs. Hill decided she no longer wanted to live there. However, Landon knew such women, well-bred and from wealthy families, would never be content residing in such a place. He thought of Orla. As nice as she was, a cabin in the middle of nowhere would not interest her.

Landon continued to the back of the house when he abruptly halted. He'd never before seen a view like the one before him.

High mountaintops in the distance met timbered hills, which met gently rolling farmland. The sun shone on the mountains, contrasting the tallest white-tipped peaks and the green prairies just below. Western white pines littered the face of the mountains.

It was God's country, plain and simple, and for Landon, the choice of whether or not to purchase it was a simple one. He'd climb back into the buggy and make an offer Mr. Woodham couldn't refuse.

But first, he'd take a perusal around the grounds.

True to the banker's description, fruit trees and raspberry bushes were in great supply. The fields of timothy and grain waved at him as if beckoning him to purchase the land forthwith before anyone else could make an offer. He climbed in the buggy and stopped at the edge of the southernmost edge of the property near the Horizon River.

Wildflowers greeted him, their perky faces smiling at the sky above. He pivoted to see the house, corrals, granary, and barn in the distance before striding alongside the rushing crystal clear waters.

Birds chirped, a woodpecker made his presence known, and a bald eagle flew overhead. Aspens whispered on the breeze, and a frog croaked. Landon closed his eyes and inhaled the aroma of a nearby lilac bush.

A crying sound caused him to fling open his eyes and peer in the direction of the noise. He traipsed amongst the tall weeds and willow trees for what he believed was a dog.

Sure enough, in a matted area by some rocks near the riverbank, a brown, black, and white animal rested, his head on his paws.

"Hey, little fellow." Landon crouched nearby, but far enough away in case the dog was unfriendly.

The animal's disheveled and dirty fur, along with abrasions, and his emaciated body struck Landon with a disturbing thought.

The creature had been neglected, abused, and left for dead.

But by whom? And when?

Landon removed his coat and slowly started toward the animal. "Easy, there. I'm going to help you."

His words were met with a sorrowful whine and woebegone brown eyes staring up at him.

He continued to talk softly and inch closer. Would the dog survive if he rescued him?

Landon smoothed his coat on the ground and prepared to lift the animal onto it. Even closer now, the bloody wounds and scruffy fur tore at his heart. *Lord, give me wisdom.*

The dog growled when Landon attempted to reach for him. "It's all right. I'm not going to hurt you."

Finally, after several minutes of coaxing, Landon lifted the wrapped dog into his arms and headed to the buggy.

Miss Greta would never allow him to keep the dog at the boardinghouse. But where else could he take him? The dog emitted a painful cry every time the buggy inadvertently hit a bump.

"You'll need a name, that's for certain," he said, doing his best to calm the animal.

When Landon was a young'un, he'd longed for a pet. Father insisted he'd never be responsible enough to care for one. Landon begged and groveled until his father punished him by sending him to his room without supper.

The boy down the street had a dog named Beans. A golden retriever who accompanied him on walks, fetched when the boy threw the ball, and provided constant companionship. Fighting the envy that settled in his heart, Landon this time attempted to persuade Mother to allow him to adopt a pet. Any pet. He'd even be content with an amphibian.

Mother deferred to Father, and Father told him to never ask again.

So Landon hadn't. But that didn't quash the yearning.

"Beans. That name suits you."

At the declaration, Beans lifted his head slowly. Was that a dog smile on his face? "You agree with me on the name, boy?"

But no matter what Landon named him, if the dog didn't survive the horrendous mistreatment he'd suffered, it would be for naught.

As he passed the Shepherdson farm, a thought occurred to him. He'd ask if they could temporarily care for the animal. As tenderhearted as Mae was, she'd presumably agree to his suggestion.

And if not? He'd have to ask around Horizon for an alternative.

Landon steered the buggy into the entrance of the farm. Mr. Shepherdson fixed the fence just on the outskirts, and Landon slowed to a stop.

"Hello, Landon." Mr. Shepherdson's gaze veered to the animal on the buggy seat.

"Hello, sir. I found this injured dog and was wondering if your family would be willing to assist in caring for him until I can find a permanent home."

Mr. Shepherdson's brow creased. "Appears he's been abused."

"Yes. Those were my thoughts as well. I found him near the river."

"By all means, bring him to the barn. We'd be happy to help."

Mae was hanging laundry, and for a moment Landon forgot all about why he was here when she smiled and waved.

The woman captivated him.

Best he concentrate on Beans.

He put on the brake and climbed down just as Mae met him. "Hello, Mae."

"Hello, Landon."

Her sweet smile stole his breath.

Beans whined, and Mae hurried to the side of the buggy. "Oh, you poor dear." Without a second thought, she scooped him into her arms and carried him to the barn. "What happened to him?"

"I found him near the river. It appears his owner—or someone—abused him."

Mae set Beans on the barn floor, and Mr. Shepherdson and Timothy joined them.

"Timothy, would you please fetch Doc?"

Mr. Shepherdson kneeled beside the dog. "We'll see what Doc has to say. We've had many pets but never one who came to us in this condition."

"I decided to name him Beans." Landon thought again of the friendly golden retriever from his youth.

"Beans?" Mae folded over part of Landon's coat and covered the animal. "The name suits him." She patted him lightly on the head. "I can't imagine why anyone would want to harm an innocent animal. I think I'll bring him some milk."

When she did, Beans lapped up the beverage as if he hadn't had something to quench his thirst in years.

An hour later, Doc arrived. "Can't say as I get a lot of dog patients," he said. Beans uttered a growl before calming. "Just going to help you feel better," Doc soothed.

He carefully cleaned Beans's fur and spread salve on the abrasions. Mae retrieved some food from the house but Beans ate so rapidly, Doc feared he'd overeat and cause further complications. He instead suggested Mae offer small portions periodically throughout the day. "Sometimes when dogs are underfed and malnourished, they will eat in excess because they've been previously forced to eat whatever they can find out of the fear food will no longer be available."

Worry creased Mae's brow. "Do you think he will be all right?"

"Thankfully Landon rescued him when he did. I'm hopeful the physical wounds will heal. The emotional ones will take longer, but with all the love and care showered on him, Beans will be just fine. Although it will take time."

When Landon left an hour later, Beans was resting his head on Mae's arm. No doubt the two had formed an immediate friendship.

He bid the Shepherdsons and Doc farewell with a promise to check on Beans tomorrow. Minutes later, Landon parked the buggy just outside the bank. He waited for the two other customers to leave before telling Mr. Woodham, "I'd like to make an offer on the Hill property."

CHAPTER FOURTEEN

MAE EAGERLY AWAITED LANDON'S arrival for supper the following Friday. Ruby had interview questions ready for Landon, this time regarding the process by which railroads were built, and after supper, Landon invited her for a stroll. He offered his arm, and they started down the road just past the barn and stopped at the bench Papa built for Mama beneath the cottonwood tree. The air smelled of hay, and an American goldfinch tweeted happily from the tree above.

"Thank you for taking the time to answer Ruby's multitude of questions."

"You're welcome. I'm happy to help her gain experience. I think with some practice, she'll do well as a reporter."

"I'll share with her that you said that." Mae thought of Ruby's tenacity when it came to writing. While only eighteen, Ruby's writing surpassed what was already published in *The Horizon Herald*, at least in Mae's opinion.

"How is Polly?"

"It's as though she'd never taken ill. Thankfully her appetite has returned as she lost so much weight while sick."

"That's good to hear. And Beans?"

As if the dog knew he was the topic of discussion, he propped his paws on Landon's leg and wagged his tail.

"He's doing well too. I am so thankful you found him. He's become a member of the family." Realization dawned. "I'm sorry. I know he's yours, but until you can care for him..." Mae had attempted not to become attached to the mild-mannered and lovable beagle, but her endeavors were for naught. She and Beans formed a bond unlike any she'd experienced with the many animals her family raised through the years.

Landon faced her. Beans tilted his head from side to side and uttered a curious bark. "When's your birthday?"

"May tenth."

"Consider Beans a belated birthday present for this year or an early one for next year."

"Oh, Landon, I couldn't."

"Sure you can. That is, *if* you want him." The teasing glint in Landon's eyes caused a flutter in her belly.

"Oh, I definitely do want him." She patted her leg, and Beans needed no further encouragement. He leaped into her lap. "Thank you."

"My pleasure. And I'm glad he found a home here."

His face was so close to hers that she could see the orange flecks in his twinkling blue-green eyes. Her heart skittered. Landon Bennick was a handsome man with his rugged charm. He was also a kindly man who cared for others. Mae had noted that from the beginning when he insisted on helping with those taken ill at the school.

She realized she was staring, and quickly averted her gaze to a loose thread on her skirt, hoping Landon didn't notice the surge of heat that climbed her face. "Oh! I almost forgot," she said once she recovered. "I have something in the house for you to borrow. Wait right here."

Without awaiting Landon's response, Mae lifted Beans from her lap then leaped from the bench and hurried to the house. She returned minutes later with a book. "You know how you mentioned your determination to learn sign language?"

"Yes."

"I thought you might want to borrow this book. Mrs. Eddington keeps a few copies on the shelf for those parents or members of the community who wish to learn the language." She situated the thick book into his waiting palms.

Landon smoothed a hand over *The Book of Sign Language.*"

"Thank you, Mae. This will be immensely helpful."

The fact that he desired to learn to communicate with the children warmed her heart even more. "The children will be so pleased, especially Hosea. He very much enjoys 'talking'."

"I best get to learning then."

They sat for a moment partaking in the golden hues of the sunset. What would it be like to sit with him each evening? Mae dismissed the fanciful notions. While she was fond of the man, she knew he wouldn't be residing in Horizon after the railroad's completion. With effort, she pushed the dismal sentiments aside. She'd not allow anything to ruin this special time together. "What made you decide to name the dog Beans?"

A shadow crossed his face before Landon answered. "When I was a young'un, I always wanted a pet. Unfortunately, my parents disagreed with me. However, a boy down the street from our home had a golden retriever named Beans. I would see him walking the dog and playing fetch with it in the yard. The two seemed inseparable. Beans sounded like the perfect name for this dog."

At his name, Beans licked Landon's hand, and Landon scratched behind his ears. "You like that name, don't you, boy?"

Beans yipped in response.

"Are you certain you want to give him to me?"

"I'm certain."

"It's a thoughtful gesture, so again, thank you."

"Again, you're welcome. On another note, I believe the Lieutenant fancies Miss Greta."

"Miss Greta certainly fancies him."

"Really?"

"Indeed."

Landon chuckled. "He asked for my advice awhile back, and I suggested he do nice things for her."

"Oh, he already does that. He fixes everything around the boardinghouse and tends to the animals and other necessary tasks. He also delivers unsuspecting visitors from the stage to Miss Greta's, thereby bringing her more customers."

"You know about that?"

The question in Landon's gaze caused Mae to giggle. "Yes, everyone in town knows all about that and also how Miss Greta pays him in three meals a day while the boarders are only fed twice. But the Lieutenant, well, he has earned a place in Miss Greta's heart. Not an easy task for even the most ambitious among us."

Landon nodded. "She is a cantankerous woman."

"She is. But deep down, Miss Greta is thoughtful and kind. When Mama first moved here, she allowed her to stay at the boardinghouse in exchange for Papa building the outhouse. Few have been able to secure a trade with her, with the exception of my parents and, of course, the Lieutenant. Not that many haven't tried. She's a woman set in her ways."

"And the Lieutenant is a man set in his ways. They both must be in their seventies, yet, he can't work up the gumption to ask her to a picnic."

"A picnic?" Mae hadn't known the Lieutenant was contemplating that, although it didn't surprise her.

"He asked me what else he could do to win Miss Greta's heart, and I suggested he take her for a buggy ride and a picnic. He had all sorts of arguments, and as far as I know, still hasn't asked her."

"Perhaps he's shy."

Landon shook his head. "The Lieutenant? The man is a war hero who was also instrumental in negotiations. I doubt he's shy."

"Perhaps with Miss Greta, he is." Mae recalled how the woman had been flustered when she saw him in the mercantile that day. "I think she's shy around him as well."

"Maybe we could aid them in realizing each other's affections."

"How so?"

A smile quirked his lips. "In Denver, we have what's called a matchmaking service. The woman, a widow in her sixties, was near destitute after losing her husband. She decided to assist those looking for a husband or wife and has been effective in many marriages."

Mae hadn't heard of a formal matchmaking service. "What would you suggest?"

"If the Lieutenant is too shy to ask Miss Greta on a picnic, perhaps he ought to place an advertisement in *The Horizon Herald.*"

"Place an advertisement?" Mae shifted so she fully faced Landon.

"Yes, he could say something like, 'Miss Greta, would you accompany me on a buggy ride and subsequent picnic this Saturday?' Miss Greta purchases a subscription to the paper for her guests, and I've seen her read it before breakfast."

"What a marvelous idea! Although, wouldn't that embarrass her? Maybe he could just include his initials."

"But what if there are others in Horizon with those initials? Besides, while Miss Greta would disagree with me, she doesn't seem like the most observant."

Mae agreed. Miss Greta would likely *consider* herself attentive, but she could be a flibbertigibbet at times. "So you would suggest the idea to the Lieutenant, and I could maybe ensure she reads the paper."

"Exactly."

"I've never been a matchmaker before."

"Nor have I." His gaze anchored hers, causing a fluttering in her belly. Landon reached for her hand and shook it. "It's an agreement then."

Her words faltered before she added, "We might just become the first matchmakers Horizon, Idaho, has ever had."

Chapter Fifteen

Sitting in the wooden chair on the boardinghouse porch, Landon inspected the ledgers on his makeshift desk—rather, a square table teetering on flimsy legs, and procured from Miss Greta's parlor. He penciled in the total amount of \$367,119.18 for equipment, land, and betterments to construct the line between Ingleville and Horizon. He then added in the proposed amount of wages for the laborers.

Tomorrow he would again travel to the location between the two towns to check on the progress. So engrossed in his work, he startled at the Lieutenant's voice.

"Hey, kid, you got a minute?"

After recovering, Landon peered up at the Lieutenant, who crouched behind the tree to the left of the porch. "Hello, sir. Yes, I have a minute." He welcomed a break from the mundane arithmetic.

"Ssh. Don't talk so loudly. I don't want her to hear."

"Who?"

"Her. That's who." The Lieutenant pointed to Miss Greta who worked in the boardinghouse garden not far away. "I know I've said before, but ain't she a sight to behold?"

Miss Greta halted from her toiling and looked about her, her attention veering toward Landon and the Lieutenant before continuing.

"Phew. That was a close one. She prit near saw me." The Lieutenant swiped a hand across his forehead.

"Doesn't she know you're doing chores around the boarding-house today?"

The Lieutenant exhaled an exasperated breath. "'Course she knows. Why wouldn't she?"

"Well, then, why...?"

The man brushed Landon's comment aside and interrupted before Landon had a chance to finish. "I been thinking about the picnic. What if she says no?"

Hadn't they already discussed this? Nonetheless, this allowed Landon to propose the plan he and Mae concocted. "I have an idea regarding that topic."

"The picnic?"

"Yes."

"All right. I reckon I could give it a listen."

"Since you're hesitant about asking her, why not print an advertisement in *The Horizon Herald*?"

The Lieutenant rubbed the back of his neck. "I'm not sure."

"You pen a sentence or two asking her on a picnic. She'll see it in the paper and agree." Or at least Landon hoped Miss Greta would agree. There really was no guarantee, but he wouldn't divulge that to the hopeful man standing beside him.

"But what if she don't agree? Besides, do I look like a writer?"

"You don't have to be a writer. It's just one sentence. I'll help you."

"In that case, I'd be much obliged. Maybe I wouldn't have to put my full name just in case her answer ain't in the affirmative."

"With all due respect, you worry too much, sir."

The Lieutenant slid him a frosty look. "You might not understand this none, but I'm not a man who cottons to being spurned."

Landon pushed the ledgers aside and reached for a clean sheet of stationery from his business notebook. "How about, 'Miss Greta, will you do me the honor of accompanying me on a buggy ride and subsequent picnic?'"

"That's sounds all right." The Lieutenant reached into his trouser pocket. "Got me a few coins. Do you reckon that'll be enough?"

"I'm not sure what the charge will be."

The Lieutenant inclined his head from further behind the tree. "Whatever the charge, Miss Greta is worth it. Best I deliver it today. Mr. O'Kane ain't known for being efficient."

Mae entered *The Horizon Herald* after school the following week. Mr. O'Kane, surly as usual, barely gave her a second of attention before growling, "If you're here in an attempt to convince me to accept your sister's stories, please refrain as such a scheme will only result in futility. Like I mentioned a thousand times before, until she becomes a more proficient writer, I'm not interested."

Mae wanted to ask how Ruby could become more proficient if she was never given the chance to hone her skills at the fledgling paper, but she refrained. "No, sir, that's not why I'm here."

With magniloquent exaggeration, Mr. O'Kane plunked the stack of newspapers on a shelf, causing a plume of dust to cloud the room. He waved it away, removed his round spectacles, and narrowed his already-thin, close-set eyes. "I doubt I'll like your stories either."

"Begging your pardon, Mr. O'Kane, but I have no ambition to write for the paper."

"Something wrong with the paper?"

"Oh, no, sir. Nothing is wrong with it." *Except that it's far too high-priced and utterly boring.* "I'm merely inquiring about an advertisement placed last week."

Mr. O'Kane replaced his spectacles. "What advertisement might that be?" As if he received many advertisements.

"The one from the Lieutenant."

The editor put a finger to his chin. "Ah, yes. I do recall that one."

"Do you know when it might be published?"

"Yes, I do. It's in today's issue as a matter of fact."

"Do you know if it's been delivered to subscribers?"

"It has." Mr. O'Kane removed his pocket watch. "About an hour ago to be exact."

"Thank you." If Mae hastened, she could ensure Miss Greta read the newspaper before starting supper.

Mae found the boardinghouse proprietress in the kitchen stirring something in the Dutch oven that smelled heavenly. "What's that decadent aroma?"

One side of Miss Greta's lips quirked upwards. "It's my famous chicken and dumplings. I didn't realize you were planning to stop by for a visit."

"I was wondering if you perchance subscribed to *The Horizon Herald*."

"I do. For my boarders. Many enjoy staying up-to-date with the latest happenings in Horizon. Why do you ask?"

"If you've already read it, might I take a quick perusal of it?"

"Do I look like I have time to read the newspaper? What a frivolous waste of time when I have a boardinghouse to manage."

"Yes, ma'am. I was just hoping to see something within the pages."

"All two of them?"

Miss Greta's comment amused Mae. If Mr. O'Kane hired Ruby, his fledgling newspaper would consist of more newsworthy items. "Yes, all two of them."

"For Ruby?"

Mae wouldn't lie; however, while not her main motivation, it would be useful to see exactly what Mr. O'Kane was publishing these days. "Yes, of course."

"All right. It's right over there on the table."

Mae flipped open the paper to the inside page. There was an update on the railroad and news about a new dress shop opening soon in a vacant building on First Street. The article encouraged townsfolk to bespeak for the dress shop a bounteous patronage. Two recipes graced the paper and a notice indicating that two subscribers to *The Horizon Herald* had not paid their subscriptions. If they wished to avoid their names in print, they best pay their overdue balances posthaste.

Mr. Salo, the blacksmith's, oversized rectangular advertisement reminded folks that horseshoeing was his specialty and that he also sold hammers for woodchoppers. Men's suits, coats, and vests were on sale for $2.50 at a business in Cornwall, and a cigar company in South Carolina wanted to hire a traveling salesman.

She then spied the Lieutenant's advert and scanned the short and succinct missive: *Miss Greta, will you do me the honor of accompanying me on a buggy ride and subsequent picnic? Signed: T.L.*

"Miss Greta?"

"Got a lot to do before supper, Mae. What is it you want?"

"I think you should see this."

The woman harrumphed before setting down the spoon and temporarily abandoning her post at the stove. "Don't tell me they're opening another boardinghouse or gonna build a hotel."

Mae wouldn't divulge that she'd heard a new hotel was imminent after the spur was completed. Instead, she said nothing and pointed at the advertisement.

Miss Greta's face turned crimson red. "Well, I'll be." She held a plump hand to her heart and tittered. "Do you think the Lieutenant feels for me the way I feel for him?"

"If he's asking you to accompany him, I imagine so."

"I'm flummoxed." Miss Greta fanned herself with her hand. "Of course, what if the initials stand for someone other than the Lieutenant?"

"I can't think of anyone else."

That seemed to satisfy the woman. "Quick, Mae! You have to help me."

"Sure, Miss Greta. Do you need me to stir the chicken and dumplings?"

"Pshaw. No, I don't need your aid with supper. I need you to deliver my response to Mr. O'Kane immediately before he closes his office for the day."

Mae had never seen Miss Greta move as swiftly as she did just now rummaging through a desk drawer in the dining room, securing a pencil, then plucking a coin from the wooden box on the shelf. She tapped Mae on the arm. "Hurry. Help me think of what to say."

"Do you wish to join him?"

"Do I look like the type of woman who would refuse such a gesture from the most handsome man in Horizon and possibly the entire United States?"

"No, ma'am."

"Good. Now, what shall I say? And make it quick. *The Horizon Herald* closes in fifteen minutes, and Mr. O'Kane isn't known for his patience or mercy."

"How about, 'Yes, T.L., I would be honored to accompany you. Signed, M.G.'"

Miss Greta's jaw went slack. "I couldn't have put it better myself. Here, you write it just like you said it."

Mae wrote the words on the plum-colored stationery. "How's that?"

"Yes, that will do." She offered the coin. "Now, go, ask Mr. O'Kane to place this advert immediately. Tell him I'll not wait until next week to see it."

Landon tethered his horse to the hitching post outside Miss Greta's and meandered to the boardinghouse. It had been a busy two days with more riding than he'd done in years to complete the round trip to assess both Humboldt and Varner City for future spurs, then to the camp just outside Horizon, then back. All he wanted was to wash up, hopefully make it in time for Miss Greta's supper, and fall into bed for a good night's sleep.

"Hey, kid!"

Landon stopped, the weariness tugging at his shoulders. The man had the poorest timing. "Hello, Lieutenant."

"I got something to show you." He waved a newspaper.

"Mr. O'Kane published your advertisement?"

"Of course Mr. O'Kane published it. Why do you ask?"

"Just thought... never mind." Landon rubbed his temples as the beginnings of a headache developed. He rolled his shoulders, hoping to release some of the tension from dealing with two wayward employees this morning.

"She wrote me back. Here. Looky at this." The Lieutenant pointed a fleshy finger at a thin, horizontal oblong advertisement. "It's there in the print. Her agreeance! I don't often buy the paper, but Mr. Pugh down at the barbershop told me about this, and I scurried on over to *The Horizon Herald* to secure my own copy."

"Now you just need to set a time and date and write back."

"No offense and all, but it'd be a whole lot cheaper if I'd just go and tell her myself."

CHAPTER SIXTEEN

JITTERS OVERWHELMED HER AS Mae organized the items for the auction on the thick wooden table Papa and Albert delivered just outside the town hall earlier that day. The school's ability to afford necessary items relied upon the success of the charity event.

Numerous baked goods, including her shoo-fly cake, awaited generous bidders. From the squares donated by Maribel and Mrs. Kleiber from the sewing circle, the children made two quilts. Velma donated a pinecone wreath she'd made, and Hans donated a round three-legged table he'd built. Lenore's hot cross buns were placed beside Mama's apple pie and Ruby's cream cookies. Wilhelmina offered two free ice creams, and Tabitha donated a new shovel from the mercantile. Other donations from Miss Greta, the Lieutenant, Doc, Sheriff Zembrodt, and the barber were also on the table.

Mayor Trabert began his announcements with his booming voice—far louder than one would imagine for a man with such a skinny frame. "Welcome to the third annual Horizon School for the Deaf benefit auction. We are thrilled to have you in attendance today and trust this will be a triumphal success in securing funds for our worthwhile school. Before we begin, I'd like to introduce you to the members of our community who make this organization possible. Mr. and Mrs. Eddington, the headmaster and headmistress, founded the school and continue to this day in managing it. Mr. Eddington provides maintenance for the school and also instructs the students in caring for the animals. Mrs. Eddington educates the pupils in gardening, cooking, and sewing. Lenore Nichols is one of the teachers and also resides at the school. Her mother is Shoshoni, and as such she learned hand signs used by her mother's tribe as a child. Lenore's knowledge of these signs is of significant benefit when teaching the children sign language. Mae Shepherdson is a teacher and has been at the school for three years. Mae teaches reading and writing.

"As many of you may or may not know, the Horizon School for the Deaf has a self-sufficient farm as well. The students learn to grow and care for crops, milk the cows, and can berries and other foods. This school is a tremendous benefit to our community and is currently awaiting state approval to receive funds. However, until then, we as a town have supported them in the additional expenses they accrue. Hence the reason for our annual benefit auction.

"Please give generously today knowing that your coins will benefit our deaf pupils and are highly appreciated. After the auction, we will commence with the baseball game. I will announce the items for bid, pupils from the school will show them to the audience, and the Lieutenant will collect the money. Let's get started!"

The crowd cheered, and Mayor Trabert began with the first item, a dozen delicious hot cross buns made by Lenore. "We'll start the bidding at fifteen cents."

Several folks offered their prices, with Reverend Marshall and Maribel placing the winning bid at twenty cents. He then offered Hans's table, Velma's pinecone wreath, and several other items, all of which received obliging bids. "Let's offer another food item, shall we? We now have up for bid this tasty shoo-fly cake made by Mae Shepherdson. Let's start the bidding at twenty-five cents."

"Twenty-five cents," shouted Papa.

"Thirty cents," added Mr. Kent from the livery.

"Thirty-five cents," countered Papa.

Mr. Woodham, the banker, added his bid. "Forty cents."

Papa appeared to be about to open his mouth when another voice joined the conversation. "One dollar."

The crowd gasped, and all heads swiveled to the speaker. Landon smiled. "I've tasted Miss Shepherdson's cake, and it's well worth every penny."

"One dollar going once, going twice, sold to Mr. Bennick!"

The Lieutenant secured the cash and delivered Mae's cake. "Not sure I can wait to eat it," joked Landon, to which the crowd laughed.

"Feel free to take it to the boardinghouse," suggested Miss Greta. "Although I cannot guarantee it'll still be there after the festivities." Her blunt honesty brought more cachinnation from the crowd.

Several more items were announced, including one of the patchwork quilts the children made. "This is a lovely blanket made from fabric squares donated by Maribel, Mrs. Kleiber, and the sewing circle. It will make a fine addition to your bed. Let's start the bidding at four dollars."

Several of the townsfolk bid until once again, a familiar voice spoke. "Eight dollars."

Mae looked across the crowd to see Landon. His gaze met hers, and he smiled.

"Eight dollars going once, going twice, sold to Mr. Bennick!"

When the auction concluded, Mae was finally able to thank Landon before the baseball game started. "I appreciate your support of the school."

"You're welcome. The shoo-fly cake may be eaten all in one fell swoop tonight, so if I can barely move at church tomorrow, that will be the reason why." He chuckled, and she joined in his merriment.

"Well, thank you again."

It was as though time stood briefly still as emotion flooded Mae with the warmth of his smile. When Lucy courted Hans, he was all she could speak of. Mae soon grew weary of Lucy's swooning about the handsome man who'd soon be her husband.

Now, several years later, Mae could more easily understand Lucy's affection for Hans, as she had begun to feel the same for Landon. For the man with the pleasing wit who so generously gave of his time and funds to assist others. For the man who sat beside her at church and lifted his voice to the Lord in worship. For the man whose image lingered in her thoughts far after she rested her head on her pillow each night.

He'd pushed up the sleeves of his forest-green shirt to reveal the sculpt of strong forearm muscles, and his broad shoulders strained against the fabric. Landon was not only kind and benevolent but dapper as well.

"I'm looking forward to the baseball game."

Landon's words jolted her thoughts. "The baseball game?"

"Yes, the one we'll play after the auction."

"The auction?"

"Mae, are you all right?"

"Oh. Yes. The auction. And the baseball game. Yes." The warmth of a blush stormed up her neck.

"Do you play baseball?"

"Do I?"

Landon threw his head back and laughed. "Yes, the game with a bat and a ball?"

If Mae didn't portray some sort of rational thought, Landon would likely think her daft. "Baseball. Oh, yes. I do play. Do you?"

"It was my favorite pastime as a young'un." He proceeded to share with her a glimpse into his life at the boarding school he attended until the Lieutenant ambled toward them, his brows in a downward "v" on his weathered face. "Are you two going to stand there talkin' about old memories all day or are we gonna get some teams ready for baseball?"

"We aim to play baseball," Landon assured him.

The Lieutenant cast a glance from Mae to Landon. He inclined toward Landon and did his best to lower his voice. "Did I tell you Miss Greta and I enjoyed our picnic?"

"You didn't tell me about that."

The older man squinted at Mae. "Reckon it's all right if you hear too, but you both gotta keep what I'm about to tell you to yourselves."

"You have our word, Lieutenant." Mae veered closer.

"I plan on asking Miss Greta to court me."

The Lieutenant's declaration came as no surprise. The boardinghouse proprietress clearly besotted the man. But he wasn't the only one besotten. It was a challenge to extract Landon's attention from the lovely Mae Shepherdson, whose rosy face, bright eyes, and slender figure commanded his attention. Would he someday entertain the thought of asking for her hand in courtship?

The crowd began to inch toward the public schoolyard for the baseball game. It was one of the first times he'd ever really been accepted by a group of people. And placing the highest bids on Mae's shoo-fly cake and the children's quilt had been one of his best decisions. By doing so, Landon had earned the townsfolk's respect. Not that he wouldn't have purchased both items anyway since he'd do just about anything for Mae.

So it should come as no surprise that he would be selected as a team captain for the baseball game.

"You ever play baseball before, kid?" asked the Lieutenant.

A flood of memories returned of perpetual games the second Landon and his classmates opened the front door of the enormous red brick building and entered recess time.

The time spent was always too short, and inevitably, they were in the middle of a game when Headmaster Mouart would summon them back inside for their tedious arithmetic class.

Landon learned early on that he would have to earn the right to play on a team because he was shyer, scrawnier, and much smaller and shorter than the other boys his age. After struggling to contrive a suitable plan the other boys accepted, Landon resorted to using his allowance to purchase a bag of marbles for each boy. But not just nondescript marbles like the ones his wealthy classmates already owned, but the most expensive glass ones with vibrant filament made of agate, each one ground by hand and made in Holland.

Alarick, the most popular boy and from the wealthiest family in New York, inspected the bag of fourteen costly marbles. He'd rolled them each around in his palm, held them up to the sunlight, and spun the shooter marble across the walkway. Landon held his breath and crossed his fingers behind his back, hoping Alarick would accept. After what seemed like hours, but was likely only minutes, Alarick nodded and slapped Landon on the back. "All right, Bennick. You can play on my team, but this is only temporary. If you prove inferior, we'll have to remove you. Do you understand?"

The much-taller boy's looming and questioning expression was etched in Landon's mind, and he'd mutely nodded. Thankfully, Landon proved to be one of the best players in boarding school history. Yet, Father and Mother had never once seen him play or even knew he'd excelled at the sport.

"Kid? You still with us?"

It took Landon a moment to return to the present and realize he was no longer ten years old, but twenty-five, and it was no longer Alarick awaiting his answer, but the Lieutenant. "Sorry, sir. Yes, When I was in boarding school."

The Lieutenant gave a clipped nod. "All right, then. You and Doc are the captains. Everyone who wants to play has paid their pennies to Wilhelmenia. Captains, make your choices."

After several rounds of choosing, Landon's team consisted of Mae, Albert, Mr. Shepherdson, Timothy, Ruby, Hans, Velma, Mr. Kent, the barber, and several children from Horizon.

Doc's team consisted of Mayor Trabert, Tabitha, the Lieutenant, three older boys from the deaf school, Wilhelmina and her husband, Hubert, Mr. Woodham, Lenore, Mr. Eddington, and several children from Horizon.

"Looks to be fair," declared the Lieutenant. Landon's team was up to bat first, while Doc's team was in the field.

The clapping from the spectators brought Landon back to boarding school days, and his heart pounded in his ears as competitiveness settled in.

Mrs. Eddington hushed the crowd. "Now, do remember, everyone, this is a game to raise money for the school. Keep in mind you are not on the Cincinnati Red Stockings team. You are not playing a tightly-contested match against New York's Mutual Baseball Club. And yes, before some of you give me a look inquiring how I would know about the Cincinnati Red Stockings, my beloved brother played for them."

Landon's jaw dropped at hearing of Mrs. Eddington's vast knowledge of the sport and the fact she'd nearly read his mind about being too ambitious. As he scanned the faces of both teams, he vowed to heed Mrs. Eddington's edict.

The batting lineup consisted of Ruby, Mr. Shepherdson, Mr. Kent, and Landon to start. Landon examined the three Snyder bats donated by Tabitha and Mayor Trabert. Ruby had already selected hers, the polished two-colored bat made of American willow. Landon lifted the white ash one and swung it before noticing a flat bat amongst the others. He'd heard of these types, legal since 1885, but had never used one.

A tug on his sleeve averted his attention to Hosea peering up at him. The boy pointed to himself with his finger, palm down, then stuck out his thumb and pinky on each hand and shook them twice in unison. While Landon had learned several hand signs, he wasn't yet aware of this particular one.

Hope filled Hosea's brown eyes, but his shoulders slumped when Landon didn't immediately answer.

He glanced up at Mae, silently seeking her help.

"He wants to know if he can play."

The little boy, small for his age with his high-water trousers held up by striped suspenders, slid his lip between his bottom teeth. While younger, something about Hosea reminded Landon of himself that day at the boarding school.

Landon balled his right hand into a fist and shook it for the sign for "yes." To Mae, he added, "Can you please tell him we just so happen to need another player, and yes, we'd love to have him on the team? Does he know how to play at all?"

Mae signed Landon's request, and Hosea jumped up and down before scurrying to stand behind Velma.

"The children often play baseball at recess, so he understands the formalities of it." Her smile drew Landon in as she continued. "Thank you for allowing him to play. He's only five so he may need some help with the bat."

"We have one that's lighter than the others, and I'll help him if need be."

Several minutes later, Doc pitched and Landon swung, sending the ball past the boardinghouse and into an empty field. He started to base one, recollections of time in boarding school once again entering his mind. With his home run, he sent Ruby, Mr. Shepherson, and Mr. Kent all home, then rounded the bases and added another run for his team.

The crowd cheered, and an outfielder finally hurled the ball to Doc for the next pitch. Mae, Timothy, and Hans were next, followed by Hosea. The boy lifted the lightest bat, its heaviness causing it to fall forward to the ground before Hosea hoisted it again.

Landon signed to him that he would help, and Hosea nodded.

They took their place, and Landon stood behind Hosea. He moved the boy's hands into perfect position on the bat, covered them with his own, then awaited the pitch.

Doc moved closer before lobbing the ball toward them. Landon swung. "Strike one!" shouted Mr. Salo, the blacksmith, who'd offered to be the umpire.

Hosea tilted his head back and peered up at Landon. Landon offered a smile that he hoped would reassure the boy.

Doc threw the next pitch. They swung, and this time the bat connected with the ball. Landon motioned for Hosea to run. He bounded to first base, easily making it before Doc threw the ball to Mayor Trabert.

Mae cheered as Hosea slid into home. For someone so young, he was quickly learning the game. He bolted toward her, the biggest grin on his face she'd ever seen. She signed to him how proud she was of him then watched as he went to stand beside Landon.

An hour later, the game concluded with their team winning by three runs. Mayor Trabert again thanked the townsfolk for their participation, and Mr. and Mrs. Eddington offered their appreciation for the generous donations.

The school would be able to continue serving students for the time being, and Mae lifted her own gratitude to the One who'd made it possible.

"Landon?"

He turned to face her, a smudge of dirt on his handsome face and a rip in the knee of his trousers from sliding across the grass to catch a fly ball the Lieutenant hit. His rugged and handsome appearance was not wasted on her, and for a moment, Mae's words faltered.

"I—thank you for allowing Hosea to play. It meant the world to him."

"You're welcome. I was glad I could help. He has a lot of potential."

"That you have confidence in him means a lot. Perhaps you could stop by the school and practice with him sometime."

"I'd be happy to."

Mae pondered whether to share her next thoughts. "Have I ever told you about how Hosea came to be a student at the school?"

"You haven't."

"It was soon after I started teaching when Mr. and Mrs. Eddington received a letter from the headmistress at an orphanage in Boise City about a two-year-old who couldn't hear. The headmistress wasn't sure what to do with the little one who'd recently lost his parents to tuberculosis. She'd heard of the Horizon School for the Deaf and wondered if we would take him. Of course, Mr. and Mrs. Eddington agreed without hesitation and traveled to Boise City. When Hosea first arrived, he was withdrawn, sorrowful, and distant. It took Mr. and Mrs. Eddington, Lenore, and myself, along with the older children, some time to help Hosea realize his new home was a safe one where he could learn to communicate, especially with others who were deaf. Unless one knew of his past, they would never know he wasn't always the smart and happy child he is now." Mae fought back the emotion that often presented itself when she thought of the children and the struggles they'd faced. Struggles some still continued to face, although to a lesser extent.

"Thankfully there are folks like you, the Eddingtons, and Lenore, who truly care about the children."

"Indeed. But we couldn't do it without God's provision. He provides for us in so many ways, including through the townsfolk each year at the charity event. Many others donate all through the year with their time and their money. So thank you for being willing to not only allow Hosea to play, but also for bidding on the shoo-fly cake and the quilt."

"You're welcome. I have to travel to the railroad camp on Tuesday, but when I return I'll stop by and spend some time with Hosea." He stepped forward and bridged the space between them before reaching for her hand and brushing a kiss on it. "I anticipate eating the shoo-fly cake. It will likely be gone before day's end."

Mae's heart stuttered. "I better go before Ruby writes an article about sisters who delay the wagon leaving for home."

"Ruby's writing has potential. She just needs to concoct some worthwhile topics." Landon laughed, and Mae was reminded how much she liked the sound of his amusement. "Have a good night, Mae, and I'll see you tomorrow at church."

If Mae could will her feet to move, she'd leave posthaste and scurry to the wagon to her waiting family. But her lead feet refused to heed her instruction. "Yes, good night."

Timothy's voice echoed through the otherwise pleasant evening. "Mae! Are you ever coming? Reckon it'll be tomorrow before we arrive home!"

Landon started toward the boardinghouse when Albert clapped him on the back. "I think we could consider that a success," he said, "although I might be a little sore after that game. And, oh, what a game it was!" Albert straightened and rolled his shoulders.

"It's been a while since I partook in a game like that. Have to say I missed it."

"You've obviously played before. Those were some hits, home runs all of them."

Landon chuckled. "I played during my boarding school years."

"On a much more professional field, I gather."

"More professional, yes, but this one easily sufficed." Landon thought of the makeshift bases and the well-used bats, neither of which would have been found at the prestigious boarding schools.

"I wanted to thank you for your donations at the auction."

"You're welcome. I think I'm finally earning the respect and friendship of the townsfolk." The thought encouraged him. "Helped that our team won."

Albert stopped and faced him. "You don't have to donate to charities or win baseball games to earn the townsfolk's respect and friendship. We already liked and respected you."

Landon shrugged. "Sometimes you have to earn that. Am I incorrect in thinking God is the same way?"

"That we have to earn His love and His favor?"

"Yes. I'll admit I would have purchased Mae's shoo-fly cake no matter the bidding amount because it's one of my favorite desserts and—"

"She made it?"

"Yes, and she made it." Landon wouldn't deny that the smile on her face when he'd purchased the cake made it all worth it.

"Landon, while people can demand that we do certain things to attain their friendship or love, God isn't like that. There is nothing we can do to earn His love or His favor. Nothing."

He exhaled a harsh sigh. "Sounds just like my father. Nothing I do earns his favor. I can work long hours, secure funds or save the business money, hire the best workers, or ensure things commence in an efficient manner, and I'm still not considered worthy in his eyes."

"I'm sorry about that."

"I've only wanted to please him. So I appreciate being accepted by the townsfolk here in Horizon." He thought of what Albert said about God's favor and how the dismal thought caused a heavy weight to settle in his chest. "So there's nothing I can do to earn God's favor or His love either? He's just like my father?"

"Do you remember when we discussed God *not* being like your earthly father in His critical nature?"

"Yes."

"This is another way God is unlike your father. There is nothing you can do to earn the love of a Holy God. You will never be good enough."

"Just like my…"

But Albert put a palm toward Landon, encouraging him to cease speaking. "You will never be good enough to earn the salvation Jesus provided when He went to the cross for your sins. Never be good enough to earn a place in Heaven. You can bid all you want on items at a charity event. You can donate money to all the most worthwhile causes. You can be the nicest and most affable fellow. Still, you won't earn God's love."

"Then what hope is there?"

"The hope is Jesus. And I know you've placed your faith in Him."

"I have."

Albert kicked at a pebble. "When Hosea asked if he could play, what was your first inclination?"

"I had no hesitation, but my first thought was that he reminded me of myself at a younger age—scrawny, smaller than the others, eager to play."

"No hesitation."

"None at all." What was Albert attempting to say?

"Hosea offered nothing to our team. He couldn't even lift the bat without help, much less hit the ball. If you hadn't stood behind him and swung, Hosea wouldn't have made it to first base. You're right. He is scrawny and small for his age. Why allow someone like that to play?" Albert shrugged. "He was more of a hindrance than a benefit."

"That's not how I saw it."

"Of course not. That's not how any of us saw it. But when Hosea came to you and asked if he could play, you didn't hesitate. You showed him mercy and grace and then assisted him in being able to effectively play the game with the others."

"Albert, I'm not sure why we're discussing Hosea. Of course, I would show him mercy."

"Just like our Heavenly Father shows us mercy. You see, Hosea could do nothing to earn his way onto the team. He couldn't hit a home run. Couldn't pitch. Couldn't catch a fly. He runs fast for a young'un, but there are those who run faster and who could catch him even before he made it on base. He couldn't offer the winning run or even cheer with the crowd since he's deaf. What could he possibly offer the team? Nothing. But you, in your mercy, didn't require that he do anything to earn his place on your team. God, in His mercy, sent His Son to die for us while we were yet sinners. Jesus did nothing to deserve the punishment He took for us. And nothing you do now or ever will secure God's love for you. He already loved you—as a matter of fact, His love was so profound that He sent Jesus for you. For me. Nothing earned. Only freely given, just as you freely gave Hosea a chance."

Landon's jaw went slack at all that Albert said. "I know we discussed not losing His love, but now you're telling me I could never have earned it in the first place?"

"That's precisely what I'm telling you. Someday if you have children, you'll do what you can to be the best pa you can be. There will be ways you'll be like the Lord, perhaps in your patience or your tender care of your young'uns. But there will be other ways you won't be like our Lord in that you will always be a sinner in need of grace, never perfect like our Heavenly Father is. Your pa is a sinner in need of grace. He won't do things perfectly. We pray for him that he someday surrenders his life to Christ, but until then, he will remain seeking the things of this world—and demanding you earn his love."

Landon reflected on all that Albert said. "You're sure I can't earn God's love? Because I'd like to. I'd like Him to think of me as worthy."

"You are worthy. He loves you more than you can ever comprehend."

"As is evidenced by Jesus' sacrifice?"

"Indeed."

"Thank you, Albert."

"You're welcome. Well, I best get home before Velma has my hide and then some for missing supper. If you ever have any other questions, let me know. I'm still learning, but I'd like to help if I can."

Landon stuck his hands in his trouser pockets and strolled to the boardinghouse. Albert's words had given him much to think about.

And Albert's friendship was the first he'd secured in a long time.

Chapter Seventeen

LANDON BRUSHED OFF HIS dark gray waistcoat and entered the Cornwall Restaurant and Hotel. Mother and Father would be waiting for him, and the train ride from Ingleville to Cornwall had taken much longer than he'd anticipated. He'd been wise and avoided the food options at the stage stop between Horizon and Ingleville, and his stomach growled, reminding him he hadn't eaten since consuming the sandwich Miss Greta packed for him.

The restaurant, with its gold-colored tin-plated ceiling, ornate silverware cart, and tables with fancy bouquets reminded Landon of a restaurant he frequented with his parents in Denver, only much smaller.

A waiter with a balding head and a thin horseshoe-styled mustache greeted him. "May I help you, sir?"

"Yes, I am here to meet Mr. and Mrs. Bertram Bennick."

"Right this way." The waiter led Bennick through an area with precisely-spaced, round tables featuring elegant, crisp white tablecloths and surrounded by black leather chairs to the far end of the room. Father peered up and nodded as Landon took a seat beside Mother. A window to his left provided a view of a stunning garden with multiple flowers and carefully pruned trees.

Mother offered a slight smile. "Hello, Landon." She held her hands in her lap, her posture impeccable. She had changed little since he last saw her. Her elegant green dress and fancy hairdo told of her wealth.

"Hello, Mother."

The waiter arrived with the menus, and for the next few minutes, the three of them stared at the food choices.

Mother glanced up at the waiter. "I'll have the fricassee of veal with the potatoes Parisienne."

"And for the vegetable?"

"Marrow squash, please."

"And the entremet?"

Mother again perused the menu. "Chocolate meringue puffs."

Landon answered next and chose the chicken saute a la financiere, boiled potatoes, and blueberry pie.

Father turned the menu over as if to peruse the other side. "There aren't more options?" He sighed. "These are meager offerings."

"Sir, we can offer a pleasing alternative if you are not able to find something of your liking on the menu. May I take your request to the chef?"

"Yes. I request boiled chicken-halibut with egg sauce, please. I would also like a gooseberry tartlet for the entremet."

The waiter fidgeted with his pencil, then tapped it on the paper on which he wrote the orders. "I will see what I can do, Mr. Bennick."

"Thank you. That will be all." Father waved the waiter away and took a drink of his coffee.

Landon had forgotten how persnickety Father could be. Apparently, Mother had forgotten as well. "Bertram, did you have a lapse in memory for a moment? This is not the Denver Opulence."

Father arced an eyebrow and straightened the lapels on his coat. "That may very well be, Gladys, but they should have more of a variety."

"It is the Wild West after all. Idaho did only become a state last year."

His parents discussed the fact that Cornwall, Idaho, would never be Denver, Colorado. Mother put on airs and Father was pompous. And together they calmly disagreed about whether the Cornwall Restaurant and Hotel should serve more than one page-worth of menu items.

Finally, the issue was laid to rest. Mother focused her attention on Landon. "You're looking a little tattered, Landon."

"It was a lengthy trip from Horizon and included a dusty ride on the stage."

Mother held a hand to her heart. "The stage? I declare. It's nearly the 1900s. They still have those?"

"Yes, Mother. In some places they do."

"Which is precisely why," said Father, "we need to ensure every town has a railroad. There is no sense in travel taking such an extreme amount of time when railways offer such expedient transit."

"I think it would be a grand adventure to travel on a stage-coach. My own mother and father, God rest their souls, frequently traveled by stage in their younger years. I've never before been on one."

Father took another drink of his coffee. "And you don't want to be on one."

"But if we pay a visit to that primitive town where Landon is supervising the new spur, we will have to travel aboard one of those modes of transport." Mother's eyes grew large. "It would be akin to an adventure. I should like to see what the Wild West truly looks like."

Landon didn't mention that it wasn't so long ago that Denver was considered the Wild West.

"Cornwall *is* the Wild West as far as I'm concerned." Father unfolded his napkin and placed it in his lap. "I have stayed here several times while preparing for the newest spurs in Ingleville and Horizon. Believe me when I say returning to Denver cannot come quickly enough."

Mother leaned toward Landon. "We do plan to come see you, dear." She deferred to Father. "I'd also delight in spending time in Maryland. It's been such a long while since we've been there."

"We'll visit there soon."

One of the Bennick family homes was on an extensive estate in Maryland—Mother's favorite of the three.

The noonday meal arrived. Landon was the only one who prayed before eating. Thankfully, Father found his meal appetizing and caused no further ado.

After the meal and dessert, Father leaned back in his chair and clasped his hands over his stomach. "Now that we've eaten, I would like a progress report of how things are proceeding on the Ingleville-Horizon line."

"It's advancing as expected."

"Will it be finished in the expected time frame?"

"Hopefully so."

Father nodded. "Good. This is a sizable investment, and promises have been made and contracts signed."

Landon shifted in his chair. "What are your thoughts about the new railroad depot in Horizon?"

"The same as was planned in Ingleville."

"With your permission, I'd like to hire some local men to build the depot."

Father exhaled a deep breath. "When I was there, I noticed a stagecoach depot. That can still be used."

"With respect, Father, that is a dilapidated building and much too small."

"Horizon doesn't need anything fancy."

Landon had prepared for this conversation. He also knew that many of the farmers in Horizon needed extra income as they were still reeling from the drought last year that had taken a toll on their crops. "Something with the Bennick name on it should be of quality, both in appearance and in structure."

"Now you are sounding like a true businessman. Since you mentioned it, I tend to agree. Bennick Railways has been providing the best in transport. That shouldn't only include the safest, fastest, and most reliable intercontinental routes, but also the best depots."

"Exactly, Father. That is why I propose we build a depot that welcomes all who travel to and from Horizon. A depot they will remember for years to come." *Not like the stage stop between Horizon and Ingleville with its filthy eating establishment.*

Mother clapped her hands. "You are sounding so much like your father. Bertram, I told you that you needn't worry about Landon. He will be more than able to assume Bennick Railways someday when you plan to retire."

"That won't be for some time, but yes, Landon is learning the importance of running a business."

That was the closest thing to a compliment Father had ever given him, and Landon reveled in the words, allowing the accolade to permeate every part of him.

"Now that we've discussed the boring aspect of business, shall we discuss Orla?"

Father's words were quickly replaced by Mother's mention of the woman she hoped he'd marry. But Landon's mind was on Mae Shepherdson, not Orla. "Mother, I don't believe Orla and I are suited for matrimony, as we discussed after our most recent supper with the Rothleutners."

"Pish posh! Won't you change your mind? The news you both shared put me in such a dither. Poor Mrs. Rothleutner nearly lapsed into melancholy.

"You and Orla would do well to reconsider," said Father, his voice firm.

"We won't be changing our minds. Both she and I are fond of others."

Mother's jaw went slack and she covered her mouth with her hand. "Someone other than Orla? Pray tell, who? Does she hail from Denver? Annapolis? Chicago?"

Landon shook his head. "No, Mother. None of those places. She's from Horizon."

"Is she at least well-bred?"

Mae's image flashed before Landon's mind. Her love for her God and her family. Her sweet face and the way it lit up when she spoke of the children at the school. Her tender heart when Polly was ill. Her immediate affection for Beans. "No, Mother, I don't believe you would consider her well-bred. Her name is Mae Shepherdson, and she does not hail from a wealthy family."

"Then you have no business considering such a woman for anything more than a dalliance."

Landon regretted he'd broached the subject, but his parents would learn of Mae if Landon decided to someday court her.

Father's voice took on an edge and he raised it slightly. "You know that any woman from a poor family will only marry you for your money. Mine and your mother's money. That is unacceptable."

"I can sense that you are blinded by what you perceive to be affection for this woman." Mother lifted the cup of tea to her lips and took a dainty sip. "However, you must understand that someone of your station does not take an interest in someone who is destitute."

"She's not destitute. Her father is a well-respected farmer in town, and Mae is a teacher. I do care deeply for her and someday, if it is the Lord's will, I would ask her to court me." Such thoughts were premature for who even knew if Mae would have him? And they hadn't known each other for long, but Landon figured while courage was on his side, he might as well mention his intentions.

"I'm not sure the Lord cares one way or another who you marry, but your mother and I *do*. I propose we completely drop this moot conversation at present. There will be no more discussion of this woman or your affection for her. If you wish to discuss a woman, discuss Orla. She hails from one of the finest families in Denver, her parents have long been friends of ours, and she is a suitable match. I'll not allow family money to be squandered away by some woman who has none of her own."

Landon knew better than to argue with Father, for he wouldn't win. So instead he would abandon the conversation as his father requested.

CHAPTER EIGHTEEN

MAE AND HER FAMILY attended church, and Landon sat next to her as he now customarily did. She found that she looked forward to seeing him.

"Good morning." He offered her one of his handsome smiles. Was she mistaken or did she notice affection glowing in his eyes? Perhaps, with such a vivid imagination, she ought to aspire to be a reporter like Ruby.

"Good morning to you."

Timothy plopped down on the other side of Mae. "Now that we've made sure everyone is having a good morning."

Mae shook her head. Brothers could be such annoyances.

Becky, Lucy's youngest daughter, dashed to Mama and flung her arms around her grandma's neck. "Can I sit with you today?" she asked.

With the exception of the little girl's blonde curls, which she'd inherited from her father, she was an exact copy of Lucy with her oval face and almond-shaped brown eyes.

Mama nodded. "If it's all right with your ma, then it's all right with me."

But even before Becky could confirm her mother's agreeance, she was in Mama's lap, and Mama's arms were wrapped tightly around her.

Oh, but to have a grandmother! Mae couldn't ask for more than what the Lord had richly blessed her with, but she did wonder from time to time what it would have been like to be a granddaughter and loved by her grandparents the way Mama and Papa loved and doted on their four grandchildren.

People milled about, greeting each other and finding their seats. Over the past couple of years, the Horizon congregation had grown. Mae spied Albert speaking with a new family. Only the Lord could have orchestrated such a perfect occupation for her brother.

Before moving to Horizon, Mae had never attended church. She'd never heard of God or how He sent His Son. She'd never even heard a hymn. The orphanage where she stayed did not cotton to such matters as the eternal security of the children under its supervision.

While the Horizon School for the Deaf wasn't an orphanage, it did house three orphans. And Mr. and Mrs. Eddington made it of utmost importance for the children to attend church each Sunday. The pupils occupied the first two pews, and Lenore sat in a chair facing them and signed the words Albert spoke. Except for a few, most of the congregation accepted the students with enthusiasm. Polly and Hosea sat side by side, rapidly signing their conversation with animation. While they hadn't known each other before they arrived at the school, they'd become close as though brother and sister.

Simon and Sherman stood on their knees in the pew in front of Mae with brown hair slicked and hazel eyes wide. Simon waved at Papa, Mae, and finally at Becky, and Sherman followed suit. Velma was fond of saying that with two twin boys, what one didn't think of, the other readily did.

Becky said, loud enough for all of Horizon to hear, "I'm a big girl now, Grandma. I 'cided I can sit all by myself on the pew." Still holding tightly to Mama's hand, she wedged herself between Mama and Ruby. "Look at me, Aunt Rube. I'm a big girl."

Ruby, of course, adored her nieces and nephews. She planted a kiss on top of Becky's head. "Yes, you are."

However, due to the little girl's insistence on sitting in her own seat, things had become quite crowded, and now Mae was sitting close to Landon. So close, in fact, that their shoulders touched.

His fingers brushed hers, and a ripple of excitement fluttered through her belly. She raised her glance to discover his gaze fixed on her, tenderness emanating from his expression.

Ruby then offered a suspicious smirk in her direction. Yes, Mae was falling in love with Landon, but she'd not share that with her sister for fear of her declaration landing in *The Horizon Herald*. It was plausible indeed that the disagreeable Mr. O'Kane would choose that story of Ruby's despite choosing no others.

With difficulty, Mae returned her focus to the front of the church just as everyone began to stand for the opening hymns. The strains of the organ sounded, and Mae joined the congregation in singing "Be Thou My Vision". The fourth stanza was her favorite, and she allowed the words to seep deep into her heart.

> *Riches I heed not, nor man's empty praise,*
> *be Thou mine inheritance, now and always;*
> *be Thou and Thou only the first in my heart,*
> *O High King of heaven, my Treasure Thou art.*

Mae had just sent the children to recess with Lenore when Mrs. Eddington requested she join her and Mr. Eddington in the school office.

A disheveled woman holding a baby on her hip, a man with black circles beneath his eyes, and a little girl with a scowl stood inside the tiny room. Another younger child stood peering behind her mother's skirts.

The man gripped his hat in his hands. "We're hoping you can help us."

"Yes, please." Tears pooled in the woman's eyes.

"We will be happy to do whatever we can," said Mrs. Eddington. She rested a hand on the woman's shoulder.

"I'm Mr. Goyette, and this is my wife. That there is our daughter, Jeralyn. She's the second oldest of our six young'uns."

Jeralyn Goyette, who couldn't have been more than five, roughly plucked the doll from her younger sister's arms and hurled it across the room, hitting Mr. Eddington square in the nose.

"Jeralyn!" exclaimed her father.

But the girl paid him no mind. Instead, she darted toward Mrs. Eddington's desk, and with an efficient swipe of her hand, relocated the paperwork and books to the floor. The crashing sound echoed throughout the room. When Jeralyn finished, she folded her arms across her chest and glowered at her father.

"We can't help her to understand that this type of behavior is unbecoming," sobbed her ma. "We've tried everything."

"But we can't communicate with her because she can't hear."

Mae had heard of this type of situation, and she correctly surmised what Mrs. Eddington would say next.

"Have you ever heard of sign language?"

Both parents shook their heads.

"It's a language that we teach deaf children so they can effectively communicate. Right now, Jeralyn is expressing herself through bad behavior because she knows no other way."

"We're sorry, ma'am, but we do not know sign language." The father attempted, without success, to rein in Jeralyn just as she took a swipe at a painting on the wall.

"We are so sorry. We feel as though we have failed her." The woman shifted the baby just as he began to whimper.

Mr. Eddington cupped the man's shoulder. "Your circumstances are not unique. We have welcomed other children with similar situations. We believe we can help Jeralyn, but it will take prayer, most importantly, but also cooperation from you and your family."

"We'll do whatever it takes. We love her and want her to succeed in life. When we heard about your school, we knew we had to make the trip from Humboldt."

"And you are welcome to stay here tonight as Jeralyn adjusts to her new home."

"So you'll help us, then?" Mrs. Goyette began to sob, which in turn caused her baby to cry.

Mrs. Eddington wrapped an arm around her. "Yes, we will help you. We don't want Jeralyn to feel as though she's been deserted, so it's imperative you visit as frequently as you can."

"We plan to do that each month, ma'am." Mr. Goyette blinked back his own emotion.

Mr. Eddington introduced Mae and Lenore, then handed Mr. Goyette a well-read copy of *The Book of Sign Language.* "The other important request after prayer and regular visits is that you and your family begin learning sign language. It will take some time for you and your wife, but your children will learn it rather quickly. At the same time, we'll be teaching Jeralyn the same signs."

Mr. and Mrs. Goyette agreed, and the Eddingtons discussed funds with the couple. Jeralyn kicked the side of the desk before plopping herself in the chair.

While teaching the little girl would be a grueling challenge, it could be done. For with prayer and the love, support, and dedication of the staff at the school, no child was beyond help.

The remainder of the day proved less eventful. Beans instantly earned the love of the children at the school. Mae brought him once a week on Fridays, on what Polly had termed "Beans Day". During recess and when the children finished their schoolwork early, they spent time with the beagle, running, playing, and...

Mae finished erasing the blackboard when she heard a yip behind her. Three little heads—Polly, Hosea, and Odin—peeked around the corner, then swiftly disappeared when she looked in their direction. Then a tap tap of paws and another yip as Beans entered the room in a vibrant red calico bonnet. He also wore a white apron, its strings tied around his middle in a gigantic bow on his back.

Giggles and sniggers persisted, and Mae lifted Beans into her arms. She lifted the wide brim of the bonnet. Beans wore spectacles, which inched down on his snout.

"Oh, poor Beans!" She laughed and held him close as he licked her face. "Are you a baker?"

Beans barked in response.

The three children came fully into view, covering their faces and tittering as Beans turned his head and caused the bonnet to flop down over his eyes and spectacles.

She set Beans on the floor and signed to the children that Beans ought to join Mrs. Eddington in the kitchen to bake supper.

In an exaggerated motion, Hosea bent in half and slapped his leg as his laughter filled the room.

Odin shook his head and signed that Beans would eat all the cookies before they got even a one. Polly untied Beans's bonnet, and Hosea replaced it with a cowboy hat. That started a whole new round of giggles.

The mantle clock on the sloping wooden shelf indicated that in fifteen minutes, Landon would be there to retrieve her. He'd sought Papa's permission last Sunday at church to bring her home each evening after school.

At first, Mae wasn't confident Papa would allow it. Whenever he was deep in thought, one eyebrow arched with two vertical lines etched on his forehead. It was the same expression he'd given whenever she, Lucy, and Albert made an outlandish suggestion as children. And between the three of them, there had been many such featherheaded propositions. Mainly conjured up by Albert, of course.

And just as Papa thought he might be liberated from such suggestions, Ruby and Timothy resumed with some half-witted ideas of their own.

Not that Landon's request was foolhardy in any way, but Papa was protective of Mae, and with the obvious difference in their stations and no feasible future for them, that only added to Papa's hesitation.

Even now, Mae continuously pondered what real future she and Landon might attain. He would no more want to reside in Horizon than she in a city. Perhaps friendship would be the appropriate direction their relationship should take.

But why then did the mere thought of that leave a stab of pain deep within her heart?

Polly interrupted her musings with a tapping on her arm and a point outside the window.

Landon climbed from the buggy, an oblong-shaped item wrapped in brown paper in his hand.

But she wasn't paying attention to the item in his hand, but rather how dapper he appeared in his green plaid shirt.

Mae followed Polly outside. Landon set the object down, propped it against his leg, and signed something to Hosea.

The young boy cocked his head to one side and shrugged.

Landon tried again, and this time Hosea clapped his hands together and advanced a few steps toward Landon.

The rest of the kids had gathered around, their curiosity besting them.

"Mae, would you mind translating for me?"

She took her place beside him. "Absolutely."

Landon handed the object to Hosea. "Would you please tell him I'm so proud of him for how well he played at the baseball game the other day? He may proceed in unwrapping the item, and while it is a gift for him, I trust he'll share it with the others."

Mae's hands flew with the words.

Hosea need not be coaxed further. He stripped away the wrap to expose a brown bat.

"It's the newest made by J.F. Hillerich and Son." Landon stood straighter as he provided the details Mae translated to Hosea and the rest of the pupils.

Hosea, meanwhile, was jumping up and down while attempting to wield the bat. Landon reached into the buggy and retrieved a ball. He tossed it to one of the older boys, and within seconds, everyone had crowded around him offering their excitable thank yous, along with a few questions.

"How did you find something in such a timely manner?" Mae asked.

Landon didn't answer, only offered the crooked grin she'd grown quite fond of.

Chapter Nineteen

THE ENTIRE DAY, LANDON anticipated retrieving Mae. It surprised him when Mr. Shepherdson agreed to his suggestion, but Landon was grateful he had.

And now, after witnessing Hosea's excitement at the new bat and ball, he counted the minutes before spending time with Mae.

He assisted her into the buggy, and Beans leaped into her lap. They waved at the children, and Landon beckoned the horses.

"Beans has had an eventful day, haven't you, Beans?"

The dog whimpered.

"My thoughts exactly. You poor thing."

"What happened to him?" Landon asked.

"Polly, Hosea, and Odin decided to transform Beans into a baker." She covered her mouth with one hand while releasing a round of contagious laughter.

"A baker?"

"Yes. They put a red bonnet on him; one I believe that belongs to Polly, along with a small child's apron from the clothesline, and a pair of spectacles, no doubt Mr. Eddington's. He'd taken a nap, providing just the opportunity to seize them. You should have seen poor Beans!"

Beans covered his face with his paws and whined at the mention of his name.

Landon chuckled, transferred the reins to one hand, and patted Beans on the head. "How did you ever survive that, boy?"

"I suppose he nearly didn't. Although he did appear rather regal in Mr. Eddington's spectacles."

Her sweet laughter and the rosy blush that tinted her cheeks mesmerized him. If only things were different and he could extend their friendship into more.

"Timothy taught him how to fetch, but when the children at the school endeavored to repeat it, Beans refused to cooperate. I think he was enjoying the attention too much to repeatedly run after the toy they'd made for him."

Landon thought of the boy down the street and his golden retriever. Had he ever dressed up the dog? Set a hat on his head or propped spectacles on his snout?

"You made mention about the dog your neighbor owned when you were a boy," said Mae, as if to read his mind. "Were you allowed to play with the dog on occasion since he lived so close?

"No, but honestly I wasn't home much. Most of the time was spent at boarding school."

"I'm sorry. That must have been disappointing to be away from your parents so often."

"My parents aren't like yours, Mae."

He regretted her shocked expression at his inadvertently abrupt tone. "I apologize. That sounded brusque. Regrettably, they were too busy with their own lives to worry much about mine, hence the reason for sending me away year after year. To their benefit, they did desire for me to have the best education possible." Landon didn't wish to cast his parents negatively and bemoaned his prior words. "Mother and Father have always provided for me, made sure I had everything I could ever need and ensured the highest of education during both my grammar and university years. I knew I was loved and that they cared for me, but they had and still do have certain expectations." *Ones I will never be able to fulfill.*

Mae's troubled countenance indicated she struggled with understanding the differences between their upbringings. He did too. But while he *did* know his parents loved him, he doubted they cherished him like Mae's parents cherished their children.

Time to change the topic. "It sounds like you had a pleasant day."

"I did. But, of course, I love working at the school."

The breeze caused a stray hair to escape from her bun, and Landon resisted the urge to brush it from her face and tuck it behind her ear.

"We welcomed a new student today."

"Oh?"

"Yes. A young girl from Humboldt. She's never learned to communicate and no one in her family knows sign language. She has some struggles, but I'm confident the Lord will provide a way to assist her."

"Most folks don't know such a language exists. I didn't until coming to Horizon." Landon thought of the book Mae loaned him and how he'd become more proficient after practicing each day, although it required considerable effort and commitment. Already he had learned to fingerspell the entire alphabet.

Mae sighed. "That's true. Fortunately, Jeralyn's parents have agreed to learn and to teach it to their other children. Such devotion will eliminate much of Jeralyn's loneliness.

"Does that happen often that the parents and families exude a willingness to learn?"

"Sometimes, but more often than not, they don't want to be burdened. This leaves the child with few resources."

Landon thought of his own parents. Would they have been amenable to learning sign language if he'd been born deaf? He respected Mother and Father but doubted they'd be willing to inconvenience themselves. He immediately chastised himself for thinking ill of his parents. The most recent time with them in Cornwall had no doubt cast them negatively in his mind.

Mother had already expressed her displeasure when they'd discussed Mae. And Father would never allow him to marry someone below his station and put the family business in jeopardy.

But Landon knew he would not be content with sharing only camaraderie with the lovely woman beside him because, in a short amount of time, he'd fallen in love with Mae.

Two weeks later, Landon met with Father, the investment partner, and the field engineers. Mr. Brillhart, a loathsome man in his forties, was one of Father's investment partners.

Father hired a wagon and driver from the Ingleville livery and they drove to where the railroad workers were busy clearing the land of brush and rocks. Duchesne, a rogue with a drinking problem, Chen, a small pleasant fellow, and Walsh, an Irishman with a thick brogue, were the supervisors.

"I'd like to ask you for a raise," said Duchesne before Father had a chance to speak.

Father dismissed him with a wave. "You don't need a raise. You're being paid plenty."

Duchesne ground his teeth and glared at Father. "We're working hard, and we deserve us a raise."

"Obviously you are deaf, dumb, or just a simpleton because Mr. Bennick has already indicated you'll receive no raise." Brillhart shoved his hands into the pockets of his suit. A suit that likely cost more than he and Father were paying Duchesne for a year's worth of work.

"Let's proceed with the reason we are here. First, we'd like to inquire as to the advancement of the spur from Ingleville to Horizon. Second, the field engineers will be determining the route for the final stretch of this line." Father strolled toward the table where one of the field engineers had placed a map of the area. "As we are all aware, usually we build the town around the line, but in the cases of both Ingleville and Horizon, we've had to build the spur around the town, or through it."

Landon bent forward and peered at the map. The field engineer had marked an "x" on the current location of the most-recently completed portion of track. They were already halfway between Ingleville and Horizon, and in his opinion, the workers had exercised diligence. Brillhart was not as complimentary and gave the supervisors a harsh lecture about the urgency to work the men harder and push them to complete the task faster.

Father said nothing, but Landon had a different view of things. He promoted safety first, and with the building of the railroad being dangerous at times, he was content with the men moving slower in areas of hazardous terrain, times of inclement weather, and situations where dynamite was used for the construction of tunnels. Both Walsh and Chen were conscientious supervisors who themselves worked hard. Duchesne, on the other hand, was an insolent cad and treated some of the employees with a complete lack of respect. He had also arrived at work drunk on more than one occasion. If it was up to Landon, he'd fire the man in an instant.

"We'll travel to Horizon and plan the remainder of the line tomorrow," suggested Father. He clicked open his gold pocket watch. "The stage leaves at eight in the morning. Landon, did you secure the rooms at the boardinghouse for us?"

"Yes, sir."

Brillhart narrowed his eyes. "Wait a minute. A boardinghouse? Is there not a hotel in the fine town of Horizon?"

"There is not. I have been there once and suffice it to say, I don't wish to return; however, due to our obligation to determine the remainder of the route, the boardinghouse is our only option. The proprietress sets aside a few rooms for those traveling through the area who wish to stay for only a night or two. It is far from the luxurious hotels found in Denver or Chicago, but it suits its purposes." Father looked at each of the men. "It is imperative we secure the final routeway."

"Landon already has a room there, but there will be four of us. Must we share a room?" Brillhart turned his nose up at the field engineers. "I propose, Bennick, that you stay with Landon, and the two field engineers room together. I require my own room."

Landon knew long ago that Brillhart had a penchant for irritating Father with his ridiculous demands. However, since they'd been friends for years, Father most often overlooked Brillhart's impositions. "Landon, how many rooms did you secure?"

"Miss Greta, the proprietress, did have two additional rooms available."

Father's mustache twitched. "Perfect!" He pointed at the field engineers. "One of you will room with me and one will room with Brillhart. It's only for a night or two, and from what I recall, Landon's room is terribly small, thereby making this the most efficient method."

"Not efficient," sneered Brillhart. "Absurd. Why not the two field engineers and you and me, Bennick? That makes more sense."

Father tilted his head back and offered a brief chuckle. "Brillhart, we have been friends for many years. So long, in fact, that I know better than to purposely subject myself to your company if I desire a good night's sleep, what with your snoring."

"Sounds a bit like the roaring of a train itself, eh?" Walsh asked.

Brillhart shot the man a contemptuous glare. "Do you wish to remain an employee of Bennick Railways?"

Walsh, a robust and jolly sort, immediately rescinded his statement. "Yes, sir, I do. Gots me a family to feed."

"Then keep your boorish comments to yourself."

The following day, the stagecoach arrived in Horizon, and after leaving their items at the boardinghouse, the men embarked on a noonday meal at Wilhelmina's Restaurant. Landon cringed when Father requested chicken okra soup rather than the meatloaf special. But Wilhelmina, always gracious, refused to allow Father's finicky eating habits to dissuade her. In all seriousness and with the utmost respect, she leaned toward Father and whispered, "Not sure I have any okra at the moment, Mr. Bennick, but I would be happy to prepare a special chicken meal just for you. It was my mother's recipe and a delicious one at that. What would you say?"

Thankfully, Father acquiesced and after the meal, he, Landon, Brillhart, and the field engineers walked along the proposed route of the railroad, map in hand. They then rented a wagon from the livery and traveled outside of town.

All was well until they stopped just near the Horizon School for the Deaf. "The route will continue through here." One of the field engineers pointed to an area that abutted the fence surrounding the front of the school.

"Just a minute," said Landon. "Are you planning to continue the tracks this close to the school?" What a preposterous plan! How would the children be safe when the second they stepped outside the front door, the train would be roaring by on the tracks? To make matters worse, they would be unable to hear it, making the situation all the more dangerous.

"The field engineers have studied the topography and other factors and believe this is the best option." Father crossed his arms, his gaze daring Landon to argue.

Brillhart held his hand palm up and shrugged. "Not sure why we would care anyway. A railroad line through here benefits more people than a school for children no one cares about."

Anger rose within Landon, and he struggled to maintain his composure. He took a step toward Brillhart and enunciated his words slowly. "People do care about the children. *I* care about the children."

A sneer formed on Brillhart's pinched face. "You're likely one of the few. As I mentioned a moment ago, we must seek to do that which benefits the most people. A school for deaf and mute children benefits no one, or..." Brillhart paused as his lips drew back into a snarl, "almost no one."

"You can't put the tracks here, Father. It wouldn't be prudent. Children could step outside and get run over by the train. It would be unsafe for them to play. It would shake the house and make living inside unbearable."

"But if deaf children reside in the house, they won't hear the train. They won't be bothered at all. The way I see it, that's another benefit to placing the tracks right here." Brillhart cracked his knuckles. "Shall we return to town?"

Landon's pulse pounded and his body tensed. "I cannot allow you to put the tracks here. Move them a mile to the north or a few miles to the south, but not directly near the school."

"You *cannot* allow it?" Brillhart took a step toward Landon and thumbed his chest. "Who cares what you will and won't allow? You are not in charge. You are not an investor. You answer to your father. You have no basis for acting as though you are the one who makes important decisions."

"Father, please, will you reconsider the location?"

"If this is what the field engineers have decided is best, then I agree with them."

"Father, this is ludicrous." Landon waved at the vast land on either side of the school. "There is plenty of area in which to build the tracks. This school belongs to Mr. and Mrs. Eddington.

You can't just take it away from them. And to build it near children—what if they were your children?"

"I highly doubt I would be the father of deaf children." Father's eyes darted between Landon and Brillhart. "Besides, we purchased this land from the seller. Unfortunately…" He offered a self-satisfied sneer. "The school's property adjoins the newly acquired property. 'Tis a shame."

How could Landon make his father see the error? "You can't build it here. Build it elsewhere, but not here."

Father pointed his finger at Landon. "You listen here, Landon Bertram Bennick, you will not tell me what I will or won't do. The track will be built here. End of discussion." Father followed the field engineers to the wagon leaving Landon and Brillhart behind.

Brillhart's eyes shot sparks at Landon, and he pasted on a fake and evil-looking grin. "Who knew you were so daft, Landon? You're just a pawn. No one, not even your father, cares what you think about any topic, let alone the railroad. You'd be easily replaceable were it not for who your father is."

Landon balled his hands into fists and felt the sweat trickle down his back. *Lord, restrain my temper. Please.*

"What's wrong? Are you suddenly speechless? Struck dumb?"

"I have wondered all my life, but never more than now."

"Wondered what?"

"Why Father would ever choose to conduct business with the likes of you."

A vein throbbed in Brillhart's narrow forehead. "At least he respects *me*."

Landon swallowed the pain Brillhart's words inflicted. Oftentimes, he wondered if Father cared about, respected, or even loved him. That uncertainty had shrouded him his entire life.

As they rode back to town in silence, concerns clouded Landon's mind. There had to be more he could say in defense of the children and the school. If only Father would listen.

And what would happen when Mae discovered Bennick Railways' plans?

CHAPTER TWENTY

MAE PLACED THE SPOOLS of thread for Mama that she'd purchased from the mercantile into her saddle bag and pulled out a knitted purple scarf. One more errand before returning home after a long day at the school.

A long, but good day. She meandered down the boardwalk, greeting passersby as she did. As a shyer individual, it had taken time for her to embrace the idea of speaking with people, especially those she didn't know well. But over time, she had come to appreciate the bonds she'd formed with many of those who resided in Horizon. This was her home. A home she hoped to remain in for the rest of her life.

Miss Greta was bent over a cast iron three-legged pot that she had converted into a planter. She fluffed the soil around, then matted it carefully around the tender green stems of what would soon be flowers.

If anyone could get a flower to grow, it was Miss Greta.

"Miss Greta?"

The woman stood, positioned a hand on her lower back as she straightened to a fully upright position, and faced Mae. "What brings you to the boardinghouse?"

"I have something for you."

Miss Greta's thin brow wrinkled. "Why would you have something for me?"

Mae did her best to stifle the giggle that threatened to erupt. Miss Greta was a crabby sort at times, but beneath her cantankerous exterior was a woman with a kind heart and generous spirit.

"I happen to know it's your birthday today."

"How do you know that?"

Mae wouldn't elaborate on who had told her the information, and with her free hand, pretended to button her lips. "I shan't tell."

"Humph. Well, when you reach my age, there isn't any use in keeping a record of birthdays. They all blend together as the years pass."

Mama would say Miss Greta's cynical statement was an excuse, and that deep down, the woman appreciated being remembered. Mae tended to agree. "Be that as it may, close your eyes and hold out your hand."

"Close my eyes?"

"Yes, Miss Greta. Close your eyes."

"Well, aren't you a bossy sort."

Mae had rarely been referred to as bossy, but she wouldn't argue with Miss Greta. "Now hold out your hand."

"My hands are a mite dirty, what with tending to my blooms." Miss Greta swiped her right hand on her faded calico apron then held it palm up.

Mae brought her right arm from behind her back and placed the scarf in Miss Greta's outstretched palm. "You can open your eyes now."

Miss Greta's eyes fluttered open and rested on the gift.

"I know it's nearly summer, but I knitted this just for you." She held her breath as the woman unfolded it.

"You're right—it is summer, so there isn't a need for a scarf." Miss Greta's voice wavered, and she blinked rapidly. The patchwork of finely-etched lines covering her face became more pronounced, and she ran a hand along the braided yarn. Tears shimmered in her eyes.

Miss Greta cleared her throat. "I love it, Mae. I do."

Mae released the breath she'd been holding. "I'm so glad. I know purple is your favorite color and…"

"How did you know purple was my favorite color?"

Should she say that Mama had told her? Or determine not to divulge her source?

Now she sounded like Ruby with the continual articles she constantly wrote in the hopes of someday being published in *The Horizon Herald.*

"I think you'll look beautiful in it come winter."

Miss Greta wrapped it around her neck, some of her frizzy red-gray hairs emerging from the yarn in a static disarray. "How does it look?"

"Lovely."

Miss Greta then removed it and wrapped it over her head as though a hat. "Lovely still?"

Mae giggled. "Lovely still."

A smile emerged on Miss Greta's lips, but as quickly as the smile emerged, she frowned and quickly pressed her lips together, removed the scarf, and patted her disheveled hair. "Did he see me?"

"Who?"

"The Lieutenant."

Mae peered over her shoulder just as Miss Greta lightly grasped her arm. "Don't look! He'll know we're talking about him."

She spun around to again peer at Miss Greta, whose plump cheeks had taken on a rosy hue. "Sorry. But why don't you want him to see you?"

"It's beyond embarrassing for a man like the Lieutenant to see me acting as though I'm a young schoolgirl with a knitted scarf on my head when it's nearly summer." The woman took a sharp intake of breath. "Isn't he just the most dapper man?"

"The Lieutenant?"

"Of course the Lieutenant," Miss Greta hissed.

Mae slowly turned and inconspicuously peered at the man old enough to be her grandfather.

"Look at him over there working so hard to stack the chopped wood. He's so strong and handsome. And he's a war hero, you know. Helped lead our Union troops to victory."

"Yes, I'd heard he was a war hero."

Miss Greta smoothed her skirt. "I have agreed to accompany him on another buggy ride and picnic tomorrow afternoon. Until a few weeks ago, I'd never been on a buggy ride. Wagons, horses, and even one train, yes. But never something as sophisticated as a buggy. And to think it was driven by such a dashing man!"

"Congratulations. I'm sure you'll again enjoy the Lieutenant's company."

"Oh, I will. For the longest time, I wasn't sure how to make him notice me."

It was the rare bird who *hadn't* noticed Miss Greta.

Without waiting for Mae's reply, Miss Greta whispered, "Now, do not tell a soul, but I do provide meals for the Lieutenant in exchange for him assisting me with fixing things around the boardinghouse and chopping wood."

Mae buttoned her lips for the second time. "You have no worries, Miss Greta. I won't tell anyone. I knew he didn't board here, as he lives in the adjacent house."

"Indeed. When he moved into the old Janvier house, I wasn't fond of him at first. He seemed a bit off-putting. A grump, if you will."

"But now?"

Miss Greta held her free hand to her heart and swooned. "I've only been in love one other time in my life. But he went off and got hisself killed in the war. The second time I've been in love..." She cleared her throat and narrowed her eyes. "You did promise not to tell anyone, right?"

"I did promise. Miss Greta, I consider you a friend, and I would never betray your confidence."

"A friend?"

"Yes. A friend."

Was it Mae's imagination or did Miss Greta's eyes glisten? "Humph. Well. At supper a few weeks ago, he acted as though he wanted to say something to me and started to do so a few times, but then he didn't. Just said 'I've been meaning to ask you...' No more words after that. He just kept right on eating as though he was half-starved. Now that I think about it, I'd bet my finest set of mismatched china—not that I'm a gambling woman, mind you, for I don't believe in such wrongdoings—but I'd bet my finest mismatched china that he was going to ask me to accompany him on a buggy ride."

"That could very well be. Perhaps you could make him his favorite cookies for the picnic. Not for the entire boardinghouse, but just for him."

Miss Greta nodded. "He does like food. I could try that. Might endear me more to him somewhat."

From what Landon insinuated, the Lieutenant was more than endeared to Miss Greta. More aptly put, the man was smitten. So much so, that he planned to ask Miss Greta to court him. It astonished Mae that the Lieutenant hadn't yet done so.

Miss Greta twisted her mouth to one side. "I haven't a clue as to why, but I'm having a case of the nerves just thinkin' about the picnic." She sighed. "Do you have a beau, Mae?"

Landon's image filled her mind. Would he someday be her beau? They came from completely different worlds, and she doubted he would ever seriously consider a woman who was below his station. In addition, he would be leaving after the railroad's completion. But what if... "No, I don't," she finally answered.

"Well, I best get to work. No sense in standing here staring at the Lieutenant all day. I can do that with more ease standing inside the house and peering through the curtains."

"Much more incognito that way."

"Indeed." Miss Greta paused. "Oh, dear. Here comes Mr. Bennick and his men. They started staying here again just last night. Thankfully their stay will be brief. Mr. Bennick's son isn't too awful, but Mr. Bennick himself complains far too often about the meals. He's always asking for something I can neither pronounce nor prepare. The tall thin one with expensive clothing—Mr. Brillhart—is a nasty sort."

Mae had never before seen Landon's father. Nor had she met the other men. "They must be here to discuss the railroad."

"Likely so. I am for being gracious, but I'll not cotton to those selfish men."

As the men neared, Mae could see the family resemblance between Landon and his pa, although Mr. Bennick's demeanor was more austere. They shared the same dark blond hair and symmetrical facial features, but Landon's build and height were taller and more muscular than that of his short and thin father.

The four men strolled toward the porch, and Mae and Miss Greta scooted aside to allow them to pass.

"Good evening," said Miss Greta, her voice strained.

"What is for supper?" Mr. Bennick asked.

"Meatloaf and baked potatoes."

"May you by chance—"

"No. You may eat at *Wilhelmina's Restaurant* if meatloaf and baked potatoes are unsuitable for your palate."

Mr. Bennick glowered at her and strode inside the house, followed by two other men. The tall thin one known as Mr. Brillhart paused and allowed his eyes to rove over Mae in a way that caused bile to rise in her throat. "Perhaps your maid here could deliver some fresh linens to my room."

"She's not the maid, and she's not going to be delivering anything to your room. All the linens you need, you already have." Miss Greta stepped between Mae and Mr. Brillhart. "Find your way elsewhere. Supper will be served soon."

A vein twitched in Mr. Brillhart's forehead. He said nothing more, only pushed his way through the door to the boarding-house.

Ten minutes later, Mae left Miss Greta's. She needed to return home soon lest Mama and Papa worry. Just as she was about to untether her horse, she spied Landon walking in her direction. Would he stop and converse for a moment? "Hello, Landon."

"Hello, Mae."

She hadn't seen much of him in recent days, and she'd missed him. "How have you been?" She offered a smile. One that wasn't returned.

"I'm fine." He paused. "Do you have a way home?"

An odd inquiry considering she was untethering her horse. "Yes, I do. I had a few errands first."

"I see. Well, I best be on my way." Landon tipped his hat, and without another word, strode past her.

Mae watched him leave, noting how his strong shoulders slumped. It was obvious something was wrong. Was he mad at her for some reason or had something else happened?

"Landon?" She started after him. Perhaps he'd share what bothered him.

But he either didn't hear her or chose to ignore her because he continued on his way in the direction of the boardinghouse.

Leaving Mae with a barrage of questions crowding her mind.

CHAPTER TWENTY-ONE

THE EXPRESSION ON MAE'S face was not one Landon would soon forget. He'd wanted to talk with her. To hear about her day at the school.

But he hadn't been able to bring himself to look her in the eye. He was certain that she would be able to detect the sorrow, regret, guilt, and frustration he carried after Father's and Brillhart's disclosure regarding the route of the railroad.

Landon wanted to be sure she had a way home, and if she needed him to accompany her, he would do so. But he was secretly relieved he hadn't had to escort her.

If Mae discovered the tracks would be built within arm's length of the fence that surrounded the school...Landon didn't want to think about her profound disappointment.

And he didn't want to think about how she would blame him for not finding a way to divert the tracks, especially when there was so much open space that could easily accommodate the construction. Space that didn't impede on the school or its grounds.

The aroma of supper permeated the air when Landon entered the boardinghouse. If his nose didn't betray him, potatoes were on the menu. He sauntered past the kitchen and up the stairs to his room. If he wasn't so hungry, Landon would prefer to spend the evening tucked inside the meager space he rented.

After supper, Father beckoned to him. "Take a walk with me."

It wasn't a request or a suggestion, but a demand.

Landon followed Father out of the boardinghouse and into the pleasant evening. "Your mother anticipates a visit to this primitive place. She'll be sorely disappointed at the lack of conveniences." Father thumbed a finger at the boardinghouse. "The food offerings at that establishment are atrocious, to say the least."

Landon disagreed with his father. As a matter of fact, he had grown to like Horizon and many of the people who called it home, including Miss Greta.

Father stopped near one of the trees at the edge of the property and turned to face Landon. "This is as good a time as any to remind you of your place."

He should have known a lecture was forthcoming after the Horizon School for the Deaf incident.

Father stood taller and straighter and pressed the wrinkles from his expensive tan plaid frock coat. "Your grandfather, Abelard Bertram Bennick, was an enterprising man. He was resourceful and ambitious. I regret that I haven't told you much about him in all these years. He and his parents emigrated from Germany when he was a baby. As a young adult, he founded A.B.B. Shipping Company, an endeavor that grew instantly from a trivial business into one of immense magnitude. Soon after I was born, he added railroads to his investments and changed the name to A.B.B. Shipping and Railway Company. His innovative practices, wise acquisitions of much smaller companies, and the accumulation of assets caused his company to be one of the most prominent in the East, if not the entire United States and her territories."

"I knew he had a hand in founding Bennick Railways, but I had no idea it was once known by a different name."

"Yes, well, he and I were not close. Nor was I close to my mother, God rest her soul. When my father passed away, I naturally took over the business, sold the shipping portion, and renamed the company to Bennick Railways. Your grandfather was a hard man. The reason I am telling you this is because while your grandfather and I disagreed on most things, I did respect him. He worked hard to start the business and maintain and grow it. Someday when your mother and I are no longer here, you will inherit Bennick Railways. Until then, I own the company and will do as I see fit. You may make occasional suggestions or request charitable funds for worthwhile causes on an infrequent basis, but you may not tell me how to run the business. Your input earlier today was unnecessary and unwarranted. You looked foolish and attempted to make me look daft in front of Brillhart. See that such an occurrence does not happen again. Am I understood?"

"Yes, sir." In nearly every discussion Landon had ever had with his father, it was the rare occasion that he was afforded the luxury of stating his own opinion. This wasn't one of those times.

Landon watched Father march back into the boardinghouse. How would he stop Father from building the tracks so close to the school, especially after this evening's admonition? What would Mae do when she found out? Should he tell her first?

He may not know the answers to those questions, but he did know that sleep would be difficult to attain tonight.

Mae was teaching her second class when she peered outside and noticed two men.

Their four-seated buggy was parked haphazardly on the side of the road and they busied themselves with a surveying tripod.

She heard the front door open and signed to her class that she would be right back. "Mr. Eddington, may I come with you?"

The older man nodded, and she followed him outside, down the stairs, and through the gate. It squeaked as he opened it, and he muttered something about needing to fix it soon.

The field engineers stood several feet away. "Excuse us, sirs." Mr. Eddington stalked toward them, and Mae struggled to keep up with him.

The shorter of the two men, a thickset man in his fifties with a graying beard, round spectacles, and a scowl, spoke first. "Yes?"

"May I ask what you are doing?"

"Surveying for the continuation of the railroad line."

Mae gasped. "The railroad line?"

"You must be mistaken. This is too close to the school." Mr. Eddington jerked a thumb toward the school.

"Makes no difference to us. We're just doing what we are told." This, from the other man, a tall lanky sort with a hunched posture and brown felt hat.

"Told by whom?" Mr. Eddington asked.

"By Mr. Bennick, of course."

Mr. Bennick would allow them to build part of the railroad so close to the school? "Which Mr. Bennick?"

The tall one shrugged. "Both of them. We've already discussed this area as the best place to continue the line."

The air whooshed from Mae's lungs. Landon would agree to such a preposterous idea? "Are you sure the young Mr. Bennick would consent to this?"

The thickset man closed his eyes and shook his head as if irritated Mae would dare doubt his words. "Yes, we're sure. As was mentioned, we discussed this idea with both Mr. Bennicks and Mr. Brillhart as well. Not that it's any of your concern, but this is the most advantageous area due to the topography and the fact there will be less preparatory work. If we move the line that way..." he pointed in the distance, "we'll have to clear all the trees. If we move the route that way..." he pointed in the area behind the school, "the workers will be hauling rocks far into the next century." He huffed. "Now, if you'll excuse us, we have work to do."

Mr. Eddington started to ask a few more questions, but the taller man shook his head and held out a hand. "If you have questions or disputes, approach either the elder or younger Bennick or Brillhart. Although I'd personally recommend the Bennicks over Brillhart. However, you'll not prevail against a company like Bennick Railways." He held out his hands, palms up. "A school few care about or a railroad that will connect Ingleville to Horizon and beyond to the Idaho border. Would seem an obvious choice."

The thickset one dismissed them with a wave of his hand. "Now, return to whatever it was you were doing and allow us to do the same."

Mr. Eddington shuffled to the house. But Mae's feet would not move. Her arms were numb and felt as though a heavy weight rested upon them. She gaped at the two men who had gone about their work as if they weren't attempting to uproot and destroy the lives of many people, most of them being children.

Lord, please. Let there be something we can do.

With effort, she lifted her eyes to scan the school. So many in town had come together to repair the home. Even now, it required further restoration. Several shingles had blown off in the last windstorm. Chipped white paint on the window frames and several missing spindles on the porch revealed the home's age. Drafty, cold air seeped into the house during cold winter days, and Mr. Eddington had placed a board over a window that one of the students accidentally broke while playing baseball.

Papa, Albert, the Lieutenant, Sheriff Zembrodt, Doc, Mr. Eddington, and many others had spent countless hours repairing the home to make it livable. Mr. Eddington attempted to do his best with the upkeep of the house and the barn while also assisting with the children, but it had become overwhelming.

Still. The Horizon School for the Deaf didn't deserve to close. Not after all the hard work, time, and devotion so many had poured into it and continued to pour into it.

Warm tears skipped down her cheeks. Yes, they could stay in the school, but it wouldn't be safe for the children. Not with a train mere feet away.

Her shoulders shook and the tears continued to silently fall. What would become of the children? Of the Eddingtons? Of Lenore? Mae had a wonderful family and she would be all right. But some of the others…

When Mr. Jeffler gifted the house to the school, no one could have foreseen the blessing it would become.

The children emerged through the door for recess, their jubilant steps reminding Mae that she ought not reveal her despondency. She swiped at a tear, straightened her shoulders, took a deep breath, and prayed once again that a solution would be found.

Polly ran to her and wrapped her arms around Mae's waist. She peered up expectantly before her hands flew with words.

Mae answered her inquiry, that yes, she was all right. And yes, she would love to play a game of hopscotch in the dirt just outside the fence.

The dirt that would eventually be prepared for a line of railroad track.

The afternoon unmercifully dragged on. Mae did her best to contain the emotions lurking so close to the surface. If only she could leave now and ride home, but she couldn't leave the teaching to Mrs. Eddington and Lenore. Not when they already had so much to do.

Nor could she just ride home. Not today. If only Papa hadn't agreed to allow Landon to retrieve her. He was the last one she wished to speak with. Indignation rose within her. How dare he agree to place the tracks so close to the school!

Mae could count on one hand the times she'd ever raised her voice or set things to right in anything but a calm manner.

Today would be one of those days.

Chapter Twenty-Two

LANDON WAITED ALL DAY to see Mae. The more he spent time with her, the more he was taken with her.

He beckoned the horses around the corner and up the slight hill to the school. When he'd first asked Mr. Shepherdson if he'd allow Landon to retrieve Mae after school, he wasn't sure her father would agree, but was thankful when he had.

Moments later, he climbed from the buggy and strode up the steps to the school. Mrs. Eddington answered the door, and he greeted her.

But the older woman's demeanor lacked its usual warmth. Instead of a friendly smile, she nearly scowled at him as she stepped aside and gestured him into the home. "Mae will be finished in a moment," Mrs. Eddington said before stalking to the kitchen.

Were the children in the backyard? Usually Hosea, at least, greeted him when he visited.

Finally, Mae appeared, and his heart did a peculiar jig in his chest. She was beautiful as usual. "Good afternoon, Mae." He offered both a smile and his arm. She didn't acknowledge his greeting, but she did place a hand through his elbow.

He assisted her into the buggy. Perhaps she wasn't feeling well. Or maybe the children had been difficult today. Or maybe her mind was on other things. Whatever the case, Landon hoped to share a pleasant conversation with her once they left the school grounds.

They passed the barn and the Horizon School for the Deaf wooden sign. "How was your day?" he asked.

"Fine."

He barely heard her nearly inaudible answer. Mae sat, hands clenched in her lap, peering to the right at the passing scenery.

What could be wrong?

Landon tugged on the reins, and the horses came to a stop. "Mae?"

Her gaze remained in the opposite direction.

Landon transferred the reins to one hand and gently tapped on her shoulder. She flinched.

"Mae? Is something wrong?"

A sniffle sounded. Was she crying?

"Mae, please. Look at me."

She turned then, and the pain in her eyes froze his heart midbeat. Tears shone in her eyes. Landon wanted to take her into his arms and reassure her that he would ease whatever caused her sorrow.

"Did someone hurt you?"

She nodded mutely, and protectiveness rose within him. He clenched his jaw and offered a prayer that the Lord would restrain the innate urge to seek revenge on whoever would seek to harm the woman he was growing to love. "Who hurt you, Mae?"

Mae didn't speak for a moment.

Landon rested his hand on her arm, as he inclined closer. "Please tell me."

Sobs choked her words then—words he was unprepared to hear. "How...how...could you?"

He'd been the one to hurt her? His chest grew tight and for a moment, he couldn't speak. A thick ache rose in him. Landon removed his hand from her arm. How had he hurt her?

Unless...

"Can you explain?" he finally asked, his voice hoarse.

More tears pooled in her eyes, and she covered her mouth with her hand. A moment later she removed it. "You're the reason the school will close."

The railroad.

He should have known she would find out. If only he'd told her when he planned to instead of avoiding the inevitable. "I have talked to my father and Brillhart about that."

A flash of anger crossed her face, but her tone remained hushed. "Yes, I'm sure you did. Apparently, you agree with them that placing the tracks so close to the school is reasonable."

"No, that's not true. I agreed with neither them nor the engineers regarding the location."

"Then why didn't you stop them?"

Her words tore at him. Anguish lodged in his throat. What could he say? That while he had attempted to reason with Father and Brillhart they hadn't listened? That Landon was a coward for not trying harder? "What do you want me to do, Mae?"

A tortured sob emitted from her mouth and her chin trembled. "What do I expect you to do?"

"Yes. I've tried talking to them."

"Do you have any idea how important the school is?"

"I do know it's important to you."

She blinked rapidly. "Not just to me. To the children. To the Eddingtons. To Lenore. To the children's parents. Do you even care about the children?"

Her accusation caused both hurt and anger. "Yes, I care for the children. Very much so."

"Polly was orphaned as an infant. When she came to the school, she could not communicate at all. *At all.*"

"I didn't know that."

"Now that her grandfather has passed, do you know what could have happened to Polly if there had been no Horizon School for the Deaf? She may have been sent to an asylum."

"Surely there are other schools."

For the first time since he'd known her, Mae raised her voice. "Other schools?"

"I'm just stating that the Horizon School for the Deaf is not the only school of its kind. I've heard of other schools across the country. Polly could have been sent to one of them."

"If only it were that easy."

Mae's shoulders shook, and Landon reached for her.

She jerked away. "Do you also know about Hosea?"

Landon realized how little he knew about the students. "No."

"Hosea is an orphan. The school is his only family. And don't suggest that someone could adopt him. Deaf children are not easy to place with permanent families. And do you know that two of the children at the school were kept from learning any kind of sign language? Their parents refused to allow them to learn any type of communication. Short of some archaic hand motions for obvious things, they could not express anything to anyone in the hearing world. Fortunately, as twins, they had each other."

Landon wanted to know how they came to the school.

"And one of our older pupils who is only nine years old, was left on the streets of Chicago at the age of five by his parents because they no longer wanted what they termed a defective child. Where would he be without the school? Some children have loving parents who only wish for the best for them. Some have parents in Horizon, Ingleville, Humboldt, Boise City, and in the northern part of the state. Those children are in the minority, yet still, their parents are grateful their children can receive a quality education. Jeralyn, our newest student and only five years old, is making amazing improvements after such a short time." Mae held up her hands and shrugged. "But don't worry about the school closing. Don't worry that it's unsafe to have the tracks adjacent to the fence."

"I've thought of all those things. As I said, I spoke to my father and Brillhart about it. To make matters worse, the land beyond the fence is not owned by the school."

Mae's eyebrows knitted together and she drew her head back quickly. "I wasn't aware the land belonged to someone else. I believe the school owns from just beyond the house in the back to the tree line in the front."

"A Mr. Lech owns that land."

"Mr. Lech?"

"Yes."

Mae's shoulders dropped and she crumbled in her seat with the appearance of defeat on her face. "Be that as it may, we must do something."

"I've tried. Nothing can be done."

"So you won't continue to try?"

How could he make Mae understand that once Father set his mind to something, nothing would change it? "I could say that the line will be moved elsewhere. I could promise you that I would persuade my father to make alternate arrangements. But what good would a promise be if it's broken?"

Mae's lower lip trembled. "Do you know what it's like to be mistreated? Do you know what it's like to know that no one wants you?"

"We can find homes for the children."

"I'm not talking about the children."

He barely heard her whispered words. "You're not talking about the children?"

Mae didn't answer him, only clasped her hands tightly together in her lap as her body continued to shake. What he wouldn't give to be able to comfort her.

"Please take me home, Landon."

He hesitated only a moment before doing as she asked.

After he assisted her from the buggy, Mae bolted to the door of her home without looking back. Should he pursue her? Speak with her father about the situation? Offer his hundredth prayer seeking God's help? So far those prayers had been anything but effective.

Landon steered the buggy toward town and to Miss Greta's. There he would see Father and Brillhart, but he had no desire to speak with either one. He was trapped in a decision, not of his own making. A decision that severely hurt Mae and those she cared about.

He would take all of that pain upon himself if allowed to do so.

The church came into view with its steeple and cross, and beside it, the parsonage.

Pastor Albert.

He would know what to do.

But would Albert refuse to listen to Landon since he'd caused his sister such pain?

Rain poured, blurring his vision, and Landon stopped the buggy, allowing it to remain stalled in the road while he hesitated. There were four options. Go back to the Shepherdson farm and attempt to rectify things, go to Miss Greta's and face Father and Mr. Brillhart, go for a drive to clear his mind—although it was likely the already-steady stream of rain would only increase—or visit Albert and seek his advice.

The last option seemed the most reasonable.

Moments later, Landon parked the buggy and rushed up the stairs to the parsonage. He was drenched in just those brief seconds.

Velma answered the door. "So good to see you, Landon."

"Is Albert here?"

"He is not. He's at the church working on his sermon for Sunday."

"Thank you."

Without waiting, Landon sprinted to the church, opened the door, and slid inside. The torrential rains pounded on the roof above, and he thanked the Lord he was out of the inclement weather for a moment. The front pew beckoned him, and he strode toward it. It was then that he noticed Albert sitting at a desk just through a doorway, hastily writing something on a piece of stationery. Should he have waited to speak with the pastor? Should he come back another time? Forego the idea altogether? After all, Albert was a busy man, likely attempting to complete the arduous task of a Biblical sermon before supper.

Landon prepared to leave when he heard a voice behind him. "Landon?"

He turned to see the pastor inching away from the desk. "Hello, Albert."

"Leaving so soon?"

"I'll come back another time when you're less busy."

"I'm never too busy to listen."

How could a man barely older than himself seem so mature? Albert's knowledge of the Bible, his wisdom about everyday things, and his servant's heart made him appear to be a man who'd preached for decades rather than years.

Landon pondered the invitation, indecision filling his thoughts. Finally, he acquiesced and sat down again in the front right-hand side pew. "If you have a few minutes, I'd sure appreciate being able to bend your ear."

"I have more than a few minutes." The pastor sat beside Landon and waited patiently while Landon attempted to gather the courage to speak.

"It's about Mae."

Albert stroked his clean-shaven chin. "I see."

"I was going to tell her about it, but I failed to do so and she learned of the tracks being built adjacent to the fence just outside the school."

"That close to the school?"

"Yes. Apparently, a man named Mr. Lech owns the land and when Mr. Brillhart, an investor in the railroad, approached him, he was fine with allowing his land to be used. Do you know Mr. Lech?"

"I do."

Albert said nothing more, but Landon had a hunch the pastor's view of the man was unfavorable.

"I have tried speaking with Father and Mr. Brillhart to no avail. They are determined to place the tracks there due to topography and other reasons."

"It's doubtful the school can remain there with the tracks so close."

"You're right. It's mere feet from the front door. It won't be safe for the children, and I completely understand Mae's concerns since I share them myself. The problem is, there is nothing I can do." Landon exhaled a deep breath. "Albert, I care deeply for Mae. I don't want her hurt, but I don't know what to do."

"Would your father be easier to persuade than Mr. Brillhart?"

"He would be, but only slightly. Usually, when Father sets his mind to something, he's not willing to change it. Mr. Brillhart…forgive me for saying so as we are in the Lord's house, but he's not an easy man to contend with."

"This calls for fervent prayer. The children in the school, some of them orphans, will have nowhere to go. There isn't an alternative building that can house the school."

Landon shifted in his seat. "I understand, sir. I have been praying."

"Perhaps if your pa could see the value of the school, he might change his mind."

It was doubtful, but Landon would welcome any suggestions. "How would you propose we do that?"

"It's something to seek God's wisdom and guidance for."

"What can I do about Mae? The way I hurt her for not telling her about the tracks—"

"Give her some time. Then you'll need to go to her and humbly ask her forgiveness."

"I'm not sure she'll forgive me."

Albert shook his head. "She likely will, provided you're sincere. Trust doesn't come easy for her."

"And I've broken that trust." The thought saddened and discouraged Landon. "I never wanted to do anything to hurt her." Mae's face flashed through his mind. The tears. The pain in her eyes. "I'd do anything to avoid having caused her any distress."

"I appreciate that you care for my sister."

"I care very much. I was hoping to someday maybe court her."

Albert pinned Landon with a gaze. "I know you're a godly and upstanding man, but I'm not sure you and Mae are suited for each other."

The words took Landon aback and for a moment the threat of pride welled within him. How would the pastor know if they weren't suited for each other? With difficulty, he tamped down his frustration before speaking. "Sir, with all due respect..." his words lingered in the air.

"I know you care for her, but you come from two different worlds. If you were to court and someday marry, would you plan to take Mae from Horizon?"

Landon hadn't thought that far into the future. Albert's words had merit.

"Mae would never be happy living in a city or traveling for any period of time. She loves Horizon, loves her family, and loves the school. Yes, the Bible tells us to leave and cleave to our spouse when we marry, which she would do, but I'm not sure that's the type of life for Mae. Nor would you be content residing in a small town in Idaho when you're accustomed to the finer things in life."

Once again, pride attempted to rear its head at Albert's insinuation. "I believe love is more important than things."

"Of course you do. All I'm saying is that if you do decide to someday ask her to court you, you'll need to have a plan in place, provided you've prayed about the decision and are assured it is God's will for both of you."

Landon tilted his head back and peered at the ceiling. "I really shouldn't give courtship a thought when I've hurt Mae as I have." He thought of her again and their conversation in the buggy. Something she said reverberated in his mind. *"Do you know what it's like to be mistreated? Do you know what it's like to know that no one wants you?"* And her subsequent answer when he mentioned the children. *"I'm not talking about the children."* Had someone in her family mistreated her? Her parents? Folks in town? No, that didn't make sense.

Perhaps he ought to ask the pastor about it. "There was something Mae said that confused me."

"Oh?"

Landon relayed the conversation. "Who would mistreat her? Your parents are godly folks. Was it someone in town?"

"It would never be my parents or anyone in our family."

"Then who?"

Albert waited a moment before he said, "That's not my story to tell."

Heaviness weighed on Mae's heart as she rested her head on her pillow that night. She'd seen firsthand the fingerprints of God's work throughout her life. He'd rescued and placed her with a family who loved her. He'd given her sisters and brothers she adored. He'd made possible the opportunity for her work at the Horizon School for the Deaf—a dream she could have only imagined before it came to fruition.

Why then was she struggling so much with not worrying about the school's future? And would He see fit to heal this broken heart she suffered at the hands of Landon's dishonesty?

Landon.

During these times spent together, she'd started to grow even fonder of him. At night when she ought to be sleeping, she'd entertained fanciful thoughts of courtship. Of resting in his arms. Of warm kisses. Not that she'd told a soul. Not even Ruby, although she knew her sister suspected her growing feelings for Landon.

But now, she attempted to rationalize how the man who'd been so caring about Polly, who sat with her at church each Sunday, and who had easily won her heart was the man who neglected to tell her about the train tracks. Surely he realized how important that would be to her.

The pain wormed itself deep inside her heart. Her vision blurred as the tears again misted her eyes.

Lord, surely there is something that can be done. Surely.

Lenore crossed her arms across her chest and levied a glare at him. "Can I help you?"

"Hello, Lenore. Is Mae here?"

"She's still teaching. You'll have to come back after classes are over."

Had the occurrence with the proposed spur not happened, he would be retrieving her this afternoon and taking her home.

Before he could respond, several children rushed past him, eager to play outside before supper and chores. Mae followed, and for a second, his heart dropped to his boots. "Mae?"

"You should come back later," Lenore said.

"It's all right. I'll speak with him."

A hefty sigh of relief left his lips. "Thank you. Can we go for a stroll?"

Lenore rested a hand on Mae's arm. "Are you sure? He could return later."

"I'm fine. Thank you."

Lenore stepped aside, and Landon held open the door for Mae. The pain in her eyes grieved him, and he prayed for the right words to say.

When they reached the barn, he stopped and faced her. "Mae, you have to believe that I'm doing all I can to halt the building of the tracks so close to the school."

"I don't understand why anyone would think it's a good idea when there are children here." She gestured in the direction of four of the older children tossing the baseball. "When Mr. Lech discussed the land with your company, surely that allowed for a diverse area that could be considered."

"The field engineers Father and Mr. Brillhart hired determined this was the best place."

"And you didn't argue?"

"Mae, I tried. I spoke to them, I spoke to my father, I suggested an alternate route…but to no avail." He lightly placed his hands on her arms, willing her to understand.

"You'll just relent?" Tears pooled in her eyes, and Landon wanted to tenderly brush them aside. To reassure her.

"No, I did not just relent. And I'm not surrendering. I will continue to discuss this matter with Father and fight for the school. For the students. You have to believe me." In his own ears, his words sounded desperate. "I care about the children. *I care about you.*"

Her shoulders trembled, and he took a step toward her. "Mae."

She fell into his arms, and he held her there, hoping he'd not stepped over any etiquette boundaries that would endanger her reputation, but knowing of no other way to comfort her. He kissed the top of her head. "Mae." He stepped back and framed her face in his hands. "I never, ever want to do anything to hurt you. Ever."

"There is so much you don't know."

"Then tell me. Please."

As if mustering courage, her voice trembled as she took a shaky breath. "I once lived in an orphanage. Before that, I resided with my first pa, a vicious, hateful man who treated me the way no child should ever be treated."

Landon wavered between grief, anger, and the desire for revenge. "I'm so sorry, Mae. I had no idea."

"Mama and Papa adopted me. They rescued a little girl who couldn't speak. Who'd been mocked for her inability to utter the words in her heart. Some thought I was deaf as well as mute. Some just didn't care. They treated me poorly because I wasn't like everyone else. Family after family passed over me in the towns we stopped at on the orphan train. At the time, I couldn't fully comprehend the lonely rejection, and with each denial of a permanent home, I continued to withdraw. Now I see that God had His hand upon me the entire time. He never left my side. Never deserted me. Never wished for me to experience mistreatment or abuse. What He did plan for from the beginning of time was that Tyler and Paisley Shepherdson would adopt me as their own. I am beyond grateful and so indebted to them for what they did. And just as they rescued me, I, too, wish to be a part of something that rescues those who need it the most. That is why the school is so very crucial."

He understood better now the story she'd held within. The one that Albert referenced. Landon comprehended now why her family protected her as they did. His throat tightened, and he again pulled her to him. He wanted to tell her he loved her, that never again would he allow anyone to hurt her the way her first father and the people at the orphanage had.

The minutes ticked by, punctuated by children's laughter, the neighing of a horse, and a busybody crow flying overhead. Finally, she stepped back. "I believe you."

Her words meant everything to him, and he blinked rapidly, fighting the emotion that threatened. "Thank you, Mae. I promise you I will do whatever I can. Father is a hard man, and he doesn't cotton to anyone challenging his authority, much less me. But you do have my word." He paused and looked into her eyes, realizing again how much Mae meant to him. "Thank you for sharing with me about your past. I know it wasn't easy to do so."

The desire to kiss her full lips and to make things right between them was intense, but he'd not do so until he properly courted her, especially not when she was so vulnerable as she was now.

Chapter Twenty-Three

LANDON FINISHED EATING SUPPER, then stepped outside into the fresh Idaho air for a meander up and down the boardwalk. He thanked God for Mae's forgiveness and beseeched the Lord again—for the one-hundredth time—to soften Father's heart about the track location.

He whistled as he ambled along, periodically pausing to peruse through the windows of a few of the shops on the main thoroughfare. Were this Denver, he might board a street car, for the moseying of the lengthy and vast streets would never be accomplished in mere minutes.

In the time while here, he'd become partial to Horizon and its townsfolk. Especially one in particular.

He surveyed the many wares inside the mercantile from his location on the boardwalk.

Yes, he could grow accustomed to the slower-paced life in Horizon, Idaho.

Raucous noises from the two saloons, ironically across the street from each other, pervaded the serenity. He contemplated reversing direction when a hand gripped his shoulder and jerked him backward, nearly causing him to lose his balance.

He righted himself and spun to face Duchesne, the unruliest of the railroad supervisors. "What's the meaning of this?" he asked.

"You owe me a raise."

Duchesne's foul breath—laced with whiskey—permeated the air. He teetered to and fro on unstable legs.

"You're drunk. Get back to camp and sleep it off."

The man gripped a wad of Landon's shirt and twisted. "Not until you give me the raise I deserve. I got me debts to pay, and I can't do it with the measly amount of wages I get."

"You having debts is of no concern to me. Besides, I have no power to authorize raises. Do a worthwhile job, you'll be noticed, and you'll receive appropriate compensation."

Duchesne released a stream of expletives through clenched teeth. "Something's gonna happen if I don't get me a fair wage."

Landon provided all of the accounting details for the Ingleville-Horizon project. While he deemed several of the men worthy of an increase in pay—Walsh and Chen among them—none of the men on this crew were being short-changed in wages as some railroads did to their employees, especially their Chinese and Japanese workers. For all of Father's faults, he was fair when it came to monetary recompense. Father's blunder was his inability to recognize those who exceeded the expectations placed upon them.

Duchesne was not one of those men.

"Did you hear me, Bennick? If I don't get me some more funds to pay a debt I got, something real bad's gonna happen."

"Are you threatening me?" Landon reached up and removed Duchesne's hand.

"It's all your fault."

"You incurring debt is your responsibility. Not mine. As I mentioned, do a worthwhile job—which means putting in a full day's work or better and not arriving to work drunk—and perhaps my father will notice your achievements and offer you further compensation. However, I offer no guarantees. As I previously stated, those decisions are my father's and my father's alone."

Duchesne's heavy breathing and visible shaking gave Landon pause for concern. Clearly, the man was inebriated and furious. Not a safe combination. "You best be on your way, Duchesne. You have work in the morning."

"I'm not done with you, Bennick." He staggered in the opposite direction, mounted his horse, and rode out of town, leaving Landon to deliberate the man's words and actions and whether he exaggerated the threat or meant every word.

Few townsfolk were on the boardwalk as Mae strolled toward *The Horizon Herald* to deliver Ruby's latest article to the editor on her way home from the school. Gratitude filled her heart at reconciling with Landon two days ago. She appreciated his consideration in attempting to resolve things between them and his vow to do all he could to prevent the line of track near the school.

She witnessed his frustration when conversing about his father, and reminded herself to never take for granted the pa God had blessed her with.

A thump behind Mae startled her. One of the men she recognized as a railroad employee was behind her—his hardened gaze on her remaining steadfast. Greasy, brown curly hair hung low past prominent earlobes. He had a narrow, elongated nose with a pronounced bump mid-bridge, hardened eyes, and a wiry and scraggly beard. Mae stopped to peer into the window of the millinery, attempting to take her mind off the shiver traveling up her spine.

The latest fashions hung in the window of one of Horizon's newest businesses, and Mae marveled at the elegant silk dress with its high neckline, puffy sleeves, and slim skirt. The gold color shimmered in the sunlight, and Mae imagined for a moment wearing such a fine piece of frippery.

A reflection in the window tore her attention from the dress.

The man she'd seen just moments before—the one she'd hoped would pass by her once she stopped to glimpse into the millinery's window—stared back at her. For a moment, her breath left her. The man stood so closely behind her that she could smell the overt stench of body odor. Why was he in her proximity and what did he want?

Mae squinted, leaned her head to one side, and perused the millinery. Would an employee see her if something were to go awry? Would someone on the boardwalk or one of the nearby businesses take note if she needed their assistance?

The man stepped even closer, nearly sandwiching her between himself and the window. Panic rose in her throat. Tight spaces and close quarters always caused alarm. Of course, it could be that the man wanted merely to see the lovely gown as well, perhaps for his wife.

For Mae had learned years ago that she was the only one who experienced trepidation when the feeling of being confined overwhelmed her.

An efficient perusal of Ruby's article in her right hand caused Mae to reluctantly release her tight hold on the paper. It wouldn't do to deliver a story to Mr. O'Kane that was crimped and soiled.

She needed to turn and continue on her way. To ignore the man standing behind her and the uneasiness he provoked.

Mae swiveled to the right and did her best to square her shaking shoulders. As she did so, she bumped into the man's upper body. "Excuse me." She regretted that her voice wavered, as it seemingly gave the man a dose of encouragement to continue intimidating her.

He said nothing, but his eyes traveled the length of her head to her toes, then back to her eyes where they remained unyielding and emotionless.

"Excuse me," she said again, this time barely hearing her own words.

In the far distance she noticed the sheriff, but his back was turned as he spoke to someone unknown to her.

A hiss sounded in her ear, and Mae froze at the jarring words. "Keep your mouth shut."

"I beg your pardon?"

The man said nothing. He stomped away as he hadn't just been harassing her.

Mae watched him swagger down the boardwalk toward one of the saloons. She expelled a deep breath and clutched the wooden window frame. A splinter lodged itself in her hand, and she quickly pulled away and bemoaned her careless action.

Why would the man tell her to keep her mouth shut? Why would he be following her? Who was he? What had she done to irk him?

Sheriff Zembrodt strolled her way. "Good afternoon, Mae. Are you all right?"

She opened her mouth, but the words stuck in her throat.

"Mae?"

She looked into the eyes of the kindly sheriff—a man who, with his family, had been friends of the Shepherdsons for years. "I—yes." Would he notice the tremor in her voice?

"Are you sure you're all right?"

"Yes. I just..." the man had turned to glance back at her before entering the saloon. Would he threaten her again if he saw her speaking with the sheriff?

His words again reverberated through her mind. *Keep your mouth shut.*

"Sheriff, do you know who that man was who was just standing here?"

The sheriff leaned closer to her. "The man?"

She raised her volume a notch, willing herself to calm. "Do you know who that man was who was just standing here?"

"I believe his name is Duchesne. He works for the railroad."

"Duchesne. All right. Thank you."

"Did he bother you, miss?"

Keep your mouth shut.

If she told the sheriff, would Duchenese harm her family? Harm her? "No. I was just wondering as he looked familiar."

Sheriff Zembrodt cocked his head to one side as if he didn't believe her. But Mae wouldn't risk something happening if she didn't obey Duchesne's demands.

CHAPTER TWENTY-FOUR

MAE PICKED AT A loose thread on her skirt. Disquietude filled every part of her. What if Mr. and Mrs. Bennick disliked her? She regretted agreeing to have supper with Landon and his parents at Wilhelmina's Restaurant. Landon's insistence prompted her to acquiesce, but she'd been nervous about it since the moment she'd agreed.

Landon placed a hand on hers. "Don't worry," he whispered.

But she could tell by his rigid posture that he was uneasy as well.

Wilhelmenia chatted with a couple two tables away. At least if things took a downturn, Mae's friend would offer abettance.

Mr. and Mrs. Bennick arrived seconds later and joined Mae and Landon at the table. "Mother, Father, this is Mae Shepherdson."

Before they could talk, Mr. Brillhart arrived. "Bertram, I need to speak with you and Landon about something of a timely manner."

Mr. Bennick continued to peruse his menu while giving little attention to the interruption. "Can't it wait, Brillhart? We're about to have supper."

"No, I'm afraid it cannot wait. It'll only take a moment."

Landon leaned toward her. "I'll return momentarily."

She nodded, but nerves overtook her. She'd never been gregarious like Ruby, or one to make others feel at ease like Mama, or one to take things calmly like Lucy. What would Mrs. Bennick think of her quiet and reticent nature?

Landon's ma was a handsome woman with auburn hair styled in a perfect coiffure with not a strand loose. She and Landon shared the same blue-green eyes, and Mrs. Bennick wore an elegant dress that caused the fancy ones at the millinery to pale in comparison. Suddenly, Mae felt drab.

"Hopefully that won't take long." Mrs. Bennick sat erect with her hands folded in her lap. "Do tell me something about yourself, Miss Shepherdson."

"Please, call me Mae." Her voice wavered, and Mae willed her heart to slow its pace.

"As you wish." Mrs. Bennick pursed her lips and the slight arc of her right eyebrow told of impatience.

Mae did her best to sit up straight and display the confidence she lacked. "My name is Mae Shepherdson…"

"Yes, we've established that. Go on."

If only she could disappear beneath the worn floorboards. "My apologies. My parents are Tyler and Paisley Shepherdson. Papa is a farmer, and we live just outside of town." Her words came in a rush despite her best attempts to slow them. "I have two sisters and two brothers, and I am squarely in the middle. My oldest brother, Albert, is a pastor and married to Velma. They have the most adorable little boys. My older sister, Lucy, is married to Hans, and they have two precious daughters and a child about to be born. My younger sister, Ruby, is vivacious and witty, and my younger brother, Timothy works alongside my pa in the fields. He's a bit ornery."

"Hmm."

Should Mae continue sharing about her family? Ask Mrs. Bennick about herself? The latter option won. "Please, do tell me about yourself."

"There's no need to discuss me."

Mae bit her lip. How was it that Landon was so affable and unassuming while his mother was so pretentious?

"So you hail from a poor farming family. Am I correct in my assumption?"

"I wouldn't say a *poor* family. I suppose if it is money you speak of, then no, we don't have a lot of it. We rely on the Lord's provision. While we may not have fine things, we do have an abundance of love, and we are all very close."

"Are you being flippant?"

Mae's jaw dropped. "No, ma'am, not at all. I just..." she took a deep breath and prayed the Lord would guide her. "I just firmly believe that wealth is not based on money and possessions. Wealth is having the joy of knowing you belong to the Lord and that nothing and no one can ever take that from you. Of having a loving family who cares about you and is there for you always. Of being richly blessed with loyal friends."

"I see." Mrs. Bennick patted her coiffure. "And yet, you have few pennies to your name?"

Never in her life had Mae ever expected to have a savings account at the bank, and that was fine with her. Earnings from the school paid her tithe, assisted Mama and Papa with expenses, and on occasion, was used to splurge on a bolt of fabric for a new dress for her, Mama, and Ruby. Mae had no complaints about working hard to help support her family. Especially at a job she loved. "I earn a wage that I use to assist my family with expenses."

"How admirable."

But Mrs. Bennick's tone did not indicate she *truly* found Mae admirable. The woman lifted her chin and stared down her nose at Mae. "You do realize, do you not, that Landon will someday be a wealthy man? As a matter of fact, he has achieved some prosperity even now at his young age."

"I hadn't really given it much thought."

"Pshaw! No woman sets her sights on a man who is destitute, homeless, or a drunkard. Instead, a woman seeks a man who can provide—and provide well."

Money had never meant more to Mae than a means to be able to have life's basic necessities. "Ma'am, I mean no offense, but I truly have not given that much thought. A love for God, kindness, and integrity are of utmost importance to me."

"That is utter foolishness. A love for God, kindness, and integrity won't buy the necessities of life. Further, a mother can always ascertain when a woman's motives are selfish and wealth-oriented. Landon has more money than the entirety of this town. His father and I will not watch as someone akin to a moocher attempts to separate him from his wealth. "

Before Mae could speak, Mrs. Bennick continued. "You would do well to find someone at your own station. Not one who is far above you. Besides, we have already arranged for—and Landon has agreed to—marry a woman from Denver whose family has considerable social standing."

Mae's eyes misted and Mrs. Bennick's pompous expression blurred through unshed tears.

"Furthermore, Landon would never be interested in someone like you. Not really." Mrs. Bennick tilted her head to one side. "Just look at that blouse and skirt. Now, mind you, they might be acceptable in this backwards, primitive town, but they'll never do in proper society."

Mae glanced down at her favorite white blouse Mama had made her with the pearl-colored buttons. Papa had saved to purchase the buttons to complete the blouse as a Christmas gift. The blue skirt, the one that reminded Mae of a perfect Idaho sky on a summer day, was one she'd sewn herself. She'd never thought of the ensemble to be anything but lovely. Sorrow closed up her throat. How could Mrs. Bennick be so cruel?

"You must realize Landon travels often for his employment. He visits not only unsophisticated towns such as Horizon but also cultured cities in the United States and Europe as well. In nearly every place he stays for a short duration, he meets new and different people. You are just one of many."

Sadness tore at Mae's chest. *Don't let her see you cry.* But a warm tear escaped and slid down her cheek. Mae brushed at it gently, hoping Mrs. Bennick wouldn't notice how her hateful words had affected Mae.

"Is everything settled?"

Mrs. Bennick's voice drew Mae from her despondency, and she peered up to see Landon and his father preparing to sit at the table.

"Yes, everything is settled. Shall we attempt to find something to order from this unrefined place?" Mr. Bennick took a seat beside his wife. "If we arrived back in Denver in an hour, it wouldn't be soon enough."

Landon sat beside Mae. "Sorry about the delay." He offered her one of his handsome smiles, the ones where the dimple in his right cheek was more prominent and his eyes shone. And that was all it took.

The tears flooded her own eyes, and Mae stood. "I'm sorry, Landon, but I remembered I must see to an errand at Albert's." She briefly faced Mr. and Mrs. Bennick. "It was nice to meet you."

"Mae, wait."

But Mae couldn't wait. She stumbled on shaky legs to the door, opened it, and rushed into the fresh air.

Landon was beside her in a moment. "At least allow me to accompany you to Albert's," he said.

Any response caught in her throat. Landon gently clasped her elbow, and together they walked to the parsonage. Mae lifted her hand to knock.

"Mae..."

"Good night, Landon."

Without a second glance, she hurried through the door the second Velma opened it.

Why had she ever thought falling in love with Landon Bennick was a good idea?

Landon stood outside the door of the parsonage. A mesh of emotions simmered through him— confusion, concern, anger, and guilt for leaving Mae with Mother while he tended to matters with Brillhart. What had Mother said to upset her?

He fisted his hands and allowed a burst of pent-up irritation to rush from his lungs. *Lord, please calm me. Please don't allow me to dash into judgment.*

Landon stalked back to Wilhelmenia's. Mother and Father were giving Wilhelmenia their order.

"And for you, Landon?"

"While I do enjoy your cooking, I'm not hungry at present. But thank you, Wilhelmenia."

The woman's shocked gaze lingered a moment before she gathered the menus and proceeded on her way. "If you change your mind, I'd be happy to prepare something for you."

But Landon wouldn't change his mind. Any appetite he'd had had vanished.

"Where did that girl go?" Father asked, his attention on his pocket watch, instead of Mae's whereabouts.

"We'll discuss it later." Landon had always respected and honored his parents, but if Mother had said something to Mae, he would need to converse with her about it. "Please excuse me. I'll be at the boardinghouse."

Mother and Father arrived an hour later, and Landon was waiting for them on Miss Greta's porch.

Mother brushed past. "I understand that the food is lackluster, but why would you wish to forego supper?"

"Mother, I respectfully request we engage in a serious conversation."

Father tugged on the lapels of his frock coat. "I'll be inside."

Mother took a seat on the chair next to Landon. "What is it you wish to discuss?"

"Mae." Landon gazed across the boardinghouse yard and to the pending sunset. Mae's red-rimmed eyes, her tear-stained cheeks, and her sadness worried him. The image of her stumbling out the door with pain etched on her beautiful face filled his mind.

"Oh, yes. Why did she leave early?"

"You truly don't know?"

Mother shrugged. "I truly don't know. We were merely having a conversation."

"She was clearly upset."

Mother blinked rapidly, her guilt obvious. "Landon, I do understand that you think you have feelings for this girl."

"I *do* have feelings for Mae."

"Your father warned me that you might be considering a courtship with her. We have both decided that such a choice would be utterly foolish. A man of your station does not consider a woman of her station. She is merely a dalliance, and the sooner you realize that, the better off we all will be."

Anger coursed through him, as heat flushed through his body. He must remain respectful and God-honoring, but such a feat would not be easy without the Lord's intervention. Landon closed his eyes, breathed a prayer, and waited as the seconds ticked by. He needed those seconds to articulate the proper words.

"Mother, I appreciate that you and Father have my best interests in mind. Please tell me what you said to Mae."

"I just mentioned she was not a suitable match for you and that you were promised to another."

"That is a bold untruth."

Mother's head jerked back, and Landon realized the harshness of his tone. He struggled to maintain his composure. "Mother, with all due respect, I am not interested in Orla. I have not ever been, nor will I ever be. Further, Orla is not interested in me. While I appreciate you and Father ensuring my future is secure, I don't appreciate unkind words spoken to a woman I deeply care about."

"Really, Landon. You care about her in such a short amount of time of knowing her?"

"Yes, Mother. Really. Mae is kind, compassionate, smart, funny, and beautiful. She loves the Lord, loves her family, and is tenderhearted. Whether my feelings for her lead to courtship or just friendship, isn't yet known, but I can't stand by and allow anyone to mistreat her."

Mother pursed her lips. "Don't forget your place, Landon."

"I haven't forgotten my place. I know I am a Bennick and proudly so. I work hard for the business, and I will continue to do so. As Father has mentioned, someday I will inherit Bennick Railways. And when I do, I'll manage it in a way that makes you both proud." He swallowed the lump that formed in his throat. "But, Mother, I will be the one to decide who I court and marry. Not you and Father. Now, with respect, I am going to leave this conversation and retire for the night."

He paused at the door. "Good night, Mother."

Chapter Twenty-Five

Sleep eluded him.

Landon paced across the floor the entire five steps it took to get from the far side of the room to the door, then back again.

He rubbed the side of his jaw, hoping to release some of the tension settling there. Then paced again and twice more.

A knock on the door sounded. He wasn't in the mood for visitors, especially if it was his parents. Would they retreat if he ignored the knock?

"Landon?"

The Lieutenant.

He opened the door. "Yes, sir?"

"Miss Greta, several of the other boarders, and myself are resting quietly in the parlor. She sent me up here to ask you to stop marching around like you're in some sort of parade. It's disrupting her and the other boarders."

"All right."

"Much obliged." The Lieutenant scrutinized him. "Something wrong with you, son?"

"Just a lot on my mind is all."

"Well, I suggest you rectify it or you'll be owing Miss Greta some of your wages to repair the floor after you wear a hole in it from all your traipsing to and fro."

"Yes, sir. I will do that. Thank you and please give my apologies to Miss Greta and the others."

The Lieutenant nodded. "Will do."

Landon closed the door and stood with his back to it. The Lieutenant suggested he rectify the matter. Perhaps he could apologize to Mae. Set things to right.

He grabbed his frock coat, left the room, and hurried down the stairs. Miss Greta stretched her neck and peered at him as he entered the foyer, but said nothing.

The warm temperatures from earlier that day had finally started to cool. Landon strolled to Pastor Albert's, praying that Mae was still there and would be willing to accept his apology for his mother's behavior.

Albert answered the door. "Hello, Landon." He stepped outside. "The children are already in bed."

"I—is Mae still here?"

"She's not. I took her home."

Landon could see Albert's furrowed brow even in the dim light. "I need to talk to her. My mother—she said some things."

"Mae told me."

Sounds of crickets, some hollering, likely from one of the saloons, and a coyote in the distance filled the silence between them. "I need to apologize to her."

"Our family is very protective of Mae."

The words and the loyalty by which they were spoken reminded Landon of the close-knit family Mae was a part of, and he buried the ache in his heart. Would Mother or Father come to his defense? If he would have had a brother or sister, would they have been as close as Mae was with her brothers and sisters? Would they each protect each other?

"Yes. I understand that, and I am sorry for what my mother said. I wasn't at the table at the time or else this never would have happened."

"It's clear you have feelings for her."

"Yes, I do."

Albert rubbed the back of his neck. "I'm a man of the cloth, but I do have to say that if you hurt my sister..."

"I would never do that."

"You do come from two different worlds. Someday when the spur is complete, you'll leave Horizon—and Mae—behind. A friendship is fine, but if you are determined to court my sister or something more, what happens when you leave?"

In the course of his developing feelings for Mae, Landon had given thought to that numerous times. Currently, they shared a close friendship. Would it someday develop into more? If so, would he ask to court her? Would she be willing to move from her family to wherever his job took him? While he had no way of knowing the future, he did know the need to ensure she was all right encompassed his every thought. "Is it too late to ride to your parents' home and set things to right?"

Albert shook his head. "It's too late tonight. However, I would pray about it and ride there in the morning. It's Saturday so Mae won't be at the school."

"I'm worried about her."

"She'll be all right. Wait until tomorrow, Landon."

He wanted to argue. To disagree and plead his side that even if the hour was late, it was imperative he see Mae. But with great difficulty, he held his tongue.

Albert extended his hand, and Landon shook it, relieved by the gesture from the man he'd come to respect and think of as a friend.

"I'm not even sure of all my mother said, but I do aim to rectify the situation."

"I'll be praying."

Landon rode toward the Shepherdson farm early the next morning. He'd rehearsed at least fifty times the words he wanted to say to Mae. Would Mr. Shepherdson allow him to speak with her?

He'd been grateful for Albert's promise to pray. While prayer still did not come naturally to him, Landon was beginning to learn more and more the importance of it. Between tossing and turning, he'd added his own petitions to the Lord.

Mr. Shepherdson mended a fence not far from the house when Landon arrived. "Hello, Mr. Shepherdson."

"Landon."

"Is Mae home?"

"She is."

Sweat slicked Landon's palms, and he wiped them on his trousers. "May I speak with her?"

Mr. Shepherdson regarded him, and Landon held his breath. Surely as close as the Shepherdson family was, they all likely knew what had transpired the previous evening.

"I would like to set things to right."

"Am I correct in assuming that you will continue to travel a fair bit with your railroad job?"

"Yes, sir."

Mr. Shepherdson leaned against the fence. "Am I also correct in assuming you have feelings for my daughter?"

"Yes, sir, I do. We've become good friends in the time I've been here." Last night for perhaps the first time, Landon realized his feelings for Mae were beginning to extend beyond friendship. Whether she felt the same, he didn't know. However, he surmised that Mr. Shepherdson was alluding to the issue of him moving on when the railroad job was completed. The thought of leaving Mae behind left him with an unsettled feeling in the pit of his stomach. Something he couldn't rightly explain. And something he didn't wish to explore at this very moment, so he proceeded with the reason he was there. "When Mae left last night from Wilhelmenia's I noticed her demeanor."

"She was quite upset when Albert brought her home."

"My mother did say some things to upset her. While I wasn't there to hear those words, Mother subsequently shared some of that conversation."

"When you asked her to supper at Wilhelmina's and you mentioned your parents would be there, Mae's ma and I saw no reason not to agree with her wish to attend with you."

Landon released a strangled breath. "Yes. I was hoping to introduce her to my parents and that we would share a pleasant evening. Such was not the case. Brillhart, a business partner of my father's, needed to speak with both Father and me. We left Wilhelmina's. While my mother can be discourteous at times when she is passionate about something, I had no idea she would upset Mae. As such, I've been concerned since I returned to the restaurant."

"I do appreciate your willingness to ride out here today and speak with her."

"Thank you, sir. I care about Mae and want to be sure she's all right. I'd also like to apologize for Mother's behavior and clear up any misunderstandings."

"I'd be the first to tell you that I know all about misunderstandings." Mr. Shepherdson nodded toward the house. "She's inside."

"Thank you."

Landon strode the short distance and raised a hand to knock.

Ruby answered. "Hello, Landon."

Landon removed his hat. "Hello, Ruby. May I speak with Mae?"

Ruby eyed him with suspicion. "I'll see if she wants to speak with you."

"Thank you. I'd be much obliged for that."

The young woman arched an eyebrow and pinned him with an unwavering gaze a moment longer before disappearing.

Would Mae be willing to talk to him and allow him to say his piece? Had she recovered from Mother's harsh words last night?

Less than a minute later, Mae emerged. The sight of her, as always, stole his breath. But today the sadness in her demeanor shook him.

And he'd caused part of that pain.

"Hello, Mae."

"Hello."

Her timid voice and the tears in her eyes unnerved him. He wanted to pull her into his arms and apologize for any word spoken that wounded her tender heart. "Can I speak with you about last night?"

Mae nodded, and he extended his elbow. She took it, and he led her outside and down the road a few paces, still within sight of the house and her father. He faced her and when she lifted her gaze to his, he witnessed the remaining sorrow. "Mae, I'm sorry about my mother's words last night."

She averted her attention to a noise just outside the house, and Landon followed her gaze. Ruby and Timothy peered out the door and in their direction. "Appears we have an audience."

A slight smile jotted across her lips. "Yes, my family is protective of me."

"So I've noticed."

Mae fixed her attention on the ground. Landon took a step forward and gently lifted her chin. "I am sorry for any pain Mother caused you."

Her shimmering dark blue eyes met his. This delicate woman had won his heart even if a future with her wasn't possible. He slowly dropped his hand by his side, aware of the spectators a short distance away, which now also included Mrs. Shepherdson hanging clothes on the line.

"Your ma mentioned that you and another woman were promised to each other."

"Another? You must be referring to Orla."

Mae shrugged slightly. "I don't know her name."

"I'm sure she was alluding to Orla. It's been a longtime objective for us to marry and combine our familys' fortunes. Unfortunately, our parents are the only ones who have this goal. Neither

Orla nor I feel we are suited for each other beyond friendship, and not a close one at that."

"I do value our friendship, Landon, but I know we come from different worlds."

"Yes, we do. And nothing says that a friendship has to be dictated by how similar or dissimilar the lives of the participants are. Longtime friendships survive whether the social standings are the same or different."

Mae shifted her feet. "Will you forget about me when the spur in Horizon is completed?"

He swallowed the emotion in his throat. If only she knew how much she meant to him. "I could never forget you, Mae."

"Your mother assumes we are preparing to court. I believe she may have arrived at that conclusion because you invited me to supper with your family."

"Mother has worried about who I may or may not court since I was a young boy. Just as your parents are protective of you, Mother and Father are protective of me, or should I say, protective of the family wealth."

"I would never do anything to jeopardize that or your relationship with your parents."

There was so much Landon wanted to say—needed to say—but he struggled with the correct words. For a man who'd excelled at speeches and was well-versed in the English language in boarding school and at the university, he failed miserably with articulation when it involved Mae. "You're not doing anything to jeopardize my relationship with my parents."

"And I would never seek to take your wealth."

His parents worried far too much about the family money. There was so much pressure on him to succeed at overseeing Bennick Railways and continuing the legacy of his father and grandfather. Landon wanted to succeed. Truthfully, he wanted to please Father, and he desired to continue the heritage of the company so much hard work and dedication had been poured into.

Mae peered up at him with expectation in her gaze as she awaited his response. "I'm not worried about that," he said.

Mother had told him often to marry at his station or above. *"In doing so, you'll never have to fear losing the lifestyle to which you've grown accustomed."*

While Landon saw the validity of Mother's statement, he'd pondered often over the years why love had never entered into the equation of importance when contemplating marriage.

Not that he contemplated marriage at present, for he didn't. Although...

The realization hit him square in the stomach. What he felt for Mae *was* more than friendship.

It might even be love.

A glimpse to the left indicated Ruby and Timothy still watching, although they'd taken to doing so by being slightly less obvious. Instead of peering at them through the doorway, Timothy was now assisting his father with the fence, and Ruby was attempting to help her mother hang the laundry. He wondered how Ruby could effectively do so given she'd held the same linen in her hands for the past five minutes. A chuckle arose in his throat.

Mae's brow furrowed and her eyes widened.

Landon needed to explain his change in temperament. "I see that we still have an audience." He jerked his chin in the direction of her brother and sister.

Mae followed his gesture and smiled.

And when she did, he was reminded all over again how beautiful she was.

"They have no qualms about being nosy."

The sweet velvety tinkle in her voice had returned. "Yes, that's true. You're fortunate to have them, even if they are overly inquisitive."

"Overly inquisitive or unabashedly meddlesome?"

Her smile warmed him, and he wanted to reach for her hands and reassure her he'd never allow anyone to be unkind to her again. But Landon could no more make that promise than promise every Idaho summer day would be as bright and sunny as today.

"But yes," she continued. "I am blessed to have them. My family means everything to me."

While Landon loved his parents, he didn't share that same depth of love for them as Mae did for her family. "I can see that."

"Papa, especially, is protective. Mama too, but it's out of love and concern, and because of—" her voice trailed.

"Because of your past?"

"Yes."

They stood in silence as the seconds passed. A comfortable silence, but then, Landon figured he could stand here with her all day without complaint. Finally, he plucked at the cuff of his shirt. Much to his chagrin, they needed to return to the reason why he was here. "Please disregard all that Mother said. I will speak with her."

"Please don't do anything to cause a rift between you and your parents on my account."

"I want to clear up any misunderstandings my parents may have. Mae…"

Ruby had slinked toward them, a linen in her hand. Had she experienced a lapse in judgment making her forget the location of the clothesline? She'd hidden her face slightly behind the sheet, although Landon could clearly see her one eye.

A rambunctious sneeze caused the sheet to flutter, but Ruby efficiently righted it.

Mae pressed her lips together and flicked her head Ruby's way. "Go away, Ruby," she said.

Only Mae Shepherdson with her sweet voice, could make such a demand without sounding rude.

Ruby pulled the linen down and wadded it in her arms. "How did you know it was me?"

"The red hair and the one eyeball were clear indicators."

Mae stifled a giggle as Ruby pivoted and returned to where Mrs. Shepherdson stood but not without glancing back twice.

"I should go."

"Thank you for coming, Landon."

"You're welcome. Mae?"

"Yes?"

"I'm glad we resolved this matter."

"Me too."

"And, Mae?"

"Yes?"

The words on his heart fell from his mouth. "You're important to me. I care about you."

A tinge of pink covered her cheeks. "Thank you."

Several minutes later when Landon rode to Horizon, a troubling thought entered his mind.

He had yet to persuade Father to alter his plans for the spur that was to be built adjacent to the school.

Mae stirred the clear soup while Ruby chopped the carrots and separated the yolks from the whites of four eggs.

"Are you fond of Landon?"

One could always rely on Ruby to unexpectedly raise a topic unrelated to the current task. "Why do you ask?"

Ruby positioned her round face directly in front of Mae's. "Your face is infused with blush."

"It's the heat of the stove."

"Hmm."

"Besides, you and Timothy really need to mind your manners and refrain from being utter pests when we have a guest."

Ruby shrugged and returned to the carrots and eggs. "It was necessary at the time."

"To converge on Landon and me all the while attempting to hide behind a sheet? Really, Rube, we could see you. Your eyeball and the top of your head, anyway."

"It's good practice for when I write articles for *The Horizon Herald*. I'm sure Mr. O'Kane may occasionally send me on a secret mission."

"Secret mission indeed. I doubt it. Horizon isn't a big city, and you aren't Nellie Bly."

Ruby lifted the knife in midair. "I may not be Nellie Bly, but I am assiduous, dauntless, and stealthy. All important traits for a successful newspaper reporter."

"Assiduous and dauntless, perhaps. But not stealthy. If memory serves, you sneezed today. Even the neighbors a mile away heard it."

"Crumbles," groaned Ruby, using one of her favorite words. "I was hoping it wasn't that noticeable. I tried to stifle it."

A heavenly aroma filled the air, and Mae bent over and opened the oven to check on the bread. When she righted herself, she caught a glimpse out the window of Mama and Papa walking hand-in-hand near the barn. "Look," she said, pointing to where their parents were.

Ruby followed her point. "They're so in love even after all these years." She held a hand to her heart. "Don't you hope someday to have a marriage like that?"

"You're such a romantic."

"I know. It's just that…all of my friends are either married, or at the very least courting someone. There isn't anyone suitable here to court." She sucked her lower lip between her teeth. "Do you ever think about marriage?"

"I do. When it's God's timing. For now, I have my family and teaching at the school. Although, I am considered a spinster at twenty-three."

"I think Landon fancies you."

Dare Mae hope that Ruby's assumption was true? "We're good friends."

Ruby wiped her hands on her apron. "I see the way he looks at you. Mama and Papa really like him. We all do. In fact, Mama and I were talking this morning before Landon arrived that we hoped you two would resolve everything."

Both Mama and Ruby knew bits and pieces of the situation from last night. They'd consoled her and prayed with her when she'd arrived home from Albert's.

"So, are you fond of him?"

"Rube, you are relentless."

"I promise I won't say a word."

Mae didn't argue with Ruby because her sister may just be correct.

CHAPTER TWENTY-SIX

LANDON SAT ACROSS FROM Mother and Father on the stage on the way to Ingleville. Both would return to Denver for a few weeks before again visiting Horizon. Father, because he would check on the progress of the spur. Mother because, in her words, she'd become slightly fascinated with the Wild West. Father then proceeded to talk nonstop about the plans to expand to Humboldt. Mother fretted and fussed about a ladies' tea she scheduled for next week.

As he listened to his parents' conversations, he appreciated it was only the three of them. As such, it was a chance to speak with Mother as a captive audience. With the memory of Mae's tearful face, he tried to squash his frustration.

Landon waited for a moment of silence before broaching the subject and worked his throat through a sandy swallow. "Mother, I need to speak with you about your conversation with Mae."

"Landon Bertram Bennick," began Father, his terse tone a clipped warning.

"Father, I will handle this respectfully, but I do wish to confer my thoughts."

His mother's face paled, and her eyes darted around the interior of the stage. "Mae?"

"Yes, Mae. I think you should know I care about her."

"You are smitten."

"Perhaps. Mae is like no one I've ever met. She's a gracious and kindhearted woman."

"And one who knows of your vast wealth yet possesses none of her own." Frown lines grooved the corner of Mother's mouth.

"Vast wealth doesn't matter to Mae. God, her family, and the children at the school where she teaches—those things are of utmost importance to her. Not money."

"And you know this to be true, how?"

"I know that if you were to remove her from her farmhouse in Horizon and transplant her in a mansion in the city, she'd flounder and beg to be returned home. Riches mean nothing to her. Helping others means everything."

Mother's forehead puckered and she firmed her lips in a straight line. "Be that as it may, she is only a dalliance."

"Not a dalliance. Right now, I value her friendship. Someday I may court her. And if I ask for her hand in marriage, you will be her mother-in-law. Whether that occurs or not, I—" Landon took a deep breath and tempered his thoughts before continuing. "I can't stand idly by as you leverage accusations at her."

"Landon Bertram Bennick," warned Father. "We are your family. Mae is not."

"You and Mother are the most important to me after the Lord, but someday I may take a wife. She will then become family too."

"You had a chance with Orla and the two other upstanding women with which your mother arranged courtship. All three women were in the same social standing. This Mae woman is significantly below."

"Yes, and those women were suitable for others, not me." Landon watched the passing scenery as the stage hit a bump in the road. "Mother, do you recall the tiny violas several years ago on the lawn at our Denver home? You discovered them growing of their own accord outside of the manicured beds and by their lonesome. They were brilliant with lavender and dark purple petals and a vibrant yellow center. No one intentionally planted them."

"Yes, I do, and I dare say the gardener accidentally cut them down with the lawnmower." Mother fingered the beads of her necklace. "Such fragile flowers struggling amidst the grass blades, and then the gardener chopped them. It was a while before they regrew."

"Seeing as how you love flowers, you were none too happy if I recall," added Father.

"I was not happy at all."

Landon lowered his voice and prayed what he was about to say would be received as it was intended and not as disrespect. "Mother, when you said those harsh words to Mae, it was like she was the violas and you were the lawnmower. She is delicate and fragile, much like the violas."

Mother's sharp inhalation of breath and her rounded eyes told Landon she understood his analogy perfectly.

Father's glower indicated Landon may have gone too far in proving his point.

"I will never do anything to cause or bring dishonor to the Bennick name. Further, I will endeavor to follow the Lord's admonition to honor my parents. Please understand my position in this matter."

Mother dabbed at her eyes with her lace handkerchief. "No, Landon, I know you wouldn't do anything to dishonor or disrespect your father or me. Please do accept my apologies for the way I treated Mae. It was out of protectiveness for you and my fear you might err in choosing a wife that motivated my behavior. I see now that I was wrong." She sniffled. "I do not want to be a lawnmower."

"I appreciate that, Mother, but it is not me who needs to hear your apology."

She leaned forward and patted his arm. "Rest assured I speak with sincerity when I say I aim to set things to right with Mae."

Mae had missed Landon and was thrilled to hear the stagecoach had arrived earlier that morning after having been away for two weeks. Perhaps he would stop by her parents' home tonight for a visit. She'd found that he'd been on her mind often in recent days.

Yes, she was falling in love with Landon Bennick.

She tethered her horse and entered the mercantile to purchase a bottle of Mr. Price's flavoring extracts for a new dessert Mama planned to make after supper. Mae giggled to herself. Mama's ambitions of baking every delicacy found within the pages of *Agusta's Kitchen* would likely come to fruition.

After she'd visited with Tabitha and completed Mama's errand, Mae unbuttoned the saddlebag to tuck the bottle of flavoring extracts inside when she heard a slightly-familiar voice behind her.

"Miss Shepherdson?"

There were many folks with whom she presumed the voice could belong. But she was completely unprepared when she turned to see none other than Mrs. Bennick.

Her stomach clenched and a gasp escaped her lips. She nearly dropped the bottle of extracts. "Mrs. Bennick?" her voice emerged as a stutter.

"May I speak with you a moment?"

While it would be uncharitable to say so, Mae would rather scrub all the floors in all the houses in Horizon without a moment's respite than speak with the cruel woman. She wished she could escape to the mercantile, Wilhelmina's, Miss Greta's, or even the barbershop. The sour taste of dread filled her mouth. "I really must—I really must return home."

"It will only take a moment. Please."

"Perhaps another day?"

"Another day is fine if you wish." Mrs. Bennick clutched a parcel in her left arm. "Would tomorrow be satisfactory?"

Mae knew that if she delayed the conversation with Mrs. Bennick until tomorrow, she'd no doubt be filled with worriment and angst from now until then. A chill zipped through her. What could Mrs. Bennick wish to discuss?

"I could hire transport to your parents' farm or we could meet at the restaurant again, or wherever is agreeable."

"Today is acceptable."

"Very well. Might we sit on that rustic bench outside the boardinghouse?"

Mae knew exactly the bench of which Mrs. Bennick spoke. "Yes, that would be fine. I just need to place this in the saddle-bag."

But would Mae's trembling fingers allow her to perform such a mundane task?

She fumbled with the bottle but was finally able to secure it. On wobbly legs, she followed Mrs. Bennick to the bench a short distance away. Mrs. Bennick gestured for Mae to sit first, then followed suit, the parcel in her lap.

"Thank you for agreeing to meet with me. Bertram, Landon, and I arrived on the stage early this morning, and I was hoping to see you."

Mrs. Bennick was hoping to see her? Why? She prepared herself for an onslaught of spiteful words.

None came.

Instead, the woman straightened her posture on the bench and fiddled with the parcel's ribbon. "On the way to Ingleville, Landon shared with me his displeasure at the way I had treated you the last time I was in Horizon."

Had such an admonition caused a rift between Landon and his parents? Mae prayed it wasn't so.

"At first, I had no mind to listen. But then I realized I was stuck inside the stage for a lengthy amount of time with no escape, so the best course of action would be to listen to his rebuke. That and Landon has rarely protested about anything. He seldom complains and is a dutiful and considerate young man. But that day, I could see the disappointment in his eyes and the respectful anger hidden in their depths."

Mae picked at a thread on her calico skirt. Should she say something?

But she didn't have the opportunity as Mrs. Bennick continued. "What I said to you was unfair and uncalled for. Landon opened my eyes to that fact. My son cares deeply for you. That was a realization I was unprepared to accept." Mrs. Bennick retied the ribbon that she'd untied with her fiddling. "Bertram knows the story I am about to tell you as we endured it together, but Landon does not."

"Mrs. Bennick, you needn't tell me anything that is uncomfortable."

"I feel you must know. While it is not an excuse for my untoward behavior, I do hope it will allow you a glimpse into the motivation behind it. You see, once upon a time, long ago when I was a young girl, I resided with my parents in Maryland. It was already planned for Bertram and I to marry, which was fine since our families had spent an extensive amount of time together and Bertram and I had become friends. I have an older brother named Hugo, and during this time, Father retired and allowed Hugo to tend to the company my father owned. We were an extremely wealthy family as my father was in the steel business." Mrs. Bennick sucked in a deep breath. "Soon after that, my parents died during a cholera outbreak."

"I'm so sorry."

"Thank you. I miss Mother terribly. Father and I were not close, but I loved my mother and had hoped for more time with her. Anyhow, after they passed, my brother was never the same. He was always a handsome man—he is where Landon got his broad shoulders and height from—and often had dalliances while traveling for our business. Our parents wanted him to marry one of several young women from wealthy families in our city. You see, to do so would combine and secure wealth, which is important."

Mrs. Bennick moistened her lips. "Hugo suffered from a severe lapse in judgment after our parents' deaths and was conned by a woman named Julene who hailed from a destitute family on the wrong side of town. She lived in the tenements, her father was a drunk, and they lived in squalor. Now, while you may not believe it to be so, I do care about the poor and make charitable donations each month to an organization that assists the impoverished. However, Julene's family was different. They took advantage of others, her father did not finish promised projects, including one for our family, and her parents were known to squander donations on alcohol, gambling, and the like, rather than food for their children. They possessed a dreadful reputation, yet Hugo fancied Julene all the same. She was a manipulative sort and it wasn't long before she and my brother married.

"I was against the marriage from the beginning, and both Bertram and I attempted to dissuade Hugo from his foolish notion that he was in love with Julene. All the while, she had another man she was seeing who just so happened to be a prominent lawyer.

"Julene convinced my brother to sell the company after they married. I wasn't concerned since Hugo had always promised to see to my care. My marriage to Bertram was, at this time, five months away. And oh, how I wished Mother could have been there. I was grateful to have the opportunity to wear her dress, but to not have her there was heartbreaking." Mrs. Bennick dabbed at her eyes. "A month or so after Hugo and Julene married, my brother died tragically when the ship he was on capsized in the ocean. He was returning from a business trip to England when he and thirty others perished at sea. While Hugo and I had our differences, it grieved me to have lost him and not have been able to say goodbye."

Mae instinctively placed a hand on Mrs. Bennick's arm. "So much loss in such a short amount of time. I'm so sorry, Mrs. Bennick."

Surprisingly, the woman did not remove Mae's hand. "Thank you. As if it wasn't enough to lose my parents and brother, I also lost my home. When Hugo died, Julene had the servants place all of my trunks on the lawn, and I was no longer welcome in my home. A home I'd lived in my entire life. The home that was my parents'. I had nowhere to go."

"Did you have any relatives?"

"I did not, save for one, an aunt in Vermont who wanted nothing to do with me. So I stood on the lawn of our family home with no idea what to do next. Yes, my parents had a summer home, but that too, had, unbeknownst to me, been sold by my brother."

"Would a judge have returned your inheritance?"

"It's possible. But instead, I stayed with a friend for a month before Bertram and I hastily married. It was not the extravagant wedding we had planned, but it was sufficient. Were it not for my husband, there is no telling what would have happened to me as I was penniless. Fortunately, Bertram convinced Julene to allow me to secure a few of my mother's possessions—her Bible, wedding ring, pearl necklace, a family painting, and a brooch my father gave her. I realized there were others like Julene, only set on taking what they could from unsuspecting individuals." Mrs. Bennick sighed. "Sadly, she lost the entire estate the following year when she squandered away my family's savings. Even the lawyer would not have her by that time, and she moved back with her parents in the tenements. After I married Bertram, I lost track of her."

"I had no idea, Mrs. Bennick."

"Only Bertram knows the entire story. And now you." Mrs. Bennick turned toward her. "What I said to you was reprehensible. I determined you to be much like Julene, and I didn't want Landon to be subject to a woman like her. To be as foolish as my brother had been in his choice of whom he fancied. I imagined Landon losing his fortune and Bertram and I penniless and homeless. Although that is irrational thinking as we have the best of lawyers; however..."

Mrs. Bennick smoothed the pleats of her elegant skirt. "Will you forgive me?"

"Yes."

"You will?"

"I forgive you, Mrs. Bennick." Mae's eyes misted as she stared at the woman who had struggled to share with her the pain she'd endured.

"Thank you. Landon said you were the most gracious and kindhearted woman he's ever met, and I see now that he was right."

"He said that?"

"He did. And other things too."

Heat traveled in a slow wave up Mae's face, and she pretended to be mesmerized by a chickadee who'd landed on the ground in front of them in search of a worm.

"My son fancies you, and having been the recipient of your grace and forgiveness, I can see why."

"Thank you, Mrs. Bennick."

"Now, I have a gift for you. Landon tells me we both love flowers. What are your favorite varieties?"

Mae tapped her chin with her forefinger. "I have many favorites. I love wildflowers and periwinkle, daisies, petunias, black-eyed Susans, lupines, violets, forget-me-nots, and buttercups. Perhaps while you are here, we can take a buggy ride and I'll show you some of the wildflowers still blooming on the prairie. Some have lost their blooms, but many others still retain them.”

“I should like that. Thank you.”

“What are your favorites?”

“Like you, too many to list. I do hope someday you can visit our home in Denver and see the extraordinary flower gardens on our property. Our rose gardens alone are magnificent. And if you are unable to visit, I shall hire a photographer to capture the flowers. You will be most amazed at their beauty.”

“I would love to see them someday.”

Mrs. Bennick handed her the parcel. “Until then, here is a gift. Do open it.”

“The parcel is far too beautifully wrapped to open.”

The woman laughed. “Yes, it is beautifully wrapped, but you will like what’s inside even more. Consider it a peace offering of sorts. Or perhaps a starting-over gift or an apology gift. Or all three.”

Mae carefully removed the paper to find an ornately-decorated wooden box with a cluster of flowers painted on the top.

“Do open it. There’s another surprise inside.”

Mae unclasped it and opened the box to find several seed packets inside. “Thank you!”

“You are most welcome. These are from the nursery in Denver. While it’s too late to plant them this season, I venture to say you’ll delight in planting them next spring.”

She held the seed packets to her chest. “It’s the perfect gift.”

Chapter Twenty-Seven

MAE ANTICIPATED MEETING LANDON when he arrived to retrieve her. Her feelings for him had grown in recent days and were cemented by the fact that he seemed to care as much about the school as she did. Such a revelation warmed her heart. Now if only his pa would agree to build the railroad spur in another area, rather than adjacent to the place that had become Mae's second home.

Beans walked alongside her, sniffing everything in his path and emitting a joyous bark on occasion.

Mae tilted her face to the sky and thanked the Lord again for all of His many blessings. Her family, her health, living in beautiful Idaho with its mountains and farms, and the school, its children, and fellow teachers. She thanked Him that He chose to pluck a little girl from the grips of an abusive and lonely existence in New York and bless her with parents and siblings who loved her. Mae stopped, closed her eyes, and allowed the sun to shine warmly on her face.

She couldn't wait to see Landon. She hoped he felt the same for her as she was beginning to feel for him.

Birds chirped, the wind rustled through the aspen trees, and in the distance, she heard a wagon. Mae squeezed her eyes shut and reveled in the day.

She was so preoccupied with her thoughts that she didn't realize the wagon had come to a stop beside her. The sound of a horse's neigh disrupted her focus, and Mae's eyes fluttered open. She blinked as a man with a cowboy hat drew closer to her. Another man sat in the wagon staring at her.

The hairs on the back of her neck stood on end. She recognized the man approaching her as Duchesne. A feeling of regret troubled her at the thought of how she'd failed to be upfront with Sheriff Zembrodt about him. And she hadn't bothered to tell Papa.

"Mr. Duschesne, how are you?" Her voice shook.

He didn't answer but instead closed the space between them in one long stride. His hardened stare did little to alleviate her concerns. Mae cast a glance behind her. The barn, empty of anything but animals, was in her direct line of vision. Mr. Eddington had gone to town, and Mrs. Eddington and Lenore were tending to the children inside the school. If Mr. Duschense had nefarious intentions, no one would be around to stop him.

A ripple of fear traveled down her spine. Should she scream and hope that her voice carried enough to penetrate the thin walls of the school?

Or perhaps Mr. Duschesne had no evil intent, but instead merely planned to ask her a question. She offered a prayer heavenward for the Lord's guidance before pasting on a fake, albeit weak, smile. "Mr. Duschene, what brings you to the school today?"

"Get in the wagon."

"I beg your pardon?"

"You heard me. Get in the wagon. Now!"

Mae didn't wait to argue with him further. Instead, she turned, lifted the hem of her skirt, and began running toward the house, Beans trailing behind her. But Mr. Duschesne was faster.

And stronger.

He clasped her arm tightly in his grasp and yanked her to him. She screamed, her voice penetrating the quiet surroundings.

Mr. Duschesne slapped his other hand over her mouth. "Get. Into. The. Wagon." His seething voice and foul breath, reeking of garlic and whiskey, filled the air between them.

Without waiting to see whether or not she would acquiesce to his demands, Mr. Duchesne jerked her arm again and dragged her toward the wagon. She resisted, pummeling him with her fists. Beans barked and clamped onto the man's pant leg. He shook the dog aside and lifted Mae off the ground. "I said get into the wagon. You're coming with me whether you want to or not."

She didn't recognize the man on the buckboard when she was ordered to sit beside him. He took one glance at her and averted his eyes to the road as he steered the wagon in the opposite direction away from the school. Beans followed a short distance, barking as he did so.

If only she hadn't decided to walk and meet Landon today.

But why had the men chosen this day to apprehend her? Would they have still found a way to execute their evil intent even if Mae *hadn't* been walking along the road by her lonesome?

She felt the hard barrel of Mr. Duschesne's gun in her left shoulder. "Make one move, utter one sound, wave, smile, or anything else, and I'll use this." Even without seeing him, she knew he gritted his yellowed teeth as he snarled the words.

Please, Lord, allow someone to pass us and wonder what is awry.

But there was no one on the empty stretch of road leading in the opposite direction of town along the Horizon River. In the distance, a farm or two dotted the landscape, but soon there was nothing but sagebrush on one side of the road and a meadow on the other.

Her heart raced in her chest and tears burned her eyes. What did the men want? What were they scheming? The driver continually looked Mae's way, but she couldn't read his expression beneath his tattered hat.

A dilapidated cabin soon came into view, one Mae had never before seen. A barn with a collapsed roof stood beside it. Water rushed by in the higher-than-usual river due to the plentiful spring rain. A porch with missing slats and splintered wood surrounded the front of the house with one broken window.

The man stopped the wagon. The barrel of the gun disappeared, only to be replaced by a tight grip on the back of her neck.

Mae flinched as fingernails dug into her tender skin. She winced as the pain seared through her.

"I could kill you right here, but I'll wait," he hissed.

Kill her? Why would Mr. Duchesne wish her such a horrible fate? She couldn't turn her neck, but she could see from her side eye that the other man had turned toward her.

"Don't think we oughta kill her."

"Gordon, no one asked what you think we ought to do. Just shut up, unless you have something worthwhile to say. I'll get her into the house while you unhitch the horses."

Gordon said nothing and Mr. Duchesne hissed in Mae's ear, "You will do exactly as I say. Do you understand?" He released his hand from the back of her neck, but the pain persisted. Mr. Duchesne leaped from the wagon and demanded she climb down from the buckboard.

"Why are you doing this?"

"You don't get to ask any questions, now get going." He shoved her toward the cabin, and she stumbled forward as her legs threatened to give way beneath her.

The cabin reeked of a musty, moldy smell combined with stale cooking odors and cat urine. Mae's heart pounded, and her arms and legs tingled with fear. Thoughts of what Mr. Duschesne may do crowded her mind, and with great effort, she attempted to push them aside. But the fear lingered.

Fear of the unknown.

And fear of being once again trapped inside a room, just like she had been all those years ago.

Lord, please help me.

Mr. Duschesne shoved her into a room with only a chair and piles of feces clumped in the corners. A mangy cat skittered away and out the door. "Get in the chair."

Mae did as he commanded. "Please tell me why you are doing this."

He raised a hand, and for a moment she feared he would strike her. But he lowered it and glowered at her. "I'm going to be seeking a ransom for your safe return."

"A ransom?"

"If only Landon Bennick would have given us the raise we deserved after all our hard work on the railroad." Mr. Duchesne's lip curled and rage lit his eyes. He began to yell, his harsh words stinging Mae's ears. "If he had done what he said he'd do, I wouldn't be in the mess I'm in." He paused, spit on the floor, and continued. "I got me a gambling debt to pay. I've also got other debts. A man needs more than the pitiful amount he's paid for all his hard work to be able to survive."

Mr. Duchesne was taking out his anger on her for the injustice he perceived was caused by Landon?

"So I'll write that ransom note, and if Bennick knows what's good for him, he'll pay it."

The lack of logic made the situation all the more dangerous. Wouldn't Mr. Duchesne be arrested when the sheriff discovered the ransom? Even more frightening, would Mr. Duchesne release her when the ransom was paid? What if it was just a ploy to get money from Landon, and the man meant to do her further harm?

"Now let's see here..." Mr. Duchesne stroked his wiry brown beard. "How much are you worth?" His eyes roved over her in a most uncouth manner, stalling before he lifted his gaze again to her face. He stroked her cheek with a rough thumb. "Not worth a whole lot, but here's the thing. I need a lot of money for my debts, so..." He tapped his chin with his finger. "Think I'll start at two thousand dollars."

Mae gasped. No one, not even Landon, could afford to pay such a steep amount.

"I'll be leaving now," said Gordon.

"Please, sir, please help me."

Gordon's gaze met hers before he shook his head and stomped from the room, leaving Mae alone with Mr. Duchesne and an uncertain fate.

Landon steered the buggy toward the Horizon School for the Deaf. He couldn't wait to see Mae again. At some point, he hoped she would agree to court him.

Would she agree?

He glanced down at the bouquet of flowers on the buggy seat beside him. Before wanting to win Mae's heart, Landon hadn't given much thought to Idaho wildflowers. Wilhelmenia suggested he meander through the area and pick a collection of violets, periwinkles, forget-me-nots, black-eyed Susans, and buttercups. Who knew that in the span of two hours he would have become knowledgeable about so many types of flowers? He had Wilhelmenia and her vast knowledge of all things plants to thank. However, such a feat had caused him to be late in retrieving Mae. Hopefully, she would forgive him when she saw the carefully-ribboned wildflowers.

Beans greeted him just before he approached the school. The beagle barked nonstop, something Beans usually didn't do, especially when seeing Landon. He stopped the buggy, and the dog leaped toward it before propping his paws on the wheel spokes.

Landon climbed from the buggy and patted Beans on the head. "What is it, boy?"

Beans continued to bay, his bark sounding more like a howl. Landon stepped from the buggy, and Beans continued to jump around. Landon stopped and the dog batted at his leg, and he scooped him up as Beans wiggled. Landon attempted to nuzzle him as he always did, but Beans would have none of it. He howled, the deafening sound threatening to damage Landon's hearing.

The dog wiggled uncontrollably until Landon set him on the ground.

He knocked on the door, and Lenore answered. "Is Mae here? I've come to take her home."

"Mae left a few minutes ago. She mentioned she was going to start walking and meet you along the way since it was such a nice day, and Beans was extra boisterous."

"She started walking? I didn't pass her."

Concern lit Lenore's face. "You didn't?"

Landon peered about the porch, his gaze lingering on the road on which he'd just driven. He should have seen Mae. Surely Lenore misunderstood Mae's intentions. "I didn't see her. Are you sure she said she'd begin walking?"

"That's what she said. Do come in, and I'll check with Mrs. Eddington. Perhaps Mae mentioned something different to her."

Landon shut the door behind him and gazed about the school he'd become so familiar with in recent days. Hosea ran through the door then, followed by Polly. When he saw Landon, the boy wrapped his arms around Landon's legs.

Landon reached down and attempted to remove Hosea's tight grip. The boy remained steadfast and began sobbing, his cries muffled against Landon's trousers. Meanwhile, Polly tucked her head and peered up at him with frightened brown eyes.

Something was amiss.

Since Hosea wouldn't release his hold, perhaps he'd get some answers from Polly. Using the signs and fingerspelling he had been practicing, he asked Polly what was wrong.

Polly looked away.

Landon crouched to eye level and again repeated the question. Hosea released his hold on Landon's legs, flew into his arms, nestled against his shoulder, and began to whimper again.

Mrs. Eddington arrived in the foyer. "What's the matter with Polly and Hosea?"

"I'm not sure. I haven't been able to procure an answer from either of them. Have you seen Mae?"

"She told us that she and Beans would start walking down the road to meet you. Lenore said you never saw her."

Guilt washed him anew at the realization he was late to retrieve Mae. "I didn't see her, and now with Polly and Hosea acting peculiar, I'm beginning to think something is amiss."

Mrs. Eddington's eyebrows furrowed. She took a seat on a nearby faded upholstered chair and beckoned Polly toward her. "Polly will be easier to obtain information from, and by the looks of it, Hosea won't be relinquishing his hold on you anytime soon."

Landon stood and held Hosea, who continued to cry into Landon's shoulder. Mrs. Eddington signed to Polly, and seconds ticked by before she finally responded. Her hands flew at a rapid pace as she signed the words, and Mrs. Eddington interpreted how Hosea, when he was standing behind the barn, had seen two men hurt Mae and take her away in a wagon.

"What?" Landon's heart pounded in his ears. "What men?"

Mrs. Eddington asked Polly for more details.

Polly tapped Hosea on the back, and Landon set the boy on the floor, where Polly signed to Hosea.

Hosea's eyes darted toward Mrs. Eddington, then to Landon, to Polly, and finally to Mrs. Eddington once again. His own hands formed the letters and words he needed to sign. His lip quivered as he recounted how he was by the barn hiding so he wouldn't have to do his chores. Hosea's attention veered to the floor, and he wrapped his skinny arms around his body.

Fear pummeled Landon. Who had taken Mae and why? Would he reach her in time to save her? What if…

His mind could wander to all sorts of places, and he tamped down the temptation to allow it to do so. He needed to do what he could to rescue Mae.

Mrs. Eddington opened her arms to the boy. He flew into them, and she hugged him briefly inquiring if he was telling the truth. He assured her he was, and the woman asked further questions about how long ago and what the men looked like.

Hosea's brown eyes, tears still lingering in their depths, grew larger. He described the man as having long curly hair and a beard.

Only one man Landon knew had curly hair, curly enough for it to be mentioned. His pulse ticked up a notch.

He asked which direction they went, and Hosea pointed westward. Landon tensed. The longer he stood here, the more of a chance Mae would succumb to Duchesne's nefarious deeds. He had to find her. When Hosea looked up at him, Landon told him he'd done the right thing and to stay and keep an eye on things. He patted the boy's shoulder and directed his attention to Mrs. Eddington. "I'm going after her. I'll stop at her parents' place first and let her father know. He can round up a search party."

Mrs. Eddington swiped at a tear. "We will be praying for our precious Mae. Please be careful, Landon."

Without hesitating a second longer, Landon dashed out the door and climbed into the buggy. Pressing the horse to go as fast as safely possible, he watched as the flowers he'd picked earlier for Mae slid off the seat and onto the floor.

Lord, please let me reach her in time.

Chapter Twenty-Eight

THINK, LANDON, THINK. WHERE would Duchesne take Mae?

Would Chen, Walsh, or one of the other men know? The sheriff likely was already inquiring of most of the workers who made one of the two saloons their second home.

She could be halfway to Ingleville by now.

A lead stone formed in his stomach. If Duchesne had already removed Mae from the area, and they were on their way to Ingleville, Landon and the others may never find her.

The disturbing thought urged him to beckon his horse faster toward the camp.

If only he'd arrived at the school sooner.

If only he hadn't taken the time to pick the flowers. While he knew Mae would love the blooms, such a gesture wasn't worth what could be happening to her.

The guilt consumed him.

Mae should not have been walking home alone. She trusted him to be there to retrieve her and hadn't taken her own horse since Landon promised to transport her.

An image of her being threatened by the likes of Duchesne—or any man who sought to bring her harm—caused bile to rise in his throat.

Did the Lord answer prayers when one's negligence caused the reason for the request?

Several drab tents amongst tall lodgepole pines came into view. Most of the men had retired for the day and rode into town, save a few, including Chen and Walsh.

"Hello, Boss, what can we do for ye?"

"Hello, Walsh. Chen. Have either of you seen Duchesne?"

Chen nodded. "He was here earlier. We saw him leave with Gordon."

Was Gordon the other man Hosea had seen? "Did either of them mention where they were going?"

Walsh tapped his chin. "I figured the saloon, but now I think no."

"They went other way from town," added Chen. "I don't pay much attention."

Landon could understand why Chen didn't give much concern to Duchesne's and Gordon's affairs. Both men, especially Duchesne, had often mistreated Chen. "I think they may have harmed someone." Just uttering the words brought about the realization of what Duchesne was capable of, and Landon balled his hands into fists. The sooner he found Mae, the better. "Can either of you think of where Duchesne might go if he wanted to hide?"

Chen shook his head. Walsh nodded. "Not sure where he might go, but he once mentioned a deserted cabin."

There could be many deserted and abandoned cabins in the area. Landon needed more information. "Can you remember where he said it was?" The anxiety radiated through him, and with difficulty, he struggled to wait patiently for Walsh's answer.

Walsh's red brows furrowed. "Ye know Duschesne does not like us much."

"I'm aware of that." Were Walsh and Chen concerned for their safety? "I won't tell him you are the ones who gave me the information."

Walsh peered from the left to the right. The other men in camp paid them no mind "Don't know for sure. Maybe something about a river?"

Landon's heart thudded in his chest as he again imagined the ill intent Duchesne may be contemplating. "Thank you for your help." He mounted his horse, and with a wave, started the opposite direction of town toward the river.

He hadn't been a man of prayer in the past, but his conversations with Pastor Albert and the reverend's sermons changed that. *"Prayer is important. It's our means of conversing with our Lord."*

Landon needed to converse with the Lord. To seek His guidance, and more importantly, to pray for Mae's protection. *Lord, please help me find her. Before it's too late.*

Had Tyler, the sheriff, or the other men found Mae yet? For a brief moment, he wrestled with perhaps going back to town to see if Mae had already been found. Or should he continue to search for her now that he had further information about her possible whereabouts?

The latter option won.

The Horizon River extended for miles and wove through forested landscape, through town, and several miles on the outskirts toward Ingleville. He beckoned his horse as he scanned the area for anything other than farmhouses and barns. About a mile from town, he noticed an abandoned cabin. Hiding his horse in the trees a short distance away, Landon slithered toward the front door, keeping careful watch over his surroundings.

The back of the house was windowless. As Landon drew closer, he recognized Duchesne's horse. The piebald mare, with its black-and-white coloring, stood in the corral with two other horses.

Landon approached the house. He crept up to the dirty window and used his shirt cuff to wipe off the grime to create a clear spot.

And that's when he saw her.

Mae sat in a chair in the gloomy room, gagged, with her hands bound behind her, and her feet tied to the chair's legs.

Landon clenched his fists, and his heart pounded in his ears. This was his fault. He should have arrived earlier. The questions mounted in his mind. Why was Duchesne holding Mae hostage? Was the man still at the cabin somewhere? Should Landon fetch the sheriff or resolve this himself?

No, he wouldn't take the time to fetch Sheriff Zembrodt. He needed to rescue Mae now. His fingers brushed the grip of his revolver. He hoped he wouldn't have to use it.

But to save Mae, he'd do just about anything.

Walking as quietly as possible, Landon inched along the porch, carefully avoiding the gaping spaces caused by missing boards. He observed Duchesne through a broken front window. The man stood at the table, his back to Landon. The door to the house was ajar, and from what Landon could see, Duchesne was the only one in the room.

Could Landon help Mae escape with Duchesne in the vicinity? Could he somehow distract him and then free Mae? But with her hands and feet bound, how could she flee? How could she evade detection by Duchesne? Was there a second door?

Landon slid further along the porch when his boot collided with a pile of empty whiskey bottles, causing a clinking sound. He held his breath and dashed to the side of the house just as he heard Duchesne's footsteps.

"Who's there?"

Landon held his breath. A wasp buzzed near his head and settled on his bare forearm. The insect chose that moment to attack. While not unexpected, the pinch of the stinger caused Landon to involuntarily grunt.

"I said, 'Who's there?'"

Landon leaned his head against the house and mulled over his options. He could wage a surprise attack on Duchesne and free Mae. He could wait until the man returned to whatever he was doing in the kitchen and somehow distract him and locate Mae. Or…? He wasn't a quick draw, like Duchesne likely was.

Several heartbeats later, Landon heard Duchesne's steps as the man returned to the house. Landon waited for the slamming of the door, but it never came. He slowly peered around the corner, noticed the door ajar again, and scanned the haphazard pile of whiskey bottles. Given the man's propensity to drink, it wouldn't surprise him if they were Duchesne's.

An idea formed in his mind then. With his back against the house, he slinked alongside the wall and glimpsed Duchesne at the table again. Landon knelt to retrieve a bottle and clutched the neck of it tightly in his grasp. Then slowly and methodically, he slipped inside.

The putrid odor of alcohol mixed with body odor and a closed-house smell filled Landon's nose, and he resisted the urge to retch.

Duchesne paused what he was doing and his shoulders stiffened. Sweat trickled down Landon's back. There was nowhere to hide. Nothing to obscure his presence if Duchesne discovered him. And for his plan to work, Landon needed to keep his arrival secret. Duchesne was a tall man, not a man of large girth, but a sturdier man nonetheless.

However, Landon was younger and faster. And more agile. And while Duchesne worked hard labor—when he worked—Landon surpassed him when it came to intelligence. Not just smarts, but also common sense.

Landon tiptoed closer, bridging the distance between him and his adversary. The floor groaned under his weight and caused Duchesne to startle. Just as the man reached for his revolver, Landon raised the whiskey bottle and brought it down hard on Duchesne's head. Glass clanged to the floor and blood spurted from Duchesne's head as he collapsed.

Landon wasted no time executing his plan. He rushed to the only other door in the house and flung it open.

Mae's eyes widened, and he held up a finger to his mouth. They needed to hurry before Duchesne regained consciousness. Landon unknotted the ropes and removed the gag.

"Landon!" she whispered.

He wanted to take her into his arms, hold her, console her, and reassure her he'd always protect her. But now wasn't the time. "I want you to take Duchesne's horse and ride home. Let your mother know you're all right, then ride into town and fetch the sheriff."

"What about you?"

"I'll be right behind you."

Her expression of uncertainty prodded him to elaborate. "You need to escape, Mae, and do it quickly."

"But…"

It wasn't like Mae to be contrary. Did she not comprehend the brevity of the situation?

"Go!" he pointed to the door, forcing himself to ignore the confusion and hurt in her eyes.

Mae turned then and rushed from the room. He watched through the window as she rode away. Once he was reassured she was safely out of Duchesne's clutches, he'd follow.

Something hard poked into his back. He needn't turn around to ascertain what it was.

"You'll be sorry you did that. Now slowly turn around and put your hands above your head."

He did as Duchesne ordered. Blood trickled down the side of the man's face, and his hardened eyes bored into Landon.

"Now toss your revolver on the floor."

Landon wouldn't be much good without his revolver.

Duchesne pulled back the hammer. "Did you not hear me? Toss your gun to the side!"

He reluctantly did as the man requested and slid his Colt across the wooden floor. Duchesne lowered his weapon and narrowed his eyes. "You always did think you was too good for the rest of us peons. Always lording it over us that you were the son of the wealthy owner." He spit to the side, his action causing his greasy brown curly hair to swish with the motion.

How had Father determined Duchesne to be an appropriate supervisor for his company? How had he not seen past the façade Duschesne so carefully erected? Not that Father paid much attention to anything that didn't suit his best interests.

Duchesne shoved Landon on the shoulder. "You always was a flannelmouth. No one ever believed a word you said. Just a bunch of taradiddle saying you were gonna get us all a raise in our wages once we reached Horizon. Ain't no one seen a cent more added to his earnings."

Landon did his best to remain calm. "Is that what this is all about? You wanted a raise?"

"You promised it!" Duchesne yelled. "Promised when we got to Horizon you'd see to it to ask your pa for more money for us workers."

"And I did. Unfortunately, Father told me after the spur into Horizon was finished, not before."

The rage in Duchesne's eyes nearly caused Landon to renege on what he'd just said. But what good would it have done? Landon knew the men wanted higher wages. Knew a few of them planned to make their actions unlawfully known. But he'd done what he could to convince Father the hardworking men were worth more than the measly pay afforded them.

Father had brushed Landon's concerns aside.

"We could settle this peacefully. I can ask Father again." Were it not for God's grace, Landon would not have been able to keep his voice calm. Not when Duchesne raised the gun and pointed at him again.

Duchesne released a stream of oaths. "You shoulda seen the ransom note I was writing for the safe return of that pretty little lady." His gaze took on a lustful glint. "That is one mighty fine woman. Mm-hmm."

Landon's body tensed and he had the urge to whack Duchesne square in the jaw in Mae's defense.

"The ransom note was gonna make me rich and help me pay off my gambling debts. But *you* had to go and ruin everything." Duchesne's lip curled. "No one would care if I wrote a ransom note for you. Not even your pa."

The words hit Landon in the gut. Father may not be the kind of pa Mr. Shepherdson and Albert were, but he *would* care if someone kidnapped Landon. If someone threatened his son.

Right?

With great difficulty, he brushed aside his own wavering thoughts about Father's concern or lack thereof. Whether Father cared or not, Duchesne needed to be stopped. "I'll see to it that you and the men get paid a fair wage."

The back of Duchesne's hand connected with Landon's face. Blackness threatened, and Landon attempted to remain standing as he reeled from the throb of the hit. Dizziness momentarily stunned him as he staggered.

"You had your chance to get us a fair wage."

The stars in his vision faded, and Landon took a deep breath. Duchesne was both drunk and crazy. Landon prayed that Mae had reached town safely and prayed that he'd emerge from this alive. *Lord, please give me wisdom.*

"Mind if I take a look at the ransom note?"

Duchesne lowered his gun and stared at Landon, likely attempting to determine Landon's sincerity.

"Reckon I could show you." Duchesne holstered his revolver and turned toward the table where a sheet of paper rested haphazardly at an angle with a pencil atop it.

Landon took action. He tackled Duchesne to the ground. His adversary reached for his revolver, and Landon knocked it from his hand, causing it to fall on the floor beside them. They tousled, Landon briefly having the upper hand before Duchesne's fist nailed his jaw. Duchesne gained the upper hand and slammed Landon's head into the floor. The breath was knocked out of him, and Landon fought the pain while struggling to breathe.

A fleeting thought occurred that if he had just turned and run after Duchesne reached for the letter, that might have been a better option. However, Landon likely would have been shot in the back.

They both grappled for the gun, Landon sliding across the floor and willing his fingers to reach the revolver. Duchesne balled his hand into a fist and slammed it down hard on Landon's hand. He winced but managed to shove the gun just out of Duchesne's reach.

Landon jumped to his feet, and Duchesne did the same. Ignoring the darkness lurking in his peripheral vision, Landon again bolted for the gun just as Duchesne stuck his foot out to trip him. Landon went down with a thud but stood again and inched toward the weapon. He grabbed it and held it on Duchesne.

The man eyed him for brief seconds before pulling a knife from his pocket and lunging at Landon. Dull pain sliced Landon's upper arm just before he pulled the trigger.

CHAPTER TWENTY-NINE

MAE URGED THE HORSE toward home. She looked back no less than six times, the thought of leaving Landon behind to contend with Duchesne filling her with apprehension. The decision of whether to do as Landon instructed or to stay and ensure he escaped warred within her.

Shouldn't she be able to see Landon in the distance? Shouldn't he be rounding the corner soon? Based on Duchesne's harsh words, the hatred the man felt for her must be unparalleled in contrast to what he felt for Landon.

She shivered despite the warm breeze. It was only the Lord's mercy and protection that she hadn't succumbed to worse treatment from Duchesne. It had only been Providence that the loathsome man hadn't violated her, killed her, or drowned her in the river as he'd threatened.

Her wrists ached from the tight ropes, and the taste of the dirty bandana stretched taut in her mouth to gag her remained. Thoughts of her days in New York with her first pa and his drunken outbursts, yelling, and shoving her into a room for hours without food or water intertwined with the treatment Duchesne wrought on her.

But God was good. He was faithful. And He had both times sent a rescuer to free Mae from the hands of evil.

Her parents' farm came into view, and Mae released the breath she'd been holding. Another glimpse behind her indicated Landon had failed to catch up with her.

Papa would know what to do, and perhaps he, Albert, and the sheriff could assist Landon if Duchesne decided to hold him hostage as well.

She dismounted and stumbled to the house, Mama flung open the door, and Mae fell into her mother's arms.

"Mae, we're so grateful you are all right!" Mama led her to the upholstered sofa Papa purchased for her for their anniversary.

Mae sat down beside her mother and rested her head on her shoulder.

It would all be all right now.

Ruby entered the house. "Mae?" She rushed toward them and sat on the other side of Mae, sandwiching her between Ruby and Mama.

After a few moments, Mama spoke. "Ruby, would you please ride into town and let the sheriff know we've found Mae? He'll know where to find Papa."

Ruby scrambled to her feet. "Yes, ma'am. And, Mae, I'm so glad you're back."

Mae swallowed hard as the tears continued to slide down her cheeks. Mama patted her hair and held her close. "I was so scared."

"Landon said someone kidnapped you."

Mae nodded and reclined against the back of the sofa. "It was Mr. Duschesne and a man named Gordon. Mr. Duschesne delivered me to a deserted cabin and locked me in a room—" The memory of the room, the gag in her mouth, and the ropes around her wrists and ankles flashed in her mind.

"Oh, Mae!" Mama wrapped her arms around Mae again as Mae sobbed.

"I was so scared. It was just like in New York when my first pa would lock me in the closet and forget about me for hours. He would be so angry when I would ask questions or speak at all. I was so hungry. So thirsty. Then he left me with that mean neighbor woman." The memories flooded her thoughts as if they occurred yesterday. The sights. The sounds. The smells. The worry that her first pa would forget about her entirely and she would starve in the confines of a room where she could barely take a few steps. Her first pa's harsh words, especially when he was drunk. The times he'd left her behind when he visited the saloon at night. The scratching of the mice scurrying across the floor in the filthy tenement closet.

Mama hugged her tighter. It was the first time Mae had ever shared with anyone everything that had happened to her those years ago. While she knew Miss Oleford from the orphanage knew some of the details, and the elderly neighbor woman knew somewhat of Mae's first pa's neglect, no one else ever really knew. Until now.

The words rushed from her lips, detailing the torn and grimy dress she wore day after day. The threats from her first pa if she spoke even one word. The realization that it benefited her to stay silent rather than to speak at all. The night he died in a saloon brawl, but Mae didn't know until two days later when she overheard the police telling the elderly neighbor. Her stomach growled, her throat was parched, her limbs ached from sleeping on the cold, hard, dirt-encrusted floor, and the cough that started a week before was the relentless beginnings of the croup.

But finally, she was free.

She told Mama of how at first she'd cried every time her first pa locked her in the closet. One cold evening he stormed through the door and yelled at her. She recalled his exact words. *"If you don't shut up, I'll throw you out the window."*

If he threw her out the window, she knew she would surely die as the building was so tall. She'd quieted immediately. He spoke spiteful words to her—words that hurt her heart. Words that she vowed to forget. Thankfully he never physically abused her, but the emotional and mental anguish he caused her would likely last a lifetime.

The children at the orphanage, all but Lucy and Albert, mocked her for her lack of words. She heard people refer to her as "dumb". But it was too terrifying to speak. For what if someone else, like her first pa, was determined to harm her because she uttered a word?

She had forgotten most of the things that happened in those days in New York. Or perhaps she'd only removed them temporarily from her mind until Mr. Duschesne kidnapped her and locked her in the cabin.

Now all those memories drowned her.

Mae's entire body shook, and Mama continued to hold her and rock her in her arms. Sweet, precious Mama—the one God had chosen for her. And Papa, strong and protective Papa, who showed her what a godly man looked like.

She pulled away then and swiped at the tears. That's when she noticed Mama crying too. "I'm so sorry, Mae," she whispered. "No child should ever have to live through that."

"Please tell no one else."

"I'll not tell a soul. But thank you for sharing with me." Mama reached for her hand. "Mr. Duchesne—did he hurt you?"

Mama's distraught expression tempted Mae not to tell her of what had truly occurred. But she'd never once told her mother a lie. Never once embellished the truth. She wouldn't start today.

"He was rough when he shoved me into the room, and he did tie my hands and legs. But no, he didn't harm me in any other way."

"Oh, praise God." Mama covered her mouth with her hand and choked back another sob as she prayed aloud, "Thank You, Heavenly Father, for keeping our Mae safe. For Your continued Providence over her life when so many things could have gone awry. You are faithful. Always faithful."

Indeed He was faithful. And just like the Lord had rescued her from New York, He'd rescued her from the clutches of Mr. Duchesne. Were it not for Landon...

"Mama, we have to help Landon. He didn't follow me from the cabin when I left. What if Mr. Duschesne harmed him or worse?"

At that moment, Papa and Sheriff Zembrodt bolted through the door. Mae ran toward Papa and allowed the safety of his arms to comfort her anew. Then she explained to him and the sheriff where the cabin was and about Mr. Duchesne and Gordon.

She'd barely finished when Papa and the sheriff exited back through the door and rode away.

While Papa was a gentle sort and a godly example in every way, Mae pitied the man who brought any harm to his family and those he cared about.

Later that evening, Landon arrived at the farm with Papa and Sheriff Zembrodt. Mae noticed the bandage around his upper arm as she rushed to him.

"Is that from Mr. Duchesne?"

"Yes, it is." He peered down at the bandage soiled with blood.

He had risked himself for her. "Are you all right?"

"I'm fine. Doc stitched me up and surmises I'll make a full recovery."

Mae reveled in the fact that the Lord had kept them both safe. "Thank you for rescuing me."

"You're welcome."

His gaze held hers, and she noticed bruising on his face. What if Duchesne had inflicted even worse injuries on him? Or if he had... She shivered despite the warm evening and wrapped her arms around herself.

Papa considered her. "Are you all right, Mae?"

"Yes, Papa."

His brows drew together, and he opened his arms to her. Mae flew into them. "I'm all right," she choked out, in between the thick emotion welling within her. When she drew back a few minutes later, she saw the concern etched on Papa's face.

"Praise God Landon was there. Otherwise, there'd be no telling—"

From her side-eye, she saw Mama shake her head. "We won't allow ourselves to think about what could have happened. Thank you, Landon."

"I'm glad I could help."

But even Landon's voice wavered.

Sheriff Zembrodt cleared his throat. "Not only did Landon rescue Mae and suffer an injury from Duchesne's knife, but he also took the man down single-handedly. Duchesne will recover—in prison."

"There was another man." Mae attempted to recall his name.

"Yep. Name's Gordon. He's in a heap of trouble too." Sheriff Zembrodt rested his hand on the revolver at his hip. "We won't have to ever worry about either of them again."

Papa and the sheriff followed Mama into the house. Before Mae could do the same, Landon put a hand on the small of her back. "When I saw you in there..."

Mae swallowed past the squeeze in her throat as her eyes flooded with tears. "It was awful, locked in that room. And then when you told me to go—"

"That was only so you could escape. I hope you can understand that."

"I did after a few minutes, but I was uneasy about leaving you behind."

Landon smiled and gently wiped the tear that slid down her cheek. "God was watching out for us both."

"Yes." Her voice shook as she again thought of the Lord's faithfulness.

"Mae, I want you to know I will always protect you. Keep you safe from harm as long as it is in my power to do so."

She fell into his arms then and rested against his firm chest as his arms folded around her.

And on that day, she knew that her feelings for Landon had indeed far surpassed friendship.

CHAPTER THIRTY

MAE GATHERED HER ITEMS and stood on the porch, awaiting Landon's arrival. It had been a long, but good day. She scratched Beans behind the ears. The air was eerily still, and an uncanny greenish-black hue lit the sky—a hue she couldn't recollect ever seeing before.

She shielded her eyes with her hand and scanned the area in the distance. No sign of Landon and no sign of the railroad workers. Had they gone back to camp for the day?

The children busied themselves with homework inside the school, and Lenore assisted Mrs. Eddington with supper preparations. Mr. Eddington was busy fixing the table leg on the well-used and worn dining room table.

The railroad workers again came to mind. Landon had tried his hardest to convince his father to move the line a greater distance from the school to no avail. Mae's own requests failed as well.

But Mae hadn't given up hope, nor had her family, Mr. and Mrs. Eddington, Lenore, and many of the townsfolk. She was convinced Landon hadn't given up on finding a solution either.

A roar of thunder sounded, startling her. Beans whined and paced. For the past half hour, he hadn't left her side. His incessant barking and restlessness did nothing to quell her unsettled feelings that something was awry.

At that moment, Landon's buggy came into view. It tilted precariously to the right as he followed the curved road to the school, driving faster than normal.

Beans began to tremble, and a flock of birds flew toward town. Except for the crunch of the buggy wheels on the hard earth, the air around her maintained its silence.

Landon climbed from the buggy and at the sight of him, her heart pitter-pattered against her ribcage. They'd grown closer in recent weeks, and she'd always be grateful for the way he rescued her from Duchesne nearly a month ago.

Landon stormed up the stairs nary giving a thought to Beans standing on his hind legs seeking attention. "Are the students and staff in the school?"

What an odd question. "Yes. Landon, is something wrong?"

"We need to get to the root cellar. Immediately."

Without waiting for her to respond, Landon rushed inside the school. She followed behind him, her heart racing for an altogether different reason than just seeing him.

Landon spoke to Mrs. Eddington, who, with Lenore, rushed from the kitchen. "Help us gather the children," she said.

Mae reached for Landon's arm. "Please tell me what's wrong."

"There's a tornado."

Mae had read of tornadoes but had never seen one.

Her feet remained firmly rooted in place. If the storms were anything like what she'd read about...

"It's a tornado! We have to seek shelter!" The terror in Landon's eyes caused a new round of fear to permeate through her.

In the far distance to the west, Mae saw a thick funnel in the shape of a gigantic "V" coming toward them.

"Get to the cellar!"

"What about the house?"

"The house isn't safe. It has to be the cellar."

Mr. and Mrs. Eddington, Lenore, and a line of children all holding hands, headed for the cellar. Beans, obviously petrified, howled while following along closely behind them.

"Mae, please, we have to seek safety."

Lightning streaked across the sky in a jagged line followed by another clap of thunder. She screamed, her voice competing with the noise. "I-I can't." She slowly plodded two steps forward, mentally coercing her legs to move.

"You have to!"

The distance to the cellar loomed in the distance. Would they even make it?

Landon clutched her hand even as the fear clawed its way through her. She struggled to force her legs to obey the command to leave the school's porch and run to the dark confines of the underground asylum.

An underground asylum.

She shuddered as memories flooded her mind.

No. She would wait here. Besides, what of Mama and Papa? What of her sisters and brothers?

Before she could contemplate following Landon, she must ensure her family was safe. "Mama and Papa."

"Your parents will see the tornado and seek shelter."

"But what if they don't? I have to go to them and warn them."

"There isn't time."

Hail pounded the porch steps, tiny ice balls of moisture mercilessly falling wherever they wished.

"There is if we hurry." Mae's eyes darted to the buggy. "We have to warn them." Why didn't Landon understand the urgency? How could she help him see that she couldn't lose them? Not after they'd rescued her.

Landon lifted her into his arms and ran to the cellar. She wrapped her arms around his neck and nestled into his shoulder seeking refuge from the pounding rain interspersed with hail.

The smell of the storm filled her nostrils. The cold damp air penetrated through her thin shirtwaist.

He set her down to open the cellar door. She hugged herself and begged the Lord to keep her family safe. To provide somewhere else for her to wait out the storm rather than the cellar.

The hail ceased for a moment, and Mae lifted her face to the west. A swirl of darkness headed toward them as the wind increased.

Landon reached for her. "Come on, Mae."

She took two more steps and stood at the edge of the cellar on the first stair. The darkness loomed below, and she again shivered, although this time not from the cold.

No, she wouldn't go down there. Not to the murkiness. Not to the isolation.

She refused to be trapped once again in a place she couldn't escape. She squeezed her eyes shut, and the memories of the room her first pa secured in for hours reappeared in her mind. The dank and musty smell. The filth. The mice skittering across the floor. The growling of her stomach because she hadn't eaten. Her mouth parched from lack of water.

The roar of the train near the tenements. Her first pa telling her that if she didn't behave herself, the train would run right into the apartments and run her over.

She had believed his words for the longest time.

Once again she relived the horror. The fear. The anxiety. The desperation to escape the confined area. The punishment should she make a sound.

No. She wouldn't go back there again. Not ever.

Hadn't she just survived a kidnapping and being trapped by Mr. Duchesne? And now this?

"Mae, we have to go into the cellar."

She shrunk away from Landon. Could she make it back to the house? Crouch on the floor in the corner and wait until the storm passed?

Why couldn't she make Landon understand that she couldn't—wouldn't take that next step that led to the unknown?

"Mae!"

This time he shouted, and she promptly clamped her hands over her ears. Why was he yelling? She squeezed her eyes shut. *Lord, please help me.*

Landon gently tugged on her right hand to remove it, but she pressed harder, resisting his attempts. She flung her eyes open and standing this close, she could see the urgency in his widened gaze. Yet, she was powerless to obey his commands.

He was saying something, but his voice was drowned out by the tornado's roaring. Its sound reminded her of not one, but two trains at once resounding near the tenements.

In a swift movement, she was again swept from her feet and into Landon's arms. She batted at him, willing him to release her.

But instead, he set her on a stair and ran back up to close the door of the cellar.

When he returned, he enveloped her into a hug and half-carried, half-dragged her down the remaining stairs. She struggled to free herself from his grasp.

A lantern flickered, and Mae could see the shadows on the faces of the scared children. Beans snuggled in Polly's lap. Mrs. Eddington turned them to face the opposite direction, and Mr. Eddington and Lenore blocked any view the children had of Mae.

She didn't want to frighten the children. She didn't. She was so embarrassed. If she relied fully on the Lord, why couldn't she find peace and calm?

Potatoes, carrots, corn, apples, and preserves all stacked nicely on shelves seemed to join the walls in closing in on her. She trembled and her throat tightened. Her arms shook and she folded herself in half as the foreboding crushed her.

"Mae."

His soothing voice brought her back to the present. Landon reached around her and pulled her to him.

She collapsed into his embrace, her heart pounding in her ears and rivaling the noise outside the cellar door.

He patted her hair, kissed her forehead, and rubbed her back. "Everything will be all right, Mae." Landon's voice calmed her and she drew closer to him. His shirt was wet from the rain, but his arms around her warmed her, and she clung to him.

"Everything will be all right," he repeated several more times.

She begged the Lord again to have mercy and spare her family.

And she thanked Him for a man named Landon Bennick.

Landon had been involved in a tornado before during the building of a major railroad in Iowa. It had been his first encounter with a storm wicked enough to destroy everything in its path.

And it had. Homes, barns, the recently-laid tracks—a town that had already existed before the railroad would also be built *around* the railroad. People lost their lives that day, including three Bennick Railway employees. Landon had been unable to save them.

Before then, Landon hadn't given much thought to the Lord. But on that day, he realized he'd only survived because of the faithful hand of God holding him in His grasp. Were it not for Landon deciding at the last minute to visit one of the farms near the new line, he would have been stuck halfway between town and the root cellar that protected him from the violent tornado.

A tornado in Idaho came unexpectedly, although Landon assumed they could happen just about anywhere.

He stroked Mae's hair and pulled her closer. He wanted to protect her. To care for her. To love her for the rest of the days he was given. He kissed the top of her head and prayed the Lord would heal the memories that haunted her.

Landon couldn't fathom all she'd been through before becoming a Shepherdson. He hoped someday she would share everything about those days. *Lord, I don't know all of the reasons for the fear that holds her so tightly in its clutches. I pray You would comfort her. Let her know of Your real presence.* Landon rested his chin on her head. *And, Father, I am falling in love with her. Please let me be worthy of her.*

Holding her in his arms, even though the scenario that led to it occurring was not one he would choose, felt right. Like she'd always belonged there.

Yes, he loved her. And to think he'd almost lost her both when Duchesne kidnapped her and again today. Those realizations devastated him.

Landon lost track of the time they'd been confined to the cellar. Mae had fallen asleep in his arms. While he didn't want to disturb her, he needed to find out if the tornado had passed and what damage it had caused. He would then need to travel to town and see if anyone was in need of assistance.

A cramp settled in his leg from sitting so long, and he gently leaned Mae against the wall holding potato bags. He shook his leg and limped to the stairs.

"Do you think it has passed?" Lenore asked.

"I hope so. I don't hear anything."

Mr. Eddington stood. "I'll come with you."

They pushed the door to the cellar open, and Landon followed Mr. Eddington.

Landon released a sigh when he saw the school. While he had hoped it would have emerged unscathed, having a damaged roof and no front door was far better than being completely destroyed. The barn was untouched, but several trees had been uprooted, and one had fallen onto the porch, cracking the railing and boards.

All of the horses were fine, and the buggy was flipped over, but otherwise in satisfactory condition. Landon hitched up the horse again, then prepared to take Mae home.

"I'll be back later this evening to assist with the school," he told Mr. Eddington.

"Much obliged. I'm praising the Lord that no lives were lost."

Landon concurred. Things could be reacquired. Schools rebuilt. But people could not be replaced. He thought of Mae and how close he had come to losing her again. The Lord was faithful indeed.

He took another glimpse at the school. While a portion of the house would now be unlivable due to the damaged roof and subsequent water damage, it could have been so much worse.

Ten minutes later, he and Mae started toward her family's farm.

During the first half mile, he noticed numerous uprooted trees, a ravaged barn with only portions of the frame still standing, and pieces of random wood and debris strewn alongside the road.

His concern for the folks of the Idaho town he'd temporarily called home increased.

Landon returned his attention to the road but periodically checked on Mae from his side-eye. Beans sat in her lap, and she absentmindedly stroked his brown-and-white fur. No doubt she was thinking about her family.

Strands of her mussed hair were plastered to her face. Hardened dirt encrusted her yellow shirtwaist, and her skirt had ripped near the bottom portion. A single tear slid down her cheek.

Landon pulled the buggy to the side of the road, put on the brake, and transferred the reins to one hand. "Mae?"

Her eyelids tipped closed, and several heartbeats passed before she reopened her eyes. He leaned toward her and gently swiped the tear and the caked mud on her chin. "I'll get you home posthaste and you can check on your family."

Mae's lower lip trembled, and Landon released the reins and pulled her to him. Beans moved into a comfortable position, and Mae nestled into Landon's chest. He wrapped his arms around her and rested his chin on her head. "We have to have faith, Mae, that the Lord brought everyone through this safely."

"I know."

Landon barely heard her weak response. He offered another prayer for Mae's family and everyone in Horizon. While he may have known what a tornado was and how to prepare for one, those who'd never seen or experienced one were at a disadvantage. Especially those who resided in a state where that type of severe weather was rare. Had the tornado veered toward town? In a completely different direction? Had it touched down again in other Idaho towns?

The smell of damp earth and the collection of piles of hail were the only indications anything had been awry just hours prior. The sun had reappeared, and only a smattering of clouds remained.

Her tears soaked his shirt, and emotion choked him at her pain. There was more to Mae Shepherdson than he knew, but what he did know was that he loved her. Wanted to care for and protect her and shield her from anything that might cause her any distress.

Mae shifted, the tension leaving her as she snuggled deeper into his embrace. While he knew she desired to check on her family, he would allow her all the time she needed.

Finally, after several minutes, Landon reclined back into the seat and cupped her chin. Her eyes met his, and for a moment he wondered—as he had numerous times since his feelings for her had grown—what it would be like to kiss her. Landon's eyes veered to her lips then back to her eyes.

Someday he would ask her if he might kiss her, but never when she was so vulnerable. "Mae?"

"I am worried about my family."

"I know. I've been praying."

"And, Landon? I'm sorry for nearly causing us not to make it to the cellar on time."

Mae was troubled by something already forgotten? "You were scared. I understand. For those who've never been in a deadly storm, the horror can make one unable to move. Even for those who have been involved in such an event, it's frightening." He thought of the time in Iowa when the tornado raged toward him, and the family invited him to seek refuge in their cellar. Many others, including his three workers, had not been so fortunate.

"It's true that I've never seen a tornado before, but there were other reasons..."

Would Mae someday feel comfortable enough to confide in Landon about all of the atrocities she'd faced? "When and if you want to share, I'm here to listen." He meant every word.

Mae looked away, and Landon could see the doubt that clouded her countenance. They hadn't known each other long, but he vowed to earn her trust.

"We best return you to your parents' home. Are you all right?"

She nodded mutely, and he gently released her before taking the reins again.

They rode in silence the remainder of the way to the Shepherdson farm, but Landon's mind remained on the delicate little bird God had placed in his life.

That evening, at Mr. Shepherdson's request, Landon followed him to the barn. "I want to thank you for again saving my daughter's life." He extended a hand.

Landon shook the man's hand. "You're welcome, sir."

"I'm forever indebted to you. Made a man feel helpless being here and not being able to ensure his daughters were safe. Mae was at the school, and Lucy was in the other direction at her house."

Landon pondered Mr. Shepherdson's words. "A man like you still worries?"

"Oh, yes. While I've been walking with the Lord for years, I still give in to the temptation to forget that God has everything under His control. Reckon I'll likely always struggle with that this side of Heaven."

"I worry that I could have done more to save workers in California when an accidental explosion killed two of my men and the three who died in a tornado in Iowa."

"Son, you will go through life with regrets. We all do. It's what we do with those regrets that matters. For years, I, too, held on to guilt. Some of it was my doing, while other things weren't. I had to learn that we can hang on to those regrets and blame ourselves for circumstances that, in your case, were beyond your control. Or we can release those remorses to our Heavenly Father. He doesn't wish for us to live lives filled with compunctions and shame."

"Thank you, sir."

Landon had formed a camaraderie with Mr. Shepherdson in the days of knowing him and this only firmed the friendship and the respect he had for a man who'd become like a second father.

CHAPTER THIRTY-ONE

LANDON MET HIS PARENTS for the noonday meal at Wilhelmina's Restaurant. He had much to discuss with them. He wiped his sweaty palms on his trousers and subsequently fidgeted with the silverware. As all discussions with Mother and Father, this one could proceed in either one of two ways: they would be agreeable or they would—in no uncertain terms—express their displeasure in Landon for proposing such a preposterous idea.

His parents entered the restaurant, and Landon stood as both were seated. "Hello, Mother, Father. I trust you slept well last night?"

"While it's far more quaint than what I'm accustomed to, I have grown rather fond of the Aspen Room where Miss Greta has placed us on the occasions we've opportunity to stay in Horizon," said Mother.

Wilhelmina arrived at their table with a pot of coffee. "Good afternoon, Mr. and Mrs. Bennick and Landon. What might I get for you today?"

"Good afternoon, Wilhelmina," said Mother as if she'd known the restaurant's proprietress for many years.

Landon and Mother ordered something from the menu, and Father requested a specially- prepared dish. After formalities, Landon prayed again for God's guidance, then proceeded to discuss the matters that had kept him awake last night.

He took a deep breath. "Mother and Father, as you may have heard, the Horizon School for the Deaf was destroyed in a recent tornado."

"Is this the same school you were concerned about with the spur?"

"Yes, Father."

"A tornado? How dreadful. Do they even have those in Idaho?"

"They're not common, Mother, but yes, they do occur. This one removed the roof from the school and caused other damage. We have temporarily fixed the school so children may still safely attend, but it won't be safe for winter with the snow and cold."

Father crossed his arms over his chest. "Allow me to guess—you wish for us to pay for the repairs?"

"No, sir. I wish for something beyond that."

Mother appeared taken aback at Landon's bold words. "Something beyond that?"

"Yes." He rolled his shoulders in an attempt to alleviate the tension. "You see, even properly repairing the school in its current location would be pointless."

"Because of the spur. Landon, we have already discussed this. We are not altering the placement of the line."

"Yes, Father, I understand. My suggestion consists of something entirely different." Landon attempted to keep his excitement contained but found it difficult to do so. He leaned forward. "I have recently purchased a plot of land and..."

Father scowled. "You've purchased land here? Whyever for? You don't purchase land in other towns where you've built spurs."

Mother waved his answer away. "I declare, Bertram. It's obviously because of a certain young woman."

The heat whooshed up Landon's face, and he loosened his collar. Best to leave that part of the discussion for later. One arduous conversation at a time. "Can you see it now?"

"See what?"

Father was going to be a challenge this morning.

"The sign that says Bennick Horizon School for the Deaf."

"No, I can't see that." Father sat back in his chair.

"I can see it," said Mother. "Do go on, Landon."

"Over the years, you both have always been exceedingly generous in your donations to worthwhile charities. What if you donated to have a brand new school built on the property I recently acquired? There's plenty of room at the far end closest to town and away from the river."

Father's scowl remained. "You've certainly thought this out."

"We have been most benevolent, Bertram." If Mother could, she'd likely pat herself on the back.

"So I thought we could donate to build the school before winter. Likely not the entire school, but enough of one so there's no disruption in the students' education. We could make any additions next spring when the weather clears. The workers here remain busy with the spur and will until at least fall, but maybe when they are in between projects, or what if we brought our workers from elsewhere—say from the northern part of the state or surrounding areas? Part of our donation would be to pay them and any individuals from Horizon we hired."

Mother's eyes widened. "You do know how Mae and I just love flowers."

"Yes."

"I can see it now." Mother faced her hands, palms out, and tilted her chin as she overly enunciated her words. "The Bennick Horizon School for the Deaf Botanical Gardens. Flowers of all varieties, meticulously planted and cared for. Petunias, pansies, forget-me-nots, daisies, geraniums, and wildflowers too. Perennials and annuals both."

"That is an extraordinary idea."

"Yes, I think so too. When do we start construction?"

A meager part of Landon's anxiety alleviated.

However, Father was not so easily swayed. "We have to be cautious when choosing charities to benefit."

"Goodness, Bertram. You've never been cautious in choosing what charities to benefit. If you wanted to offer funds, you did. How is this any different from the countless other instances of benevolence?"

Landon wanted to agree with Mother and further argue his point, but after years of studying Father's response to requests, he'd learned to wait patiently rather than speak further.

Wilhelmina brought their food and Landon said grace, thankfully without any resistance from his parents. He was about to take a bite of his pork chop when Father spoke.

"All right. I will agree, but I will have conditions to set forth."

Not a surprise. Father always had conditions to set forth. "Thank you, Father. With your permission, I'll take care of the arrangements."

"May I take care of arrangements regarding the botanical garden?" Mother took a sip of her coffee.

"That would be most welcome, Mother."

"Fabulous! I am so ecstatic I can barely eat."

The next topic for discussion would have to wait until Father had digested what he'd just promised. But at least the children would have a fully-funded new school. Landon attempted to slow his eating so as not to choke, but the next issue he needed to broach had more to do with his heart than his money.

When they'd finished eating and Wilhelmina had cleared the dishes and poured more coffee, Landon sought the Lord's help for courage. "Since you are both in Horizon for the next couple of days, I find it prudent to discuss one other matter with you."

Mother's brow furrowed. "We will be back to Horizon again, Landon. I've become partial to this backwards and uncivilized Wild West town. Not that I desire to visit it frequently, mind you, but on occasion until the spur is complete.

If Mother knew what he was about to say, she might change the frequency of her visits. "When I bought the property, I had other plans in mind for it than just the new school."

"Why would you buy property here if not for the school?" Father asked.

"Could it be because of a certain young lady?"

Mother could be perceptive, but her words came out as more of an insinuation than a cheerful inquiry. "Yes, it does have to do with Mae." He attempted to release a tight breath. "You see, I—well, I love Mae. I want to spend the rest of my life with her—if she'll have me."

Father's lips pressed into a grim line and Mother gasped.

This wasn't going well.

"We've had this discussion about this woman already," growled Father.

"And, Landon, you know she is far below your station, as much as I like her."

"Yes, Mother and Father, you've shared your sentiments on the matter." Landon's voice shook. "But I do truly love her. I still have to ask for permission from her father to court her, and from what I know of her parents, they'll require a lengthy courtship."

"Well, that's good to hear." Mother held a hand to her heart. "Landon, we have such hopes and dreams for you. You'll not throw it all away by marrying a peasant girl and living in a primitive town."

"With your permission, Father, I plan to build one of the headquarters for Bennick Railways here in Horizon. I will continue to do my job as I always have. There will be travel, yes, but when Mae and I do marry—if that is God's will for us—then I won't be traveling far distances nearly as much. With the railway underway to be complete from Cornwall to Horizon, I can easily journey to Cornwall for any pressing matters. However, with a wife and a family, I aim to put them first, so I—"

"A wife and a family?" Mother's mouth fell open.

"If Mae and I marry, we will hope to have a family someday. I'm merely thinking of the future."

Mother's face retained its startled expression as if she were frozen in time or her image captured in a tintype. Finally, she recovered. "Well, I suppose I would like to be a grandmother someday."

"Yes, I think you'd make a fine grandmother."

Father said nothing, only offered the disapproving look he'd perfected since Landon had learned to walk.

So Landon took advantage of no interruptions. "What with the courtship, marriage and a family are far into the future. However, I have been thoroughly assessing the situation. When I ought to be sleeping, I might add." He offered a nervous chuckle but was alone in his merriment. "I will be plenty busy running the company from one of our headquarters here in Horizon as well as managing the depot. During those times when I cannot travel, I fully trust two of my men, Walsh and Chen, to take up the reins and handle matters in distant locations."

The room was thick with silence as if even the other patrons were intent on listening, although Landon knew that wasn't the case. He worked his lip between his teeth and willed his legs not to shake beneath the table. His heart pounded in his ears as the seconds ticked by.

Father straightened in his chair. "You do know I am of the age where I could have a heart condition, what with all of this nonsense."

Not the answer Landon wanted, but not an entirely unexpected one. At least Mother seemed somewhat agreeable. "Father, the last thing I would want is for you to have a heart condition."

"Well, then you could do what you wish with the company."

"He couldn't because I would still be here, and I don't plan on having a heart condition." Mother tossed a prideful glance at her husband.

This was not going well. Landon accidentally bumped the table and the remaining coffee in his cup nearly sloshed over the edge. *Lord, please help me.* "Please do understand what I am attempting to articulate," he said, doing his best to keep his quivering thoughts from escaping through his words. "I have no desire to take over the company. I have no desire to fully run Bennick Railways until such time as I am required to do so. Lord willing, that will be decades from now. I have some ideas for managing it from Horizon, hopefully in a way that is agreeable to you. There are other ideas, including a shipping portion I'd also like to discuss with you at a more pertinent time. However, for now, I am anticipating and eagerly yearning for your and Mother's blessing to court and marry Mae Shepherdson. And further, for my permanent home to be in Horizon. Not that we won't come see you in Denver, because we will." With the words that tumbled from his mouth, so did a shaky exhalation.

"I see."

That was all Father had to say? Landon waited for him to say more, but he only drank more of his coffee while staring vacantly ahead.

"Mother, do you understand my position?"

"I do. I don't agree with much of it, however"

Leave it to Mother to express how she really felt.

"I will take all you have said under advisement."

"Thank you, Father."

The awkward silence between them made Landon wonder if he ought to have broached the subject at a more opportune time. But there was no better time. His parents were leaving town Monday, and Landon wished to speak with Mr. Shepherdson soon about courting Mae. As it was, Landon found she filled his thoughts more hours than not.

The bell above the restaurant door jingled, and Mr. Shepherdson entered with a crate, likely full of pies Mrs. Shepherdson made for Wilhelmina to serve her customers. He set the crate on the counter, conversed with Wilhelmina, then turned and waved at Landon before striding over to the table. "Hello, Landon."

"Mr. Shepherdson, I'd like you to meet my parents. Mother, Father, this is Mae's father."

Mr. Shepherdson shook hands with Father and nodded at Mother. "Pleasure to meet you both." He gripped Landon's shoulder. "You two must be quite proud of your son."

"Oh?" Father retained his irritable countenance.

"When we heard the railroad was first coming to Horizon, most of us, myself included, were amenable to the fact. However, some weren't so agreeable. Landon handled things in a manner that brought our town together rather than divided it. Much more importantly, he saved my daughter's life during the tornado and possibly the lives of others as well. There was another situation as well, for which I am greatly indebted to him for."

Emotion flickered in Mr. Shepherdson's gaze, and Landon knew it was the situation with Duchesne of which he spoke.

Mother's eyes rounded "Is that so?"

"You've raised yourself a fine son."

"Yes, well we do know that." Mother brushed the compliment aside.

"I best be on my way. Will you be at the church potluck Sunday?"

Landon was still attempting to regain the use of his voice after Mr. Shepherdson's meaningful words. "Uh, yes, sir. I do aim to be there."

"Reckon I'll see you then. Mr. and Mrs. Bennick, if you're staying in town on Sunday, you're welcome to come to the potluck. There'll be bountiful food and pleasant company."

"I doubt there would be any food I would like," muttered Father.

"Yes, doubtfully so," agreed Mother.

"Even the pickiest eaters have found something to eat at our church potlucks. I'm sure the townsfolk would appreciate meeting you. I know my family would. We've all grown fond of Landon in the past weeks."

Father's mouth gaped open and Mother, the voice for them both, spoke again. "We'd be delighted to attend. Do count on us."

"See you then. Pleasure to meet you both. Landon."

Mr. Shepherdson exited the restaurant before Father finally spoke. "It appears you've endeared yourself to that family."

The fact that Mr. Shepherdson spoke so highly of Landon in his presence—and more importantly, in the presence of his parents—had evoked gratitude and further appreciation for the family he'd spent so much time with in recent days. A family he longed to be a part of.

Father cleared his throat. "We'll attend the potluck and church, even though it's not Christmas or Easter. Further, Landon, you do realize that I—we—" Father pointed to Mother then himself. "That we both are—" Clearly, Father could not express his thoughts.

"What your father is attempting to say is that we both are—well, we're thankful for the way you are running the business."

"Yes. What your mother said."

A surge of emotion filled every part of him, and Landon blinked rapidly before regaining his composure. How long had he waited for those words?

True to their word, Mr. and Mrs. Bennick arrived at church, although Mr. Bennick's restlessness gave evidence to his discomfort. Landon, however, sat a little straighter, and Mae could see the pride of having his parents in attendance.

After the services, everyone met outside for the potluck. Introductions abounded, and Papa, Landon, Mr. Bennick, and several others engaged in a conversation about the spur. Mae, Mama, Lucy, and Mrs. Bennick met beneath one of the trees, and Mama welcomed Landon's ma. While different in nearly every way, the two women shared a camaraderie, not completely unexpected given Mama's gift of hospitality.

The children from Horizon families as well as the children from the school mingled together and played in the open field beside the church. Polly, Carrie, and Becky, all carrying handfuls of dandelions and wildflowers, sprinted toward the women. "All of you close your eyes and hold out your hands," demanded Carrie. "You too, ma'am." She nodded to Mrs. Bennick.

The girls presented them with the beautiful bouquets, Polly giving some of her blooms to Mrs. Bennick.

"You can open your eyes," said Becky.

A chorus of thank yous sounded, and Mama folded all three girls into a hug. When she released them, Polly stared up at Mrs. Bennick and smiled.

"The flowers are lovely, thank you," she said.

"This is how you sign, 'thank you'," directed Carrie. She demonstrated the open hand extending from her chin.

"Oh, but I've never done these types of gestures before." Mrs. Bennick's hesitancy failed to dissuade Polly. She took Mrs. Bennick's free hand in her own and demonstrated the sign.

Landon joined them at that moment. "Very good, Mother. You're an efficient learner."

"Oh!" Mother's grin covered her entire face and color splotched her cheeks.

Polly answered, "You're welcome".

"I'd like to learn that one too."

Landon signed to Polly to show Mrs. Bennick the sign, and Polly happily obliged. The woman practiced the sign at least six times, and all three girls giggled at Mrs. Bennick's serious demeanor as she did so.

Mrs. Bennick nodded toward Polly. "She is such an adorable child."

Mae agreed. "Yes, she is. She's so smart and so willing to learn."

"I daresay this is my first time ever meeting a deaf individual, and most certainly my first time speaking in their language."

"You're learning quickly," Landon said.

Mrs. Bennick offered a superior lift of her chin. "Did I ever tell you, Landon, that I learned how to speak French as a young girl?"

"No, I don't believe you did."

Hosea interrupted Mrs. Bennick's diatribe about French lessons when he tapped on Landon's arm and asked if Landon would throw the ball with him and the other boys. Landon affirmed his request that he would join them in a few minutes.

"Oh, but that little boy reminds me so much of you at that age, Landon. Just a slip of a boy. For how many treats you would sneak from Cook's kitchen, you remained scrawny and lanky. Now, you've far surpassed your father's height and are tall and strong like my brother, Hugo, was. God rest his soul."

"You knew about me sneaking treats?"

"Yes, I did, especially the cinnamon-and-sugar mixture you gleefully devoured." Mrs. Bennick raised an eyebrow.

Her dramatic presentation and Landon's feigned surprise caused a round of laughter among Mae, Mama, and Lucy.

"Well, I best make good on my word to join the boys to play catch." His gaze met Mae's, and her heart skipped several beats.

God had blessed her with a good and kind man when He allowed Landon Bennick to enter her life.

Chapter Thirty-Two

MAE REVELED IN THE time spent with Landon on their buggy ride. The spur from Ingleville to Horizon was scheduled for completion in a month. Trepidation regarding Landon's future plans consumed Mae's thoughts. Would he leave Horizon? Stay while the Horizon to Humboldt spur was completed? What of winter when work was stalled? But while they needed to discuss such matters, Mae refused to allow any dismal thoughts to interrupt the highly anticipated time together. So instead, she raised another topic.

"Did you hear that the Lieutenant and Miss Greta are courting?"

From the expression on his face, Landon had not yet heard the news. "No, but that doesn't surprise me."

"Miss Greta informed me when I took the children on a visit to the mercantile yesterday. Apparently, they have planned for a July wedding next year."

"Seems our matchmaking machinations worked."

Mae glanced at their surroundings and assumed they were traveling on a road past her house she'd not yet been on for a picnic near the river. She'd packed a freshly-baked shoo-fly cake along with sandwiches and carrots for that very purpose.

So when Landon halted the buggy near a cabin on a well-kept clearing, she thought perhaps he mistakenly did so.

He assisted her from the buggy and held her hands in his. "Mae?"

"Yes?"

"I purchased this land a few months ago. What do you think?"

She scanned the nearby fields, the aspen grove, and the mountains covered in western white pines in the distance. A cabin hovered nearby, a pot of flowers on its porch. The entire setting was unlike any she'd ever seen. "Landon, it's breathtaking. But why did you purchase it?" She held her breath, hoping his answer was what she anticipated.

"I plan to make Horizon the new headquarters for Bennick Railways."

Her pulse ticked up a notch. "Horizon?"

"Father and I have been negotiating. Once a month or so, I'll travel to Denver for a few days. Journey time is significantly shorter with the railroad now spanning the entire distance. I'll travel periodically to the camp near Humboldt as the spur is being built there next spring. All other business can be completed from here in Horizon."

She inhaled a shocked gasp of breath. "Really? But what about…?"

He gently pressed a finger to her lips. "No other feasible option exists when the woman I love lives here."

The woman he loved? Her mouth dropped open.

"Besides, I've grown fond of the town and the townsfolk."

"You're staying in Horizon?"

"I am. I'm hoping the lovely woman I spoke of will do me the honor of courting me. I'd be remiss if I didn't mention I aim to make her my wife if she'll have me. And before you ask, yes, I've already secured permission from your father."

"Yes."

"Yes?"

"Yes, I'll court you and yes, I'll marry you, and yes, I'll live in this cabin with you." Her words emerged in an exhilarated jumble. How long had she wondered if a future with Landon was possible?

He swept her into his arms and spun her around until they were both dizzy. "Thank you for saying yes," Landon said as returned her to solid ground and took a step toward her. "There is something you should know."

"Oh? Surely your parents are in agreement?"

"They are in agreement. Look closely through the grove of trees, just beyond the hill in the far distance. You'll see a clearing."

She did as he requested.

"That is the new home of the Bennick Horizon School for the Deaf. We've already ordered lumber, and the railroad crew and others in town, whom Father has hired at his expense, will construct it. The school will be completed before winter."

"Landon, really?"

"Really. No child will be refused, and income from the crops here on this farm and the school's farmland will all go to feed the children and aid in school expenses."

The tears fell before she could stop them. "Thank you."

"You're welcome."

They stood, their faces just inches from each other. Would he kiss her?

"Mae?" He stroked her cheek with his finger.

"Yes?" she whispered.

"May I kiss you?"

She nodded because words would not come. She raised on tiptoe in anticipation. Joy rippled through her as he first brushed her forehead with a kiss before his warm lips found hers.

Their first kiss was interrupted by a second one with only a brief interlude in between.

Epilogue

One year later

POLLY AND HOSEA RACED each other down the road, Beans following them until they reached the pine tree at the edge. They bowled over, their laughter carrying on the breeze.

Landon squeezed Mae's hand. "Should we tell them?"

Her smile in response stole his breath. Was it possible to love someone the way he loved her?

"I can't wait for their reaction."

Landon gestured to Polly and Hosea, and the two dashed toward them. Their faces were flushed from the warm summer day, and Hosea put his hands on his hips and exaggeratedly attempted to catch his breath. Beans chased his tail before his attention shifted to a monarch butterfly flitting past.

Mae gazed up at him, and Landon considered foregoing telling the children the news until after kissing her again.

"Our children are going to be so excited," said Mae, her words interrupting his thoughts.

Our children.

They'd adopted Polly and Hosea shortly after marrying, and while Landon experienced some trepidation regarding how best to be a father, God had alleviated many of his worries.

Landon watched their responses when Mae signed that Polly would soon be a big sister, and Hosea, a big brother.

Polly's eyes flickered in Hosea's direction before she responded that she was already a big sister. Hosea scrunched his nose and signed that he thought Polly was older, so how could he be a big brother?

Mae's sweet laughter filled the air, and he joined in her amusement before wrapping his arms around her. She explained to the children about the baby to be born in five months.

"A baby?" signed Polly.

When Mae nodded, Polly and Hosea jumped up and down, joined hands, and spun around in a circle. Beans forgot all about the butterfly and added his own opinion with a series of barks.

Polly signed that she wanted to sew the baby a new blanket.

Hosea signed that if the baby was a boy, he could live with Hosea in his new room.

Landon's attention veered to their new house, a tasteful and sizable home amidst the breathtaking scenery. The former house was now Landon's office where he conducted work for Bennick Railways and Shipping, the latter being a new business venture Father reluctantly agreed to.

Beyond the houses were productive fields, fruit trees, and the glorious Idaho mountains. In the distance, loomed the new Bennick Horizon School for the Deaf, surrounded by Mother's botanical gardens.

The children rushed off to play again, leaving Landon alone with his wife.

The sun began to set in the west, a spectacular combination of purples, pinks, and blues.

"So many dreams have come true." Mae gently patted her stomach. "And so many more dreams on the horizon yet to come.

She faced him, and he started at the top of her head and kissed her hair before nuzzling her ear, and finally capturing her mouth with his.

Never would he have anticipated all the blessings God had bestowed on him, the most precious being the woman in his arms.

PENNY
ZELLER
Beyond the
HORIZON
HORIZON SERIES, BOOK THREE

BEYOND THE HORIZON
SNEAK PEEK

FOR A MOMENT, SHE was the world-famous reporter, Ruby Shepherdson, author of the latest award-winning article.

Ruby closed her eyes and imagined seeing her name below the numerous articles and stories she submitted to the editor Mr. O'Kane, the editor of *The Horizon Herald.* The editor from the prestigious *Boise City Chronicle*, who was just happening to visit his mother in Horizon, would peruse the pages of *The Horizon Herald* and become engrossed in one of Ruby's engaging articles. He would then invite her to submit a story each month to his well-read publication.

But alas, such a fanciful dream would have to wait.

Ruby resumed scrubbing one of Papa's shirts on the washboard. There was no fictional editor from the *Boise City Chronicle* visiting his mother in Horizon. And until Ruby's shipment of her Smith Premier typewriter arrived from the R. Altman & Company in St. Louis, Missouri, she would continue to dip her pen in ink and handwrite each and every composition she submitted to the cantankerous gloomy Gus who'd become her boss just one year ago last week.

Not that she minded tending to everyday chores, including laundry on Mondays, for she didn't. As a matter of fact, Ruby's highest aspirations were to someday marry and be a wife and mother. But until the Lord saw fit to allow a suitable gent into her life, she would continue on the path of writing.

Ruby hung the shirt on the line, then proceeded with washing the next item when she noticed a buggy rounding the curve to their farm. She stood tall and placed her hands on her lower back to stretch the tightness from hunching over the washboard. A closer perusal indicated Wilhelmina, one of Mama's best friends, was paying them a visit.

Wilhelmina, a permanent smile on her round face, folded Ruby into a hug. "It's so nice to see you. Your ma and I are planning some new recipe ideas, but first, I was asked to deliver a message."

It didn't surprise Ruby that Mama and Wilhelmina would be experimenting with recipes. After the Bible, Mama's favorite book was *Recipes from Augusta's Kitchen*, a book she'd purchased when she and Papa first married. "A message?"

"Yes. Tabitha said to tell you that your special purchase has arrived."

The air caught in Ruby's lungs. "My special purchase? It has arrived?"

"That's what she said."

Not caring how unladylike it might be, Ruby let out an enthusiastic yelp, threw up her hands in excitement, and danced a little jig.

"Might be that you are thrilled to hear this news," teased Wilhelmina.

"Oh, yes. Not only thrilled, but exhilarated. I've waited forever for this momentous occasion."

"Congratulations."

"Thank you." Ruby plopped the unwashed clothes in a pile. She'd finish the daunting chore later, but for now, she'd seek Papa's permission to take the wagon into town and retrieve the item that would change her life forever.

Wilhelmina put an arm through Ruby's, and together they marched to the house, albeit more slowly than Ruby would have preferred. She attempted not to be impatient as Mama and Wilhelmina greeted each other and acted as though they hadn't just seen each other at church yesterday. Finally, Ruby was able to edge in a word.

"Mama, may I please borrow the wagon? My shipment has arrived at the mercantile."

Mama's eyes widened. "So soon?"

For Mama, it may be soon, but for Ruby, it had been an eternity since she'd sought a loan from the bank and ordered her soon-to-be prized possession.

"It's fine with me, but check with Papa and see if he'll need the wagon in the meantime. And would you mind gathering some provisions while you're there?"

"Not at all."

After Mama handed her a list, Ruby bounded out the door and to the farthest northern corner of the field to secure Papa's permission. She lifted her dress and ran, being sure to dodge the numerous muddy puddles from last night's rain. The spring breeze whipped her skirts and blew wisps of hair from her once-secure chignon.

"Ruby? Is there an emergency?" Papa stood from fixing the plow, concern in his eyes.

"Oh, no, I just was hoping to borrow the wagon to retrieve my shipment."

"I'm going to town tomorrow for some lumber. I can fetch it for you then."

"Thank you, but if it's all the same, I'd like to retrieve it today. Posthaste."

Timothy, her younger brother, shook his head. "What's the rush, Rube? You've been waiting for the shipment for this long. One more day won't make a bit of difference."

"On the contrary, dear brother. It makes *all* the difference. Papa, please may I borrow the wagon? I fear Tabitha will close the mercantile for the day if I tarry."

"Judging from the sun's placement in the sky, reckon you have plenty of time," offered Timothy, who was constantly set on offering unsolicited advice.

"Not everyone is a dawdler, Timothy. I prefer not to lollygag as time is of the essence."

Papa chuckled. "You two and your squabbling. Yes, Ruby, you can take the wagon to town. Would you mind stopping by the mill for the lumber? It will save me a trip tomorrow. Vernon will load it for you."

"Yes, absolutely, I will stop by the mill." She waited two more seconds in case Papa had more to add. When he said nothing, she added, "Thank you, Papa. I'll be back as soon as possible."

She hitched the horses, and with her notebook, pencil, and Mama's list in hand, Ruby climbed into the wagon. She beckoned the horses and headed to town, excitement filling every part of her.

Once at the mercantile, Ruby gathered everything into a crate from Mama's list and stood in line behind three other customers, all of whom, while dear people, seemed to have a penchant for prattling on. Finally, she reached the counter.

"Hello, Ruby. You must have received my message."

"Yes, I'm here for my shipment." Her breathless words bespoke of her anxiety to secure her order.

"Jimmie will load it for you. It's a sizable crate." Tabitha's face lit. "You're well on your way to becoming an established journalist now that you'll be the proud owner of a Smith Premier. I noticed in the catalogue that there's even a new version now."

Ruby was content with the previous version, especially given the cost. Tabitha put Mama's items on her account and beckoned her husband to hoist the crate hidden in the back room.

"Say, Ruby, I thought you should be the first—well, second to know, seeing as how I told Tabitha first—that I'm planning to run for another term as mayor."

"That's delightful news, Mayor Trabert."

"Thank you." He pushed the crate to the front of the wagon beside Mama's provisions. "I love serving this town. Perhaps you could write an article about my plans to run again."

"I'd be happy to ask Mr. O'Kane if he'd be amenable to me doing just that."

Mayor Trabert tipped his hat. "Tell your folks I said hello."

Ruby stopped next at the mill where Vernon loaded the lumber for Papa after assisting two other customers.

And finally, Ruby was on her way home.

All was well until an idea struck her for a story she hoped to approach Mr. O'Kane with. Since she knew that if she didn't stop to write down the thought it would escape her overcrowded mind forever, Ruby pulled to the side of the road, set the reins beside her, and reached for her notebook and pencil, which had fallen off the seat.

But there was one small problem.

In her haste, she'd forgotten to set the brake.

The horses advanced forward, jolting Ruby from her once-comfortable spot on the buckboard. The reins, also jolted by the sudden movement slithered just beyond her reach.

Mud flew up on the sides of the wagon as the horses determined their route—a route off of the road and into the muddy weeds.

"Whoa!" she yelled as the wagon bumbled along and the pieces of lumber rattled in the back. A quick glance told her the typewriter remained secure, but some of Mama's provisions rolled throughout the wagon.

Ruby clamored again for the reins and finally secured them, but not before the wagon immersed itself in a thick pile of dark brown mud. It screeched to a halt, propelling her forward.

Several minutes later, she righted herself and heaved a deep breath of relief. "Thank You, Lord," she gasped, noting she could have fallen headfirst beneath the horses' feet or the wagon and been trampled.

She may have emerged unscathed from her adventure, but the wagon had firmly rooted itself in the mud. Taking a minute to catch her breath, she determined she was halfway home, although far from the road.

Ruby had two choices. Attempt to dislodge the wagon wheels from the mud or walk home and fetch Papa and Timothy.

She could hear her brother's voice now, *"Reckon I'm not surprised it happened the way it did, Rube. You can be such a knucklehead sometimes, what with you in such a rush to retrieve your shipment and all."*

No, she wouldn't walk home and seek Papa's and Timothy's assistance, prideful as it may be. Instead, she would endeavor to liberate the wagon.

Mud caked the hem of her dress as she attempted to pry the wheels loose with a piece of Papa's lumber. Her arms ached from the laborious undertaking, and after what seemed like hours, she paused and climbed back into the wagon.

Perhaps she would have to rethink her options and overlook and ignore Timothy's insolent admonishments.

Just as she'd uttered her fifteenth prayer for wisdom and was about to embark on the journey toward home, she saw a passing wagon. Help had arrived!

As ladylike as possible, Ruby climbed into the back of the wagon. She stood on tiptoe and waved her arms. "Over here!"

The driver of the wagon peered in her direction. Would he stop?

Surely he would. The residents of Horizon, most of them anyhow, were kindly folks.

"Help!" she yelled again, her voice echoing on the vacant stretch of land.

The man reversed direction and drove his wagon toward her, and Ruby released the breath she'd been holding. He stopped on the road away from the muddy patch and disembarked.

"What seems to be the problem?"

While his hat was pulled low over his eyes so she couldn't see much of his face other than a scraggly and unkempt brown beard, Ruby was quite certain she'd never seen him before. As any perceptive reporter would do, she attempted to ascertain his age. Given his hands were not gnarled or arthritic, he must not be an elderly man. He wore a red plaid shirt stretched over broad shoulders, tan trousers, and boots, indicating he was likely a farmer. Dark brown hair curled beneath his hat, and a portion of his neck was sunburned.

"Yes, I seem to have taken an accidental adventure by departing from the road and finding myself plumb stuck in the middle of a muddy field." She laughed, noting her voice sounded nervous in her own ears.

"I see that."

"Yes, well, I hadn't meant to. You see, I had this most amazing idea for one of my articles, and while I was reaching…"

"Miss, with all due respect, I'll just assist you and be on my way."

"Oh. All right."

He was obviously one of few words.

"I was attempting to use a piece of the lumber—"

But the man was not listening. Instead, he strode to his own wagon and reached for a shovel from the back. When he returned, he said, without so much as a lift of his head, "You might want to remove yourself and stand over there."

His voice was deep and clipped, and Ruby did as he requested. The man dug the wheels from the mud, coaxed the horses, and freed Ruby from her predicament in a matter of minutes.

"Thank you so much. I appreciate your help. Might I ask your name?"

"No."

How abrupt! Such a peculiar man. "Oh. All right. Well, thank you again."

"You should be able to continue to wherever it is you're going. Next time, I would suggest you mind yourself while driving the team. You're fortunate you weren't injured or worse."

"Oh, yes, sir. I will be more mindful in the future. You see, when these ideas hit me, I have to—well, never mind." The man likely would not care to hear her flimsy excuse for being so careless.

"If that's all, I'll be on my way."

He tipped his hat and strode to his wagon.

Ruby tapped her chin as she watched the unusual stranger drive away. Perhaps Mr. O'Kane would allow her to investigate the man's identity. After all, who could resist a mystery?

If you want to be among the first to hear about the next Horizon installment, sign up for Penny's newsletter at www.pennyzeller.com. You will receive book and writing updates, encouragement, notification of current giveaways, occasional freebies, and special offers.

A

WYOMING
SUNRISE
NOVELETTE

If you enjoyed this glimpse into the lives of Mae and Landon,
please consider leaving a review on your social media, Amazon,
Goodreads, Barnes and Noble, or BookBub. Reviews are critical
to authors, and those stars you give us
are such an encouragement.

Author's Note

Dear Reader,

When I set out to write *Dreams on the Horizon*, I knew I'd be conducting plenty of research. While I did take some fictional liberties, many things were influenced or inspired by real events.

The scene with the contaminated milk due to the rattlesnake biting the cow was based on a true story from the 1800s. A family in Wyoming suffered when the milk they drank was given by a cow who'd been bitten by a rattler. As in *Dreams on the Horizon*, the milk had been mixed with other milk, making it less potent. The real-life story indicated that the numerous afflicted children would have died were it not for the diluted milk. Also in the real-life story, a colt died within minutes when it was fed the contaminated, undiluted milk.

I also researched marbles, the price of rent, and of course, railroads. The figure $367,119.18 in chapter fifteen was based on a figure from my research of a fifty-mile stretch built in Idaho in the late 1800s. Landon's memory of an explosion killing two workers in California was based on a true event. Building railroads was dangerous work.

Deaf history was also on my research radar. American Sign Language, or ASL, was developed in 1814 by Dr. Thomas Hopkins Gallaudet, a minister. Alexander Graham Bell argued that the oralism method was superior, to which many did not agree, including the fictional characters in *Dreams on the Horizon*, who were huge ASL proponents.

During my research, I found a recipe for clear soup from President Benjamin Harrison's wife, Caroline. It inspired me to mention it in the book as the recipe Mae and her younger sister, Ruby, are making for supper in a fun scene where Ruby tries her feeble attempts at matchmaking. Shoo-fly cake was also a real recipe. The farm prices were taken from actual research, and there truly was a cigar company in South Carolina seeking "agents" (salesmen) willing to sell their product. Finally, I learned that timothy is a type of hay. Having grown up surrounded by farmland, I previously had no idea of this type of crop.

I thoroughly enjoyed writing *Dreams on the Horizon* and mixing in the funny parts with the more somber parts. Ever since writing *Over the Horizon*, I knew Mae would need her own story. How could a little girl go through so much and come out unscathed? It was a wonderful way to show God's faithfulness and His plan for her life, even when things looked dismal.

A book wouldn't be complete without a few bloopers. Thankfully these have been edited out, but I thought you'd enjoy knowing that there was once a "font of the church" (Times New Roman or Arial, anyone?) instead of "the front of the church". And there was once a sentence talking of the "lives of man people" instead of "lives of many people".

Characters in my books come to life and are always so much more than figments of my imagination. There is nothing quite like being able to create characters and give them personalities, motivations, good traits, and flaws. They become real and fill my thoughts nonstop during the writing process.

So, what's next on the agenda? Ruby will have her own story in *Beyond the Horizon*, and I'll introduce you to a new Horizon character—the hunky recluse, Jake Lynton. Mae, who is shy, timid, reserved, and gentle is quite the opposite of her spunky and vivacious sister, who doesn't hesitate to speak her mind.

I recently learned that Timothy will also have his own story, *Love on the Horizon*, which will complete the series. We'll fast forward a bit and give him a love interest who will be perfect for his ornery personality.

Thank you, as always, for joining me as I weave the stories together and transfer them from my mind—or what my family calls an overactive imagination—to paper. Your dedication to reading my books means the world to me, and I am humbly grateful.

Until we meet again, happy reading!

Blessings,

Penny

Acknowledgments

As always, a book couldn't be written without the help of so many.

To my family. I can never thank you enough for your encouragement, support, and patience as I put words to paper. I'm so grateful for you.

To my oldest daughter. What would I do without you to constantly bounce crazy ideas off of? Thank you for all you do to help me stay sane during the writing process and all you do to aid me in making sure release day goes off without a hitch. Thank you also for naming Beans. The name fits him perfectly!

To my Penny's Peeps Street Team. Thank you for spreading the word about my books. I appreciate your encouragement and support!

To Marie Concannon, Head, Government Information & Data Archives University of Missouri Library and her graduate student assistant, Catherine. You two were amazing at helping me with railroad research. Thank you, thank you, thank you!

To Brian Darcy, Administrator of the Idaho School for the Deaf and Blind. Your help was invaluable. Thank you for taking the time to talk with me about your school and answer my multitude of questions.

To veterinarian, Wim Sherman, for all of your assistance with detailing information about rescue dogs. Because of you, I was able to more accurately create my dog character, Beans.

To Con Trumbull, Author of *Wyoming Central Railroads*, and archivist at the Northern Nevada Railway Museum, for taking the time to answer my questions about railroads. I appreciate your help and vast knowledge of historical railways.

To Teri Easterling for inspiring me to make Beans, the dog character in *Dreams on the Horizon*, a rescue dog. I loved how you and your husband, in the course of your 47 years of marriage, have rescued numerous dogs.

To my readers. May God bless and guide you as you grow in your walk with Him.

And, most importantly, thank you to my Lord and Savior, Jesus Christ. It is my deepest desire to glorify You

About the Author

Penny Zeller is known for her heartfelt stories of faith-filled happily ever afters and her passion to impact lives for Christ through fiction. Her books feature tender romance, steady doses of humor, and memorable characters that stay with you long after the last page.

While she has had a love for writing since childhood, Penny began her adult writing career penning articles for national and regional publications on a wide variety of topics.

Today Penny is a multi-published author of over two dozen books and is represented by Tamela Hancock Murray of the Steve Laube Agency. She is also a fitness instructor, loves the outdoors, and is a flower gardening addict. In her spare time, she enjoys camping, hiking, kayaking, biking, birdwatching, reading, running, and playing volleyball.

Penny resides with her husband and two daughters in small-town America and loves to connect with her readers at her website at www.pennyzeller.com, her blog, www.pennyzeller.wordpress.com, and her Facebook page at www.facebook.com/pennyzellerbooks where she posts faith, funnies, writing updates, and encouragement. All of her socials can be found at https://linktr.ee/pennyzeller.

HORIZON SERIES

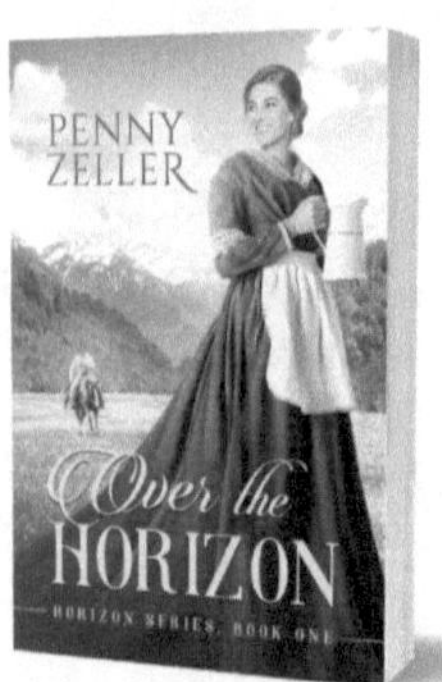

PENNY ZELLER
Over the HORIZON
HORIZON SERIES, BOOK ONE

PENNY ZELLER
Dreams on the HORIZON
HORIZON SERIES, BOOK TWO

PENNY ZELLER
Beyond the HORIZON
HORIZON SERIES, BOOK THREE

PENNY ZELLER
Love on the HORIZON
HORIZON SERIES, BOOK FOUR

WYOMING SUNRISE SERIES

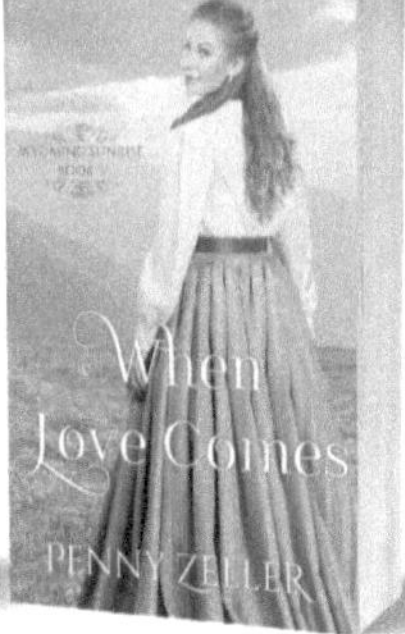

HOLLOW CREEK

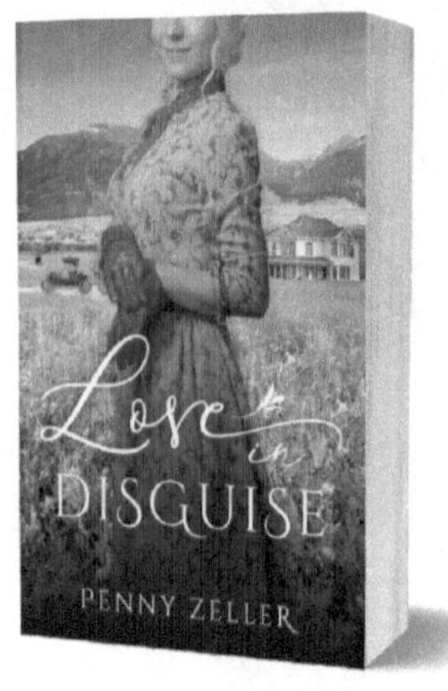

LOVE LETTERS FROM ELLIS CREEK

PENNY ZELLER
Love
FROM AFAR

PENNY ZELLER
Love
UNFORESEEN

PENNY ZELLER
Love
MOST CERTAIN

STANDALONE BOOKS

SMALL TOWN SHENANIGANS

PENNY ZELLER
Love in the
Headlines

PENNY ZELLER
recipe for
LOVE
SMALL TOWN SHENANIGANS

Chokecherry Heights